EVERYMAN,

I WILL GO WITH THEE,

AND BE THY GUIDE,

IN THY MOST NEED

TO GO BY THY SIDE

EVERYMAN'S POCKET CLASSICS

RIVER STORIES

EDITED BY HENRY HUGHES

EVERYMAN'S POCKET CLASSICS
Alfred A. Knopf New York London

THIS IS A BORZOI BOOK
PUBLISHED BY ALFRED A. KNOPF

This selection by Henry Hughes first published in
Everyman's Library, 2025

Illustrations by Paul Gentry

A list of acknowledgments to copyright owners appears at the back of this volume.

Published by Alfred A. Knopf, a division of Penguin Random House LLC, 1745 Broadway, New York, NY 10019 and distributed by Penguin Random House LLC. Published in the United Kingdom by Everyman's Library, 50 Albemarle Street, London W1S 4BD and distributed by Penguin Random House UK, One Embassy Gardens, 8 Viaduct Gardens, London SW11 7BW.

everymanslibrary.com
www.everymanslibrary.co.uk
penguinrandomhouse.com

ISBN 979-8-217-00717-2 (US)
978-1-84159-639-6 (UK)

A CIP catalogue reference for this book is available from the British Library

Typography by Peter B. Willberg

Typeset in the UK by Input Data Services Ltd, Bridgwater, Somerset

Printed and bound in Germany by GGP Media GmbH, Pössneck

The authorized representative in the EU for product safety and compliance is Penguin Random House Ireland, Morrison Chambers, 32 Nassau Street, Dublin D02 YH68, Ireland, https://eu-contact.penguin.ie

Contents

DRAMA AND DANGER

LOVE AND LOSS

MYSTIC RIVERS

FOREWORD

Rivers speak to us, and we speak to rivers. In this collection you will hear rivers cascading down mountains; rolling through deserts, forests, and fields; bound and gagged behind dams or roaring open-mouthed to the sea. They flow through wilderness and city, through countries and cultures, inspiring the rhythms, settings, and symbols of some of our greatest stories.

Whether it's an escape to freedom across the frozen Ohio River, a dangerous flood in Ukraine, or whispered promises of love and loss on the Ganges, many a life-changing scene is driven by watery currents. "I reviewed my life," says the main character in Hermann Hesse's lyrical novel *Siddhartha*, "and it was also a river."

Siddhartha learns during his time with a ferryman that "the river has very many voices." In this volume, you will hear the young, hopeful voice of Huynh Quang Nhuong in a remarkable Vietnamese story of survival, and that of E. M. Forster's misunderstood elderly man who yearns for the fountain of youth in rural Greece. The agonized wails of a grieving mother in the Mexican legend "La Llorona" contrast with the unease of Guy de Maupassant's boatman losing his nerve one foggy night on the Seine. The freedom of water incites the exuberant desires of adolescent girls in "The Found Boat" by Nobel Prize-winning Canadian author Alice Munro and sustains the marginalized lives of Melbourne's homeless in "Ghost River" by Australian author Tony Birch.

In times of trouble, rivers can be mystical sources of hope, from the fluvial fantasy of ancient China's "Peach Blossom Spring," where a wayward fisherman finds his Brigadoon, to the Native American trickster tale, "Coyote Frees Water from the Frog People," in which those who would hoard water meet a just fate. If we take care of rivers and their inhabitants, they will take care of us, suggests the eerie moment when Rat and Mole behold the powerful and benevolent Pan in "Piper at the Gates of Dawn" from Kenneth Grahame's classic, *The Wind in the Willows*. The sacred, healing powers of a river help restore Ernest Hemingway's character, Nick, just returned from the horrors of World War I, while Salwa Elhamamsy's resilient heroine, Laila, defies both the traditional marriage expectations for modern Egyptian women and the ancient myth of a sacrificial Nile Bride: "This river would never allow that to happen."

Darker currents abound as well. In Elizabeth Jane Howard's "Three Miles Up," tourists on a canal barge drift into geographically and psychologically ominous territory, and in Kunikida Doppo's tale of a long-deferred homecoming, a Japanese man who grew up by a river finds that "the spring of his spirit had dried up." In "The Lazy River," Zadie Smith brings a brilliantly discomfiting metaphor to life in a Spanish resort hotel where the tourists float in endless circles on an artificial river. On a much larger scale, the dire consequence of enraging the goddess of rivers is dramatized in the fable "What Is a Volcano?" by Lesley Nneka Arimah.

Even in their most quiet and invisible depths, rivers can be eloquent. In a powerful chapter from Elif Shafak's novel, *There Are Rivers in the Sky*, the hydrologist Zaleekah honors London's "ghost streams," paved-over waterways that endure deep underground, as she seeks to unlock the mysteries of "aquatic memory" – the possibility that a drop of water remembers everything it has touched over its millennia of existence.

Sometimes rivers address the reader directly, as in Zora Neale Hurston's "Magnolia Flower," a parable of interracial love overcoming hate and violence. Sometimes writers speak directly to rivers, as when Ovid asks the goddess Arethusa, "How did you become a sacred spring?" It is to be hoped that in this gathering of richly varied tales from around the world there is something that will speak to everyone.

Henry Hughes

RIVER STORIES

The face of the water, in time, became a wonderful book . . . which told its mind to me without reserve, delivering its most cherished secrets as clearly as if it uttered them with a voice. And it was not a book to be read once and thrown aside, for it had a new story to tell every day.

MARK TWAIN
Life on the Mississippi

FREEDOM ON THE WATER

MARK TWAIN

IT'S LOVELY TO LIVE ON A RAFT

from *The Adventures of Huckleberry Finn*

TWO OR THREE days and nights went by; I reckon I might say they swum by, they slid along so quiet and smooth and lovely. Here is the way we put in the time. It was a monstrous big river down there – sometimes a mile and a half wide; we run nights, and laid up and hid day-times; soon as night was most gone, we stopped navigating and tied up – nearly always in the dead water under a tow-head; and then cut young cotton-woods and willows and hid the raft with them. Then we set out the lines. Next we slid into the river and had a swim, so as to freshen up and cool off; then we set down on the sandy bottom where the water was about knee-deep, and watched the daylight come. Not a sound anywheres – perfectly still – just like the whole world was asleep, only sometimes the bull-frogs a-clattering, maybe. The first thing to see, looking away over the water, was a kind of dull line – that was the woods on t'other side – you couldn't make nothing else out; then a pale place in the sky; then more paleness, spreading around; then the river softened up, away off, and warn't black any more, but grey; you could see little dark spots drifting along, ever so far away – trading scows, and such things; and long black streaks – rafts; sometimes you could hear a sweep screaking; or jumbled up voices, it was so still, and sounds come so far; and by and by you could see a streak on the water which you know by the look of the streak that there's a snag there in a swift current which breaks on it and makes that streak look that way; and you see the mist curl up off of the water, and the east reddens up, and the river, and you make out a log cabin in the edge of the woods, away on the bank on t'other side of the river, being a wood-yard, likely, and piled by them cheats so you can throw a dog through it anywheres; then the nice breeze springs up, and comes fanning you from over there, so cool and fresh, and sweet to smell, on account of the woods and the flowers; but sometimes not that way, because they've left dead fish laying around, gars, and such, and they do get pretty rank; and next you've got the full day, and everything smiling in the sun, and the song-birds just going it!

A little smoke couldn't be noticed, now, so we would take some fish off of the lines and cook up a hot breakfast. And afterwards we would watch the lonesomeness of the river, and kind of lazy along, and by and by lazy off to sleep. Wake up, by and by, and look to see what done it, and maybe see a steamboat, coughing along up stream, so far off towards the other side you couldn't tell nothing about her only whether she was stern-wheel or side-wheel; then for about an hour there wouldn't be nothing to hear nor nothing to see – just solid lonesomeness. Next you'd see a raft sliding by, away off yonder, and maybe a galoot on it chopping, because they're most always doing it on a raft; you'd see the axe flash, and come down – you don't hear nothing; you see that axe go up again, and by the time it's above the man's head, then you hear the *k'chunk!* – it had took all that time to come over the water. So we would put in the day, lazying around, listening to the stillness. Once there was a thick fog, and the rafts and things that went by was beating tin pans so the steamboats wouldn't run over them. A scow or a raft went by so close we could hear them talking and cussing and laughing – heard them plain; but we couldn't see no sign of them; it made you feel crawly, it was like spirits carrying on that way in the air. Jim said he believed it was spirits; but I says:

"No, spirits wouldn't say, 'Dern the dern fog.' "

Soon as it was night, out we shoved; when we got her out to about the middle, we let her alone, and let her float wherever the current wanted her to; then we lit the pipes, and dangled our legs in the water and talked about all kinds of things – we was always naked, day and night, whenever the mosquitoes would let us – the new clothes Buck's folks made for me was too good to be comfortable, and besides I didn't go much on clothes, nohow.

Sometimes we'd have that whole river all to ourselves for the longest time. Yonder was the banks and the islands, across the water; and maybe a spark – which was a candle in a cabin window – and sometimes on the water you could see a spark or two – on a raft or a scow, you know; and maybe you could hear a fiddle or a song coming over from one of them crafts. It's lovely to live on a raft. We had the sky, up there, all speckled with stars, and we used to lay on our backs and look up at them, and discuss about whether they was made, or only just happened – Jim he allowed they was made, but I allowed they happened; I judged it would have took too long to *make* so many. Jim said the moon could a *laid* them; well, that looked kind of reasonable, so I didn't say nothing against it, because I've seen a frog lay most as many, so of course it could be done. We used to watch the stars that fell, too, and see them streak down. Jim allowed they'd got spoiled and was hove out of the nest.

Once or twice of a night we would see a steamboat slipping along in the dark, and now and then she would belch a whole world of sparks up out of her chimbleys, and they would rain down in the river and look awful pretty; then she would turn a corner and her lights would wink out and her pow-wow shut off and leave the river still again; and by and by her waves would get to us, a long time after she was gone, and joggle the raft a bit, and after that you wouldn't hear nothing for you couldn't tell how long, except maybe frogs or something.

After midnight the people on shore went to bed, and then for two or three hours the shores was black – no more sparks in the cabin windows. These sparks was our clock – the first one that showed again meant morning was coming, so we hunted a place to hide and tie up, right away.

HARRIET BEECHER STOWE

THE MOTHER'S STRUGGLE

from *Uncle Tom's Cabin*

IT IS IMPOSSIBLE to conceive of a human creature more wholly desolate and forlorn than Eliza, when she turned her footsteps from Uncle Tom's cabin.

Her husband's suffering and dangers, and the danger of her child, all blended in her mind, with a confused and stunning sense of the risk she was running, in leaving the only home she had ever known, and cutting loose from the protection of a friend whom she loved and revered. Then there was the parting from every familiar object, – the place where she had grown up, the trees under which she had played, the groves where she had walked many an evening in happier days, by the side of her young husband, – everything, as it lay in the clear, frosty starlight, seemed to speak reproachfully to her, and ask her whither could she go from a home like that?

But stronger than all was maternal love, wrought into a paroxysm of frenzy by the near approach of a fearful danger. Her boy was old enough to have walked by her side, and, in an indifferent case, she would only have led him by the hand; but now the bare thought of putting him out of her arms made her shudder, and she strained him to her bosom with a convulsive grasp, as she went rapidly forward.

The frosty ground creaked beneath her feet, and she trembled at the sound; every quaking leaf and fluttering shadow sent the blood backward to her heart, and quickened her footsteps. She wondered within herself at the strength that seemed to be come upon her; for she felt the weight of her boy as if it had been a feather, and every flutter of fear seemed to increase the supernatural power that bore her on, while from her pale lips burst forth, in frequent ejaculations, the prayer to a Friend above – "Lord, help! Lord, save me!"

If it were *your* Harry, mother, or your Willie, that were going to be torn from you by a brutal trader, tomorrow morning, – if you had seen the man, and heard that the papers were signed and delivered, and you had only from twelve o'clock till morning to make good your escape, – how fast could *you* walk? How many miles could you make in those few brief hours, with the darling at your bosom, – the little sleepy head on your shoulder, – the small, soft arms trustingly holding on to your neck?

For the child slept. At first, the novelty and alarm kept him waking; but his mother so hurriedly repressed every breath or sound, and so assured him that if he were only still she would certainly save him, that he clung quietly round her neck, only asking, as he found himself sinking to sleep,

"Mother, I don't need to keep awake, do I?"

"No, my darling; sleep, if you want to."

"But, mother, if I do get asleep, you won't let him get me?"

"No! so may God help me!" said his mother, with a paler cheek, and a brighter light in her large dark eyes.

"You're *sure*, an't you, mother?"

"Yes, *sure*!" said the mother, in a voice that startled herself; for it seemed to her to come from a spirit within, that was no part of her; and the boy dropped his little weary head on her shoulder, and was soon asleep. How the touch of those warm arms, the gentle breathings that came in her neck, seemed to add fire and spirit to her movements! It seemed to her as if strength poured into her in electric streams, from every gentle touch and movement of the sleeping, confiding child. Sublime is the dominion of the mind over the body, that, for a time, can make flesh and nerve impregnable, and string the sinews like steel, so that the weak become so mighty.

The boundaries of the farm, the grove, the wood-lot, passed by her dizzily, as she walked on; and still she went, leaving one familiar object after another, slacking not, pausing not, till reddening daylight found her many a long mile from all traces of any familiar objects upon the open highway.

She had often been, with her mistress, to visit some connections, in the little village of T—, not far from the Ohio River, and knew the road well. To go thither, to escape across the Ohio River, were the first hurried outlines of her plan of escape; beyond that, she could only hope in God.

When horses and vehicles began to move along the highway, with that alert perception peculiar to a state of excitement, and which seems to be a sort of inspiration, she became aware that her headlong pace and distracted air might bring on her remark and suspicion. She therefore put the boy on the ground, and, adjusting her dress and bonnet, she walked on at as rapid a pace as she thought consistent with the preservation of appearances. In her little bundle she had provided a store of cakes and apples, which she used as expedients for quickening the speed of the child, rolling the apple some yards before them, when the boy would run with all his might after it; and this ruse, often repeated, carried them over many a half-mile.

After a while, they came to a thick patch of woodland, through which murmured a clear brook. As the child complained of hunger and thirst, she climbed over the fence with him; and, sitting down behind a large rock which concealed them from the road, she gave him a breakfast out of her little package. The boy wondered and grieved that she could not eat; and when, putting his arms round her neck, he tried to wedge some of his cake into her mouth, it seemed to her that the rising in her throat would choke her.

"No, no, Harry darling! mother can't eat till you are safe! We must go on – on – till we come to the river!" And she hurried again into the road, and again constrained herself to walk regularly and composedly forward.

She was many miles past any neighborhood where she was personally known. If she should chance to meet any who knew her, she reflected that the well-known kindness of the family would be of itself a blind to suspicion, as making it an unlikely supposition that she could be a fugitive. As she was also so white as not to be known as of colored lineage, without a critical survey, and her child was white also, it was much easier for her to pass on unsuspected.

On this presumption, she stopped at noon at a neat farmhouse, to rest herself, and buy some dinner for her child and self; for, as the danger decreased with the distance, the supernatural tension of the nervous system lessened, and she found herself both weary and hungry.

The good woman, kindly and gossipping, seemed rather pleased than otherwise with having somebody come in to talk with; and accepted, without examination, Eliza's statement, that she "was going on a little piece, to spend a week with her friends," – all which she hoped in her heart might prove strictly true.

An hour before sunset, she entered the village of T—, by the Ohio River, weary and footsore, but still strong in heart. Her first glance was at the river, which lay, like Jordan, between her and the Canaan of liberty on the other side.

It was now early spring, and the river was swollen and turbulent; great cakes of floating ice were swinging heavily to and fro in the turbid waters. Owing to the peculiar form of the shore on the Kentucky side, the land bending far out into the water, the ice had been lodged and detained in great quantities, and the narrow channel which swept round the bend was full of ice, piled one cake over another, thus forming a temporary barrier to the descending ice, which lodged, and formed a great, undulating raft, filling up the whole river, and extending almost to the Kentucky shore.

Eliza stood, for a moment, contemplating this unfavorable aspect of things, which she saw at once must prevent the usual ferry-boat from running, and then turned into a small public house on the bank, to make a few inquiries.

The hostess, who was busy in various fizzing and stewing operations over the fire, preparatory to the evening meal, stopped, with a fork in her hand, as Eliza's sweet and plaintive voice arrested her.

"What is it?" she said.

"Isn't there any ferry or boat, that takes people over to B—, now?" she said.

"No, indeed!" said the woman; "the boats has stopped running."

Eliza's look of dismay and disappointment struck the woman, and she said, inquiringly,

"May be you're wanting to get over? – anybody sick? Ye seem mighty anxious?"

"I've got a child that's very dangerous," said Eliza. "I never heard of it till last night, and I've walked quite a piece today, in hopes to get to the ferry."

"Well, now, that's onlucky," said the woman, whose motherly sympathies were much aroused; "I'm re'lly consarned for ye. Solomon!" she called, from the window, towards a small back building. A man, in leather apron and very dirty hands, appeared at the door.

"I say, Sol," said the woman, "is that ar man going to tote them bar'ls over tonight?"

"He said he should try, if 't was any way prudent," said the man.

"There's a man a piece down here, that's going over with some truck this evening, if he durs' to; he'll be in here to supper tonight, so you'd better set down and wait. That's a sweet little fellow," added the woman, offering him a cake.

But the child, wholly exhausted, cried with weariness.

"Poor fellow! he isn't used to walking, and I've hurried him on so," said Eliza.

"Well, take him into this room," said the woman, opening into a small bed-room, where stood a comfortable bed. Eliza laid the weary boy upon it, and held his hands in hers till he was fast asleep. For her there was no rest. As a fire in her bones, the thought of the pursuer urged her on; and she gazed with longing eyes on the sullen, surging waters that lay between her and liberty.

Here we must take our leave of her for the present, to follow the course of her pursuers.

"Course," said Sam, "Mas'r can do as he'd ruther, go de straight road, if Mas'r thinks best, – it's all one to us. Now, when I study 'pon it, I think de straight road de best, *deridedly*."

"She would naturally go a lonesome way," said Haley, thinking aloud, and not minding Sam's remark.

"Dar an't no sayin'," said Sam; "gals is pecular; they never does nothin' ye thinks they will; mose gen'lly the contrary. Gals is nat'lly made contrary; and so, if you thinks they've gone one road, it is sartin you'd better go t' other, and then you'll be sure to find 'em. Now, my private 'pinion is, Lizy took der road; so I think we'd better take de straight one."

This profound generic view of the female sex did not seem to dispose Haley particularly to the straight road, and he announced decidedly that he should go the other, and asked Sam when they should come to it.

"A little piece ahead," said Sam, giving a wink to Andy with the eye which was on Andy's side of the head; and he added, gravely, "but I've studded on de matter, and I'm quite clar we ought not to go dat ar way. I nebber been over it no way. It's despit lonesome, and we might lose our way, – whar we'd come to, de Lord only knows."

"Nevertheless," said Haley, "I shall go that way."

"Now I think on 't, I think I hearn 'em tell that dat ar road was all fenced up and down by der creek, and thar, an't it, Andy?"

Andy wasn't certain; he'd only "hearn tell" about that road, but never been over it. In short, he was strictly noncommittal.

Haley, accustomed to strike the balance of probabilities between lies of greater or lesser magnitude, thought that it lay in favor of the dirt road aforesaid. The mention of the thing he thought he perceived was involuntary on Sam's part at first, and his confused attempts to dissuade him he set down to a desperate lying on second thoughts, as being unwilling to implicate Liza.

When, therefore, Sam indicated the road, Haley plunged briskly into it, followed by Sam and Andy.

Now, the road, in fact, was an old one, that had formerly been a thoroughfare to the river, but abandoned for many years after the laying of the new pike. It was open for about an hour's ride, and after that it was cut across by various farms and fences. Sam knew this fact perfectly well, – indeed, the road had been so long closed up, that Andy had never heard of it. He therefore rode along with an air of dutiful submission, only groaning and vociferating occasionally that 't was "desp't rough, and bad for Jerry's foot."

"Now, I jest give yer warning," said Haley, "I know yer; yer won't get me to turn off this road, with all yer fussin' – so you shet up!"

"Mas'r will go his own way!" said Sam, with rueful submission, at the same time winking most portentously to Andy, whose delight was now very near the explosive point.

Sam was in wonderful spirits, – professed to keep a very brisk lookout, – at one time exclaiming that he saw "a gal's bonnet" on the top of some distant eminence, or calling to Andy "if that thar wasn't 'Lizy' down in the hollow;" always making these exclamations in some rough or craggy part of the road, where the sudden quickening of speed was a special inconvenience to all parties concerned, and thus keeping Haley in a state of constant commotion.

After riding about an hour in this way, the whole party made a precipitate and tumultuous descent into a barn-yard belonging to a large farming establishment. Not a soul was in sight, all the hands being employed in the fields; but, as the barn stood conspicuously and plainly square across the road, it was evident that their journey in that direction had reached a decided finale.

"Wan't dat ar what I telled Mas'r?" said Sam, with an air of injured innocence. "How does strange gentleman spect to know more about a country dan de natives born and raised?"

"You rascal!" said Haley, "you knew all about this."

"Didn't I tell yer I *knowd*, and yer wouldn't believe me? I telled Mas'r 't was all shet up, and fenced up, and I didn't spect we could get through, – Andy heard me."

It was all too true to be disputed, and the unlucky man

had to pocket his wrath with the best grace he was able, and all three faced to the right about, and took up their line of march for the highway.

In consequence of all the various delays, it was about three-quarters of an hour after Eliza had laid her child to sleep in the village tavern that the party came riding into the same place. Eliza was standing by the window, looking out in another direction, when Sam's quick eye caught a glimpse of her. Haley and Andy were two yards behind. At this crisis, Sam contrived to have his hat blown off, and uttered a loud and characteristic ejaculation, which startled her at once; she drew suddenly back; the whole train swept by the window, round to the front door.

A thousand lives seemed to be concentrated in that one moment to Eliza. Her room opened by a side door to the river. She caught her child, and sprang down the steps towards it. The trader caught a full glimpse of her just as she was disappearing down the bank; and throwing himself from his horse, and calling loudly on Sam and Andy, he was after her like a hound after a deer. In that dizzy moment her feet to her scarce seemed to touch the ground, and a moment brought her to the water's edge. Right on behind they came; and, nerved with strength such as God gives only to the desperate, with one wild cry and flying leap, she vaulted sheer over the turbid current by the shore, on to the raft of ice beyond. It was a desperate leap – impossible to anything but madness and despair; and Haley, Sam, and Andy, instinctively cried out, and lifted up their hands, as she did it.

The huge green fragment of ice on which she alighted pitched and creaked as her weight came on it, but she staid there not a moment. With wild cries and desperate energy she leaped to another and still another cake; stumbling

– leaping – slipping – springing upwards again! Her shoes are gone – her stockings cut from her feet – while blood marked every step; but she saw nothing, felt nothing, till dimly, as in a dream, she saw the Ohio side, and a man helping her up the bank.

"Yer a brave gal, now, whoever ye ar!" said the man, with an oath.

Eliza recognized the voice and face for a man who owned a farm not far from her old home.

"O, Mr. Symmes! – save me – do save me – do hide me!" said Eliza.

"Why, what's this?" said the man. "Why, if 'tan't Shelby's gal!"

"My child! – this boy! – he'd sold him! There is his Mas'r," said she, pointing to the Kentucky shore. "O, Mr. Symmes, you've got a little boy!"

"So I have," said the man, as he roughly, but kindly, drew her up the steep bank. "Besides, you're a right brave gal. I like grit, wherever I see it."

When they had gained the top of the bank, the man paused.

"I'd be glad to do something for ye," said he; "but then there's nowhar I could take ye. The best I can do is to tell ye to go *thar*," said he, pointing to a large white house which stood by itself, off the main street of the village. "Go thar; they're kind folks. Thar's no kind o' danger but they'll help you, – they're up to all that sort o' thing."

"The Lord bless you!" said Eliza, earnestly.

"No 'casion, no 'casion in the world," said the man. "What I've done's of no 'count."

"And, oh, surely, sir, you won't tell any one!"

"Go to thunder, gal! What do you take a feller for? In course not," said the man. "Come, now, go along like a likely, sensible gal, as you are. You've arnt your liberty, and you shall have it, for all me."

The woman folded her child to her bosom, and walked firmly and swiftly away. The man stood and looked after her.

KUNIKIDA DOPPO

RIVER MIST

Translated by Naoko Ishikura Smith

IT WAS ABOUT twenty years ago that Toyokichi Ueda left his hometown. He was twenty-two years old, and nearly everyone celebrated his assured success. With dreams of great undertakings in the golden mist of his imagination, he departed the old castle town and set off for Tokyo, without even bothering to visit Osaka or Kyoto. Friends, relatives, and siblings all got together and cheered the news of his safe arrival, speculating about his promising future.

One old man, Zenbe Namiki, nicknamed Cedar Forest Whitebeard, had his doubts, however. "What can Toyokichi do? I'm sure within five or ten years he will come back home looking pale as a ghost. You just wait and see."

"Why would you say that?" asked a friend of Toyokichi's. The old man did not answer, he just grinned wickedly and twisted a hank of his snowy beard.

Let me tell you a bit about this old Whitebeard. It's reasonable to say there was no one in Iwakuni who didn't know this strange old-timer. Having gained that nickname from his remarkable whiskers, he was just a small, filthy old man, and yet he had a strong and sturdy physique for someone in his seventies. Standing silently with his small round eyes beaming brightly in the dim shadow of the cedar forest, people found him creepy. But it wasn't just the old man. Long before he was born, the cedar forest had already become a spooky place among the samurai haunts of Iwakuni. So now, hundreds of years later, a single cedar tree

– which at its base would take five men, with their arms outstretched, to fully encircle – stands at the corner of the old man's house, forming a lonely crossroad. Whitebeard had been eccentric, rude, and foul-mouthed ever since he was young. But he became even more vulgar as he got older. He made ominous prophecies regarding the lives of others, crudely blurting out, "That chap will die before long." Strangely enough, his predictions often came true. He was equipped with a kind of supernatural vision, and to put it frankly, he had an innately sharp intuition. Even though Toyokichi had no real relationship with Whitebeard, Whitebeard made one of these prophecies about Toyokichi. That's all there is to say, but remember the three parts to this prophecy: "What can Toyokichi do?" "I'm sure he'll come home," and "Within five or ten years." I have shared Whitebeard's predictions from the shadow of the cedar forest with his eyes shining like a weasel's, but it must be noted that Toyokichi was a talented person who lacked patience; or rather, he had too much patience and rarely hit his mark. He was like a sturdy staff which is struck hard against something, producing only a dull thud rather than a resounding crack. Toyokichi was a good, compassionate man, but he was chicken-hearted, or rather, he was spineless like a sea anemone.

For twenty years, Toyokichi tried many things, mainly in the Tohoku region around Tokyo, sometimes succeeding, but mostly failing. Finally, the spring of his spirit had dried up, and he turned back toward his hometown, which he never forgot. No matter how hard he fell, he would not settle like dust on the streets of the distant capital, relying only on cheap saké for companionship. Admittedly, Whitebeard's prediction of his returning "within five or ten years" was not accurate. It was twenty years before he returned. But

Toyokichi was not the kind of man who would retreat immediately after defeat.

So, for the most part, Whitebeard's prophecies were realized, but there is one prophecy that even that old soothsayer missed. This is something perhaps only the cedar grove itself could have known, drawing from its many centuries of observing the fates of humans.

Around one o'clock on a Sunday afternoon in mid-September, a man stood aimlessly at the crossroads of the cedar grove. He was around forty, dark-skinned and long-faced, with a salt-and-pepper head and sunken cheeks. Crumpled, faded, sweat-soaked clothes hung off him; his once blue leggings were worn and discolored, his straw sandals were in tatters. He looked like a fugitive from the capital. Yes, it was Toyokichi Ueda.

His hometown had changed quite a bit after twenty years. All over Japan, castle towns were undergoing modern development, and yet the old samurai lanes outside city-centers remained rustic – Iwakuni was no exception. New buildings and glittering shops had opened downtown, and yet the samurai mansions still held an ancient charm and an indescribable sense of tranquility.

Toyokichi rested in the shade of the cedars. Having fallen so low and being a chicken-hearted man, he could not shout out greetings upon his return, he could not stride through the old streets in triumph, he could not go immediately to his older brother's house – that is, the house in which he was born. He wandered in a dreamy trance, tracing the edges of old memories. Things have changed, he thought. But some things are the same. The hole in the wall from twenty years ago that Toyokichi mischievously poked with the end of a stick, was still there, it had just gotten a little bigger.

In his eyes, however, the road seemed to be narrower than before, and there were more trees, more desolation. Cicadas buzzed their monotonous, soporific voices; lonely sunlight beat down; and a venerable samurai house appeared sound asleep. As he walked around the cedar hedge, a crepe myrtle reflected against the blue sky at the end of the mud-and-tile wall, and the wall was almost completely covered in ivy. The gate was shadowed by oaks, plums, and oranges, and inside the gate were two or three palms, their thick, fan-shaped leaves shone brightly, undulating in the wind.

He nodded and looked at the weathered name on the gate: "Shiro Katayama." He was Toyokichi's childhood friend.

"He must be doing quite well," he thought. "Perhaps he has children." He took a peek inside and saw, from the direction of the mulberry garden, six or seven hens led by a rooster. Suddenly he heard the sound of a well's pulley, and a voice that seemed to be the master of the house: "Come and bring me the metal wash basin, Oyasu."

Toyokichi looked nervously around as if he feared attack, then quickly turned the corner of the wall. There was not so much as a shadow in sight.

"Shiro, Shiro," Toyokichi spoke his friend's name, squinting and staring blankly into the distance along that narrow, tree-shaded road. Far away down the lane, a shimmering heat haze hovered. A dog suddenly appeared from between the bamboo hedges, right where Toyokichi was standing. The dog looked at the stranger and raised his ears suspiciously, but as soon as two high-pitched whistles were heard inside the fence, the dog ran back inside. Toyokichi's eyes widened, as if he had just emerged from a dream, and a sad smile appeared on his face. Then, a boy of about twelve or thirteen came out of the shade with a fishing rod in his hand. He didn't seem to notice Toyokichi, didn't even look his way;

he softly chanted something that sounded like a military song and strode past. The same dog trailed the boy, sniffing the ground. Toyokichi followed at a hundred paces or so, watching closely the boy's shadow, the distance between them transformed into thirty years – his old self before his eyes. Just when he thought that the shadows of the boy and the dog had vanished, he recognized the old plum tree with cicadas drumming amid its branches, just as it always had been. He smiled happily and said, "I see, that kid is going to our old place." He looked cheerily up at the plum tree and turned the corner.

Soon he came upon a creek about six feet wide, shaded by willows. Toyokichi grinned and hurried over to where four boys were gathered. This little creek, which is a tributary of the Okawa River, has long been the fishing spot for local kids. Toyokichi sat in the shade of a grand willow, and for the first time in ages, he saw the reflected shadow of himself on that old familiar stretch of water where the stream becomes wider, deeper, quieter and darker. Beams of sunlight filtered down through the willows, casting golden rays into the water and on the clear, pebbly bed that sparkled like silver and jasper.

The boys were fishing, stationed on willow tree stumps here and there, and they turned towards the lad who had just joined them. A boy of twelve or thirteen shouted, "Hiyama! Look at this!" He laughed proudly, holding up a fish with a bright red belly that was almost the size of a fine trout.

"Ueda, don't brag!" shouted one boy. Toyokichi suddenly stood up and turned to the boy called Ueda. The weathered man furrowed his eyebrows, narrowed his eyes, and looked at the boy's face. He approached the boy who now looked suspiciously at Toyokichi and raised the lid of the creel basket.

"I see, I see." Toyokichi glanced inside the basket, then stared at the boy's face and tilted his head.

The boy said sharply, "It's big, isn't it?" He closed the lid and plunged the basket back into the water, gazing at the stream as if he'd already forgotten the curious man.

Toyokichi was stunned. *It's definitely my brother's son*, he thought. *Not only do they look alike, but his voice is just like my brother's*. He continued studying the boy's face in profile. They made a fine picture, these two. The long green leaves of the willows glittered in the sunlight, mingling together with black shadows as the wind blew. At the water's edge, in the cool shade, a plump boy was fishing, staring intently at the surface of the deep, clear water. Sitting on a willow stump a little way off, the worn and shabby Toyokichi gazed dreamlike. Above the willows upstream of the creek, the crumbling stone walls of the Jozan Mountain Castle could be discerned in the distance. It was the beginning of autumn; the day was clear and bright. It made for quite a picture – a deeply meaningful picture. Toyokichi's eyes filled with tears, though he blinked and swallowed, and tried to choke them back. Then, he felt an indescribable sense of nostalgia rise up in his heart: "This is where I was born, this is where I will die, so happy, so happy, so relieved." And somehow, he felt like his long agonies and tribulations were suddenly shed like an old skin.

Toyokichi approached the boy in a friendly manner and asked, "What is your father's name?" The boy's eyes widened and he looked warily at the stranger.

Toyokichi went on, "His name is Kan'ichi, isn't it?"

The astonished boy stared at Toyokichi's face. The man smiled a little. "Is Kan'ichi doing well?"

"Yes," the boy said. "He's fine."

"Oh, I'm relieved to hear that. You must have heard about your Uncle Toyokichi."

The boy stood up in blank surprise.

"What is your name?" asked the man.

"Genzo," said the boy.

"Genzo, I am your uncle, Toyokichi."

The boy turned pale and dropped his fishing rod. Without saying another word, he ran in the direction of the mansion. The other boys looked at Toyokichi suspiciously. They quickly wound up their fishing lines, retrieved their baskets, and took off. The deserted man stood there bewildered, looking into the shadows into which the boys bolted.

Toyokichi Ueda had returned. People who remembered and gossiped about him were all surprised. All of Toyokichi's acquaintances from when he was twenty were now in their forties and fifties, some had children, some even had grandchildren. Many came to visit, especially women who were once beautiful maidens and were now old ladies. One after another, folks came by, surprised at how decrepit Toyokichi had become, but also happy that he was safe. People felt sorry that he had come down in the world, returning home without succeeding. They talked, laughed, cried, and consoled him until they ran out of words.

Oh hometown! Toyokichi never forgot his hometown for a single day during those twenty years of ups and downs. And now, he'd come back a ruined man, never imagining people would be so kind. He was surprised at how sympathetic people were, including his brother. And he wept, feeling happy and sad for no particular reason. Yes, he felt old and disappointed, having drifted ashore from a hopeless, miserable sea to a hopeless, secure island. But his brother cared for this unfortunate drifter with all his heart.

His brother Kan'ichi had three children: Ohana, who was fifteen years old; followed by Genzo, mentioned earlier; and the youngest was Isamu, a cute seven-year-old boy. Ohana consoled her uncle, Genzo played with him, and Isamu was spoiled by his uncle. Toyokichi would lean against the tea room window, dozing, while Ohana sat on the stone steps in front of the storehouse singing her school songs. At Genzo's invitation, Toyokichi went fishing; and there on the stream bank he would also fall asleep. At home he became Isamu's horse, sluggishly crawling around the tatami room. Asked to make the sound of a horse's neigh, Toyokichi misheard and bellowed the deep moo of a cow. Isamu got mad at him, making the whole house laugh.

During this time, he taught Ohana and Genzo the basics of reading Chinese, as well as mathematics and English. His success as a tutor led people to believe that playing all the time was not good for Toyokichi. Maybe if he gathered all the children together and started something like a private school, it would be good for both himself and others. Kan'ichi recommended this idea to Toyokichi – and he agreed, feeling a secret sense of joy. It was an unhappy prospect to live out his days without any challenges, doing nothing, accomplishing nothing, and ending his life in vain while depending on others.

A month of this safe, dull and hopeless life had elapsed and he stopped lazing around and dozing off. On autumn evenings, when the sky was clear and starlit, he accompanied Ohana along the banks of a small creek. While listening to her sing a mournful tune in her low voice, he felt his sinking heart skip a beat. Despite past failures, he felt it was better to put his heart into some meaningful work than to rest on safe and uneventful security. Perhaps his past failures were due to the cruelty of the people around him. If he set out to do something among the kind people of his hometown, he was sure to achieve something.

But Toyokichi did not know himself. He did not see the darkness of his shadow. He had agreed to establish this private school because he wanted to do some kind of work, but he wasn't sure how to broach the subject. Now it was happening.

So, one might say, up to that point, much of Whitebeard's prophecy had come true. But no one could predict what would happen next.

It was around ten o'clock on a moonlit night, and the Okawa River seemed to wrap around the foot of the castle hill. Toyokichi was alone, chasing his own shadow up a wooded path. Leaving the path through the bushes, he came upon a cemetery. The ancient, moon-bleached tombs rose in mounds along the cliff. Toyokichi weaved his way through the graves, stopping in front of the smallest, set beside the roots of a little pine tree. It was marked "Zenbe Namiki – Cedar Forest Whitebeard." Toyokichi noted that Whitebeard had died seven years ago.

Earlier that day, Kan'ichi and the others worked on the new private school. They rented the Katayama family dojo to serve as a classroom. This wood-floored dojo, once used for kendo before the Meiji Restoration, provided an ample 700 square feet of space. It was where Toyokichi once tumbled recklessly with the Katayama boy on his way home from elementary school. Kan'ichi and the others made every effort to gather enough desks and chairs for twenty anticipated students. They had to make some repairs, piecing together surplus furniture from the town hall and elementary school storage rooms. It was hard work, but they got it all done in time. The school's opening ceremony was to be held the next day, and Toyokichi had made various preparations and even drafted a speech. The old houses in Iwakuni bubbled with chatter and laughter that day, and even the lonely cedar forest felt more animated. All that week at school, Genzo felt proud because his uncle would be his new teacher. Ohana would sing the national anthem for the ceremony, and little Isamu hadn't the slightest idea why everyone was making such a fuss.

That night, Toyokichi went to Katayama's dojo to finish his preparations for the big day. On his way home, he suddenly changed direction and headed out to the banks of the Okawa River and up to the old cemetery. He sat down on the grave of Whitebeard and gazed at the moon. Surely, Whitebeard did not know what was happening to Toyokichi, and Toyokichi didn't know the prophecies of Whitebeard. Toyokichi's eyes took in the flowing river and the pleasant features of his hometown. After a while, he let out a sigh of disappointment. Having exhausted all his energies, he now felt an unbearable fatigue. *Establishment of a private school.* He no longer felt any elastic force in these words. The mountains, rivers, and moon remained the same. Some of his old acquaintances were buried in this cemetery. At that moment, Toyokichi felt that the flow of his life had also nearly reached the vast and endless ocean, and that only a translucent veil separated him from his dead friends. It was not true, of course, he was just exhausted. But he couldn't even summon the energy to dip his cup into the water to quench his thirst.

Toyokichi quietly stood up and went down to the river bank. Then he trudged along the water's edge, following the incessant current. The moon shone bright and clear, and Jozan Mountain cast its pitch-black shadow over the river. The quieter pools were mirror-like, and the faster riffles glittered with shattered moonlight. He felt dreamy, and continued downstream. A small boat was tethered to the shore. Toyokichi jumped in, untied the line, and picked up the long push pole. His old boating skills had not deserted him, and as he pushed off, the punt glided smoothly into the channel. Toward the far-off estuary, everything seemed bathed in moonlight, and river mist floated over the water's glowing surface – like a dream. Toyokichi desired this dream, and he poled the punt farther downriver. As the boat descended, the mist gradually receded, and the river opened to the sea. Toyokichi never returned to his home in Iwakuni. All the people expressed great sorrow, but Ohana and Genzo were saddened the most.

ERNEST HEMINGWAY

BIG TWO-HEARTED RIVER

PART I

THE TRAIN WENT on up the track out of sight, around one of the hills of burnt timber. Nick sat down on the bundle of canvas and bedding the baggage man had pitched out of the door of the baggage car. There was no town, nothing but the rails and the burned-over country. The thirteen saloons that had lined the one street of Seney had not left a trace. The foundations of the Mansion House hotel stuck up above the ground. The stone was chipped and split by the fire. It was all that was left of the town of Seney. Even the surface had been burned off the ground.

Nick looked at the burned-over stretch of hillside, where he had expected to find the scattered houses of the town and then walked down the railroad track to the bridge over the river. The river was there. It swirled against the log spiles of the bridge. Nick looked down into the clear, brown water, colored from the pebbly bottom, and watched the trout keeping themselves steady in the current with wavering fins. As he watched them they changed their positions by quick angles, only to hold steady in the fast water again. Nick watched them a long time.

He watched them holding themselves with their noses into the current, many trout in deep, fast moving water, slightly distorted as he watched far down through the glassy convex surface of the pool, its surface pushing and swelling smooth against the resistance of the log-driven piles of the bridge. At the bottom of the pool were the big trout. Nick did not see them at first. Then he saw them at the bottom of the pool, big trout looking to hold themselves on the gravel bottom in a varying mist of gravel and sand, raised in spurts by the current.

Nick looked down into the pool from the bridge. It was a hot day. A kingfisher flew up the stream. It was a long time since Nick had looked into a stream and seen trout. They were very satisfactory. As the shadow of the kingfisher moved up the stream, a big trout shot upstream in a long angle, only his shadow marking the angle, then lost his shadow as he came through the surface of the water, caught the sun, and then, as he went back into the stream under the surface, his shadow seemed to float down the stream with the current, unresisting, to his post under the bridge where he tightened facing up into the current.

Nick's heart tightened as the trout moved. He felt all the old feeling.

He turned and looked down the stream. It stretched away, pebbly-bottomed with shallows and big boulders and a deep pool as it curved away around the foot of a bluff.

Nick walked back up the ties to where his pack lay in the cinders beside the railway track. He was happy. He adjusted the pack harness around the bundle, pulling straps tight, slung the pack on his back, got his arms through the shoulder straps and took some of the pull off his shoulders by leaning his forehead against the wide band of the tump-line. Still, it was too heavy. It was much too heavy. He had his leather rod-case in his hand and leaning forward to keep the weight of the pack high on his shoulders he walked along the road that paralleled the railway track, leaving the burned town behind in the heat, and then turned off around a hill with a high, fire-scarred hill on either side onto a road that went back into the country. He walked along the road feeling the ache from the pull of the heavy pack. The road climbed steadily. It was hard work walking up-hill. His muscles ached and the day was hot, but Nick felt happy. He felt he had left everything behind, the need for thinking, the need to write, other needs. It was all back of him.

From the time he had gotten down off the train and the baggage man had thrown his pack out of the open car door things had been different. Seney was burned, the country was burned over and changed, but it did not matter. It could not all be burned. He knew that. He hiked along the road, sweating in the sun, climbing to cross the range of hills that separate the railway from the pine plains.

The road ran on, dipping occasionally, but always climbing. Nick went on up. Finally the road after going parallel to the burnt hillside reached the top. Nick leaned back against a stump and slipped out of the pack harness. Ahead of him, as far as he could see, was the pine plain. The burned country stopped off at the left with the range of hills. On ahead islands of dark pine trees rose out of the plain. Far off to the left was the line of the river. Nick followed it with his eye and caught glints of the water in the sun.

There was nothing but the pine plain ahead of him, until the far blue hills that marked the Lake Superior height of land. He could hardly see them, faint and far away in the heat-light over the plain. If he looked too steadily they were gone. But if he only half-looked they were there, the far-off hills of the height of land.

Nick sat down against the charred stump and smoked a cigarette. His pack balanced on the top of the stump, harness holding ready, a hollow molded in it from his back. Nick sat smoking, looking out over the country. He did not need to get his map out. He knew where he was from the position of the river.

As he smoked, his legs stretched out in front of him, he noticed a grasshopper walk along the ground and up onto his woolen sock. The grasshopper was black. As he had walked along the road, climbing, he had started many grasshoppers from the dust. They were all black. They were not the big grasshoppers with yellow and black or red and black wings whirring out from their black wing sheathing as they fly up. These were just ordinary hoppers, but all a sooty black in color. Nick had wondered about them as he walked, without really thinking about them. Now, as he watched the black hopper that was nibbling at the wool of his sock with its fourway lip, he realized that they had all turned black from living in the burned-over land. He realized that the fire must have come the year before, but the grasshoppers were all black now. He wondered how long they would stay that way.

Carefully he reached his hand down and took hold of the hopper by the wings. He turned him up, all his legs walking in the air, and looked at his jointed belly. Yes, it was black too, iridescent where the back and head were dusty.

"Go on, hopper," Nick said, speaking out loud for the first time. "Fly away somewhere."

He tossed the grasshopper up into the air and watched him sail away to a charcoal stump across the road.

Nick stood up. He leaned his back against the weight of his pack where it rested upright on the stump and got his arms through the shoulder straps. He stood with the pack on his back on the brow of the hill looking out across the country, toward the distant river and then struck down the hillside away from the road. Underfoot the ground was good walking. Two hundred yards down the hillside the fire line stopped. Then it was sweet fern, growing ankle high, to walk through, and clumps of jack pines; a long undulating country with frequent rises and descents, sandy underfoot and the country alive again.

Nick kept his direction by the sun. He knew where he wanted to strike the river and he kept on through the pine plain, mounting small rises to see other rises ahead of him and sometimes from the top of a rise a great solid island of pines off to his right or his left. He broke off some sprigs of the heathery sweet fern, and put them under his pack straps. The chafing crushed it and he smelled it as he walked.

He was tired and very hot, walking across the uneven, shadeless pine plain. At any time he knew he could strike the river by turning off to his left. It could not be more than a mile away. But he kept on toward the north to hit the river as far upstream as he could go in one day's walking.

For some time as he walked Nick had been in sight of one of the big islands of pine standing out above the rolling high ground he was crossing. He dipped down and then as he came slowly up to the crest of the bridge he turned and made toward the pine trees.

There was no underbrush in the island of pine trees. The trunks of the trees went straight up or slanted toward each other. The trunks were straight and brown without branches. The branches were high above. Some interlocked to make a solid shadow on the brown forest floor. Around the grove of trees was a bare space. It was brown and soft underfoot as Nick walked on it. This was the overlapping of the pine needle floor, extending out beyond the width of the high branches. The trees had grown tall and the branches moved high, leaving in the sun this bare space they had once covered with shadow. Sharp at the edge of this extension of the forest floor commenced the sweet fern.

Nick slipped off his pack and lay down in the shade. He lay on his back and looked up into the pine trees. His neck and back and the small of his back rested as he stretched. The earth felt good against his back. He looked up at the sky, through the branches, and then shut his eyes. He opened them and looked up again. There was a wind high up in the branches. He shut his eyes again and went to sleep.

Nick woke stiff and cramped. The sun was nearly down. His pack was heavy and the straps painful as he lifted it on. He leaned over with the pack on and picked up the leather rod-case and started out from the pine trees across the sweet fern swale, toward the river. He knew it could not be more than a mile.

He came down a hillside covered with stumps into a meadow. At the edge of the meadow flowed the river. Nick was glad to get to the river. He walked upstream through the meadow. His trousers were soaked with the dew as he walked. After the hot day, the dew had come quickly and heavily. The river made no sound. It was too fast and smooth. At the edge of the meadow, before he mounted to a piece of high ground to make camp, Nick looked down the river at the trout rising. They were rising to insects come from the swamp on the other side of the stream when the sun went down. The trout jumped out of water to take them. While Nick walked through the little stretch of meadow alongside the stream, trout had jumped high out of the water. Now as he looked down the river, the insects must be settling on the surface, for the trout were feeding steadily all down the stream. As far down the long stretch as he could see, the trout were rising, making circles all down the surface of the water, as though it were starting to rain.

The ground rose, wooded and sandy, to overlook the meadow, the stretch of river and the swamp. Nick dropped his pack and rod-case and looked for a level piece of ground. He was very hungry and he wanted to make his camp before he cooked. Between two jack pines, the ground was quite level. He took the ax out of the pack and chopped out two projecting roots. That leveled a piece of ground large enough to sleep on. He smoothed out the sandy soil with his hand and pulled all the sweet fern bushes by their roots. His hands smelled good from the sweet fern. He smoothed the uprooted earth. He did not want anything making lumps under the blankets. When he had the ground smooth, he spread his three blankets. One he folded double, next to the ground. The other two he spread on top.

With the ax he slit off a bright slab of pine from one of the stumps and split it into pegs for the tent. He wanted them long and solid to hold in the ground. With the tent unpacked and spread on the ground, the pack, leaning against a jack pine, looked much smaller. Nick tied the rope that served the tent for a ridge-pole to the trunk of one of the pine trees and pulled the tent up off the ground with the other end of the rope and tied it to the other pine. The tent hung on the rope like a canvas blanket on a clothesline. Nick poked a pole he had cut up under the back peak of the canvas and then made it a tent by pegging out the sides. He pegged the sides out taut and drove the pegs deep, hitting them down into the ground with the flat of the ax until the rope loops were buried and the canvas was drum tight.

Across the open mouth of the tent Nick fixed cheesecloth to keep out mosquitoes. He crawled inside under the mosquito bar with various things from the pack to put at the head of the bed under the slant of the canvas. Inside the tent the light came through the brown canvas. It smelled pleasantly of canvas. Already there was something mysterious and homelike. Nick was happy as he crawled inside the tent. He had not been unhappy all day. This was different though. Now things were done. There had been this to do.

Now it was done. It had been a hard trip. He was very tired. That was done. He had made his camp. He was settled. Nothing could touch him. It was a good place to camp. He was there, in the good place. He was in his home where he had made it. Now he was hungry.

He came out, crawling under the cheesecloth. It was quite dark outside. It was lighter in the tent.

Nick went over the pack and found, with his fingers, a long nail in a paper sack of nails, in the bottom of the pack. He drove it into the pine tree, holding it close and hitting it gently with the flat of the ax. He hung the pack up on the nail. All his supplies were in the pack. They were off the ground and sheltered now.

Nick was hungry. He did not believe he had ever been hungrier. He opened and emptied a can of pork and beans and a can of spaghetti into the frying pan.

"I've got a right to eat this kind of stuff, if I'm willing to carry it," Nick said. His voice sounded strange in the darkening woods. He did not speak again.

He started a fire with some chunks of pine he got with the ax from a stump. Over the fire he stuck a wire grill, pushing the four legs down into the ground with his boot. Nick put the frying pan on the grill over the flames. He was hungrier. The beans and spaghetti warmed. Nick stirred them and mixed them together. They began to bubble, making little bubbles that rose with difficulty to the surface. There was a good smell. Nick got out a bottle of tomato catchup and cut four slices of bread. The little bubbles were coming faster now. Nick sat down beside the fire and lifted the frying pan off. He poured about half the contents out into the tin plate. It spread slowly on the plate. Nick knew it was too hot. He poured on some tomato catchup. He knew the beans and spaghetti were still too hot. He looked at the fire, then at the tent, he was not going to spoil it all by burning his tongue. For years he had never enjoyed fried bananas because he had never been able to wait for them to cool. His tongue was very sensitive. He was very hungry. Across the river in the swamp, in the almost dark, he saw a mist rising. He looked at the tent once more. All right. He took a full spoonful from the plate.

"Chrise," Nick said, "Geezus, Chrise," he said happily.

He ate the whole plateful before he remembered the bread. Nick finished the second plateful with the bread, mopping the plate shiny. He had not eaten since a cup of coffee and a ham sandwich in the station restaurant at St. Ignace. It had been a very fine experience. He had been that hungry before, but had not been able to satisfy it. He could have made camp hours before if he had wanted to. There were plenty of good places to camp on the river. But this was good.

Nick tucked two big chips of pine under the grill. The fire flared up. He had forgotten to get water for the coffee. Out of the pack he got a folding canvas bucket and walked down the hill, across the edge of the meadow, to the stream. The other bank was in the white mist. The grass was wet and cold as he knelt on the bank and dipped the canvas bucket into the stream. It bellied and pulled hard in the current. The water was ice cold. Nick rinsed the bucket and carried it full up to the camp. Up away from the stream it was not so cold.

Nick drove another big nail and hung up the bucket full of water. He dipped the coffee pot half full, put some more chips under the grill onto the fire and put the pot on. He could not remember which way he made coffee. He could remember an argument about it with Hopkins, but not which side he had taken. He decided to bring it to a boil. He remembered now that was Hopkins's way. He had once argued about everything with Hopkins. While he waited for the coffee to boil, he opened a small can of apricots. He liked to open cans. He emptied the can of apricots out into a tin cup. While he watched the coffee on the fire, he drank the juice syrup of the apricots, carefully at first to keep from spilling, then meditatively, sucking the apricots down. They were better than fresh apricots.

The coffee boiled as he watched. The lid came up and coffee and grounds ran down the side of the pot. Nick took it off the grill. It was a triumph for Hopkins. He put sugar in the empty apricot cup and poured some of the coffee out to cool. It was too hot to pour and he used his hat to hold the handle of the coffee pot. He would not let it steep in the pot at all. Not the first cup. It should be straight Hopkins all the way. Hop deserved that. He was a very serious coffee drinker. He was the most serious man Nick had ever known. Not heavy, serious. That was a long time ago. Hopkins spoke without moving his lips. He had played polo. He made millions of dollars in Texas. He had borrowed carfare to go to Chicago, when the wire came that his first big well had come in. He could have wired for money. That would have been too slow. They called Hop's girl the Blonde Venus. Hop did not mind because she was not his real girl. Hopkins said very confidently that none of them would make fun of his real girl. He was right. Hopkins went away when the telegram came. That was on the Black River. It took eight days for the telegram to reach him. Hopkins gave away his .22 caliber Colt automatic pistol to Nick. He gave his camera to Bill. It was to remember him always by. They were all going fishing again next summer. The Hop Head was rich. He would get a yacht and they would all cruise along the north shore of Lake Superior. He was excited but serious. They said good-bye and all felt bad. It broke up the trip. They never saw Hopkins again. That was a long time ago on the Black River.

Nick drank the coffee, the coffee according to Hopkins.

The coffee was bitter. Nick laughed. It made a good ending to the story. His mind was starting to work. He knew he could choke it because he was tired enough. He spilled the coffee out of the pot and shook the grounds loose into the fire. He lit a cigarette and went inside the tent. He took off his shoes and trousers, sitting on the blankets, rolled the shoes up inside the trousers for a pillow and got in between the blankets.

Out through the front of the tent he watched the glow of the fire, when the night wind blew on it. It was a quiet night. The swamp was perfectly quiet. Nick stretched under the blanket comfortably. A mosquito hummed close to his ear. Nick sat up and lit a match. The mosquito was on the canvas, over his head. Nick moved the match quickly up to it. The mosquito made a satisfactory hiss in the flame. The match went out. Nick lay down again under the blanket. He turned on his side and shut his eyes. He was sleepy. He felt sleep coming. He curled up under the blanket and went to sleep.

PART II

IN THE MORNING the sun was up and the tent was starting to get hot. Nick crawled out under the mosquito netting stretched across the mouth of the tent, to look at the morning. The grass was wet on his hands as he came out. He held his trousers and his shoes in his hands. The sun was just up over the hill. There was the meadow, the river and the swamp. There were birch trees in the green of the swamp on the other side of the river.

The river was clear and smoothly fast in the early morning. Down about two hundred yards were three logs all the way across the stream. They made the water smooth and deep above them. As Nick watched, a mink crossed the river on the logs and went into the swamp. Nick was excited. He was excited by the early morning and the river. He was really too hurried to eat breakfast, but he knew he must. He built a little fire and put on the coffee pot.

While the water was heating in the pot he took an empty bottle and went down over the edge of the high ground to the meadow. The meadow was wet with dew and Nick wanted to catch grasshoppers for bait before the sun dried the grass. He found plenty of good grasshoppers. They were at the base of the grass stems. Sometimes they clung to a grass stem. They were cold and wet with the dew, and could not jump until the sun warmed them. Nick picked them up, taking only the medium-sized brown ones, and put them into the bottle. He turned over a log and just under the shelter of the edge were several hundred hoppers. It was a grasshopper lodging house. Nick put about fifty of the medium browns into the bottle. While he was picking up the hoppers the others warmed in the sun and commenced to hop away. They flew when they hopped. At first they made one flight and stayed stiff when they landed, as though they were dead.

Nick knew that by the time he was through with breakfast they would be as lively as ever. Without dew in the grass it would take him all day to catch a bottle full of good grasshoppers and he would have to crush many of them, slamming at them with his hat. He washed his hands at the stream. He was excited to be near it. Then he walked up to the tent. The hoppers were already jumping stiffly in the grass. In the bottle, warmed by the sun, they were jumping in a mass. Nick put in a pine stick as a cork. It plugged the mouth of the bottle enough, so the hoppers could not get out and left plenty of air passage.

He had rolled the log back and knew he could get grasshoppers there every morning.

Nick laid the bottle full of jumping grasshoppers against a pine trunk. Rapidly he mixed some buckwheat flour with water and stirred it smooth, one cup of flour, one cup of water. He put a handful of coffee in the pot and dipped a lump of grease out of a can and slid it sputtering across the hot skillet. On the smoking skillet he poured smoothly the buckwheat batter. It spread like lava, the grease spitting sharply. Around the edges the buckwheat cake began to firm, then brown, then crisp. The surface was bubbling slowly to porousness. Nick pushed under the browned under surface with a fresh pine chip. He shook the skillet sideways and the cake was loose on the surface. I won't try and flop it, he thought. He slid the chip of clean wood all the way under the cake, and flopped it over onto its face. It sputtered in the pan.

When it was cooked Nick regreased the skillet. He used all the batter. It made another big flapjack and one smaller one.

Nick ate a big flapjack and a smaller one, covered with apple butter. He put apple butter on the third cake, folded it over twice, wrapped it in oiled paper and put it in his shirt pocket. He put the apple butter jar back in the pack and cut bread for two sandwiches.

In the pack he found a big onion. He sliced it in two and peeled the silky outer skin. Then he cut one half into slices and made onion sandwiches. He wrapped them in oiled paper and buttoned them in the other pocket of his khaki shirt. He turned the skillet upside down on the grill, drank the coffee, sweetened and yellow brown with the condensed milk in it, and tidied up the camp. It was a good camp.

Nick took his fly rod out of the leather rod-case, jointed

it, and shoved the rod-case back into the tent. He put on the reel and threaded the line through the guides. He had to hold it from hand to hand, as he threaded it, or it would slip back through its own weight. It was a heavy, double tapered fly line. Nick had paid eight dollars for it a long time ago. It was made heavy to lift back in the air and come forward flat and heavy and straight to make it possible to cast a fly which has no weight. Nick opened the aluminum leader box. The leaders were coiled between the damp flannel pads. Nick had wet the pads at the water cooler on the train up to St. Ignace. In the damp pads the gut leaders had softened and Nick unrolled one and tied it by a loop at the end to the heavy fly line. He fastened a hook on the end of the leader. It was a small hook; very thin and springy.

Nick took it from his hook book, sitting with the rod across his lap. He tested the knot and the spring of the rod by pulling the line taut. It was a good feeling. He was careful not to let the hook bite into his finger.

He started down to the stream, hooking his rod, the bottle of grasshoppers hung from his neck by a thong tied in half hitches around the neck of the bottle. His landing net hung by a hook from his belt. Over his shoulder was a long flour sack tied at each corner into an ear. The cord went over his shoulder. The sack flapped against his legs.

Nick felt awkward and professionally happy with all his equipment hanging from him. The grasshopper bottle swung against his chest. In his shirt the breast pockets bulged against him with the lunch and his fly book.

He stepped into the stream. It was a shock. His trousers clung tight to his legs. His shoes felt the gravel. The water was a rising cold shock.

Rushing, the current sucked against his legs. Where he stepped in, the water was over his knees. He waded with the current. The gravel slid under his shoes. He looked down at the swirl of water below each leg and tipped up the bottle to get a grasshopper.

The first grasshopper gave a jump in the neck of the bottle and went out into the water. He was sucked under in the whirl by Nick's right leg and came to the surface a little way down stream. He floated rapidly, kicking. In a quick circle, breaking the smooth surface of the water, he disappeared. A trout had taken him.

Another hopper poked his face out of the bottle. His antennae wavered. He was getting his front legs out of the bottle to jump. Nick took him by the head and held him while he threaded the slim hook under his chin, down through his thorax and into the last segments of his abdomen. The grasshopper took hold of the hook with his front feet, spitting tobacco juice on it. Nick dropped him into the water.

Holding the rod in his right hand he let out line against the pull of the grasshopper in the current. He stripped off line from the reel with his left hand and let it run free. He could see the hopper in the little waves of the current. It went out of sight.

There was a tug on the line. Nick pulled against the taut line. It was his first strike. Holding the now living rod across the current, he brought in the line with his left hand. The rod bent in jerks, the trout pumping against the current. Nick knew it was a small one. He lifted the rod straight up in the air. It bowed with the pull.

He saw the trout in the water jerking with his head and body against the shifting tangent of the line in the stream.

Nick took the line in his left hand and pulled the trout, thumping tiredly against the current, to the surface. His back was mottled the clear, water-over-gravel color, his side flashing in the sun. The rod under his right arm, Nick stopped, dipping his right hand into the current. He held the trout, never still, with his moist right hand, while he unhooked the barb from his mouth, then dropped him back into the stream.

He hung unsteadily in the current, then settled to the bottom beside a stone. Nick reached down his hand to touch him, his arm to the elbow under water. The trout was steady in the moving stream, resting on the gravel, beside a stone. As Nick's fingers touched him, touched his smooth, cool, underwater feeling he was gone, gone in a shadow across the bottom of the stream.

He's all right, Nick thought. He was only tired.

He had wet his hand before he touched the trout, so he would not disturb the delicate mucus that covered him. If a trout was touched with a dry hand, a white fungus attacked the unprotected spot. Years before when he had fished crowded streams, with fly fishermen ahead of him and behind him, Nick had again and again come on dead trout, furry with white fungus, drifted against a rock, or floating belly up in some pool. Nick did not like to fish with other men on the river. Unless they were of your party they spoiled it.

He wallowed down the stream, above his knees in the current, through the fifty yards of shallow water above the pile of logs that crossed the stream. He did not rebait his hook and held it in his hand as he waded. He was certain he could catch small trout in the shallows, but he did not want them. There would be no big trout in the shallows this time of day.

Now the water deepened up his thighs sharply and coldly. Ahead was the smooth dammed-back flood of water above the logs. The water was smooth and dark; on the left, the lower edge of the meadow; on the right the swamp.

Nick leaned back against the current and took a hopper from the bottle. He threaded the hopper on the hook and spat on him for good luck. Then he pulled several yards of line from the reel and tossed the hopper out ahead onto the fast, dark water. It floated down towards the logs, then the weight of the line pulled the bait under the surface. Nick held the rod in his right hand, letting line run out through his fingers.

There was a long tug. Nick struck and the rod came alive and dangerous, bent double, the line tightening, coming out of water, tightening, all in a heavy, dangerous, steady pull. Nick felt the moment when the leader would break if the strain increased and let the line go.

The reel ratcheted into a mechanical shriek as the line went out in a rush. Too fast. Nick could not check it, the line rushing out, the reel note rising as the line ran out.

With the core of the reel showing, his heart feeling stopped with the excitement, leaning back against the current that mounted icily his thighs, Nick thumbed the reel hard with his left hand. It was awkward getting his thumb inside the fly reel frame.

As he put on pressure the line tightened into sudden hardness and beyond the logs a huge trout went high out of water. As he jumped, Nick lowered the tip of the rod. But he felt, as he dropped the tip to ease the strain, the moment when the strain was too great; the hardness too tight. Of course, the leader had broken. There was no mistaking the feeling when all spring left the line and it became dry and hard. Then it went slack.

His mouth dry, his heart down, Nick reeled in. He had never seen so big a trout. There was a heaviness, a power not to be held, and then the bulk of him, as he jumped. He looked as broad as a salmon.

Nick's hand was shaky. He reeled in slowly. The thrill had been too much. He felt, vaguely, a little sick, as though it would be better to sit down.

The leader had broken where the hook was tied to it. Nick took it in his hand. He thought of the trout somewhere on the bottom, holding himself steady over the gravel, far down below the light under the logs, with the hook in his jaw. Nick knew the trout's teeth would cut through the snell of the hook. The hook would imbed itself in his jaw. He'd bet the trout was angry. Anything that size would be angry. That was a trout. He had been solidly hooked. Solid as a rock. He felt like a rock, too, before he started off. By God, he was a big one. By God, he was the biggest one I ever heard of.

Nick climbed out onto the meadow and stood, water running down his trousers and out of his shoes, his shoes squelchy. He went over and sat on the logs. He did not want to rush his sensations any.

He wriggled his toes in the water, in his shoes, and got out a cigarette from his breast pocket. He lit it and tossed the match into the fast water below the logs. A tiny trout rose at the match, as it swung around in the fast current. Nick laughed. He would finish the cigarette.

He sat on the logs, smoking, drying in the sun, the sun warm on his back, the river shallow ahead entering the woods, curving into the woods, shallows, light glittering, big water-smooth rocks, cedars along the bank and white birches, the logs warm in the sun, smooth to sit on, without bark, gray to the touch; slowly the feeling of disappointment left him. It went away slowly, the feeling of disappointment that came sharply after the thrill that made his shoulders ache. It was all right now. His rod lying out on the logs. Nick tied a new hook on the leader, pulling the gut tight until it grimped into itself in a hard knot.

He baited up, then picked up the rod and walked to the far end of the logs to get into the water, where it was not too deep. Under and beyond the logs was a deep pool. Nick walked around the shallow shelf near the swamp shore until he came out on the shallow bed of the stream.

On the left, where the meadow ended and the woods began, a great elm tree was uprooted. Gone over in a storm, it lay back into the woods, its roots clotted with dirt, grass growing in them, rising a solid bank beside the stream. The river cut to the edge of the uprooted tree. From where Nick stood he could see deep channels, like ruts, cut in the shallow bed of the stream by the flow of the current. Pebbly where he stood and pebbly and full of boulders beyond; where it curved near the tree roots, the bed of the stream was marly and between the ruts of deep water green weed fronds swung in the current.

Nick swung the rod back over his shoulder and forward, and the line, curving forward, laid the grasshopper down on one of the deep channels in the weeds. A trout struck and Nick hooked him.

Holding the rod far out toward the uprooted tree and sloshing backward in the current, Nick worked the trout, plunging, the rod bending alive, out of the danger of the weeds into the open river. Holding the rod, pumping alive against the current, Nick brought the trout in. He rushed, but always came, the spring of the rod yielding to the rushes, sometimes jerking under water, but always bringing him in. Nick eased downstream with the rushes. The rod above his head he led the trout over the net, then lifted.

The trout hung heavy in the net, mottled trout back and silver sides in the meshes. Nick unhooked him; heavy sides, good to hold, big undershot jaw, and slipped him, heaving and big sliding, into the long sack that hung from his shoulders in the water.

Nick spread the mouth of the sack against the current and it filled, heavy with water. He held it up, the bottom in the stream, and the water poured out through the sides. Inside at the bottom was the big trout, alive in the water.

Nick moved downstream. The sack out ahead of him sunk heavy in the water, pulling from his shoulders.

It was getting hot, the sun hot on the back of his neck.

Nick had one good trout. He did not care about getting many trout. Now the stream was shallow and wide. There were trees along both banks. The trees of the left bank made short shadows on the current in the forenoon sun. Nick knew there were trout in each shadow. In the afternoon, after the sun had crossed toward the hills, the trout would be in the cool shadows on the other side of the stream.

The very biggest ones would lie up close to the bank. You could always pick them up there on the Black. When the sun was down they all moved out into the current. Just when the sun made the water blinding in the glare before it went down, you were liable to strike a big trout anywhere in the current. It was almost impossible to fish then, the surface of the water was blinding as a mirror in the sun. Of course, you could fish upstream, but in a stream like the Black, or this, you had to wallow against the current and in a deep place, the water piled up on you. It was no fun to fish upstream with this much current.

Nick moved along through the shallow stretch watching the banks for deep holes. A beech tree grew close beside the river, so that the branches hung down into the water. The stream went back in under the leaves. There were always trout in a place like that.

Nick did not care about fishing that hole. He was sure he would get hooked in the branches.

It looked deep though. He dropped the grasshopper so the current took it under water, back in under the overhanging branch. The line pulled hard and Nick struck. The trout threshed heavily, half out of water in the leaves and branches. The line was caught. Nick pulled hard and the trout was off. He reeled in and holding the hook in his hand, walked down the stream.

Ahead, close to the left bank, was a big log. Nick saw it was hollow; pointing up river the current entered it smoothly, only a little ripple spread each side of the log. The water was deepening. The top of the hollow log was gray and dry. It was partly in the shadow.

Nick took the cork out of the grasshopper bottle and a hopper clung to it. He picked him off, hooked him and tossed him out. He held the rod far out so that the hopper on the water moved into the current flowing into the hollow log. Nick lowered the rod and the hopper floated in. There was a heavy strike. Nick swung the rod against the pull. It felt as though he were hooked into the log itself, except for the live feeling.

He tried to force the fish out into the current. It came, heavily.

The line went slack and Nick thought the trout was gone. Then he saw him, very near, in the current, shaking his head, trying to get the hook out. His mouth was clamped shut. He was fighting the hook in the clear flowing current.

Looping in the line with his left hand, Nick swung the rod to make the line taut and tried to lead the trout toward the net, but he was gone, out of sight, the line pumping. Nick fought him against the current, letting him thump in the water against the spring of the rod. He shifted the rod to his left hand, worked the trout upstream, holding his weight, fighting on the rod, and then let him down into the net. He lifted him clear of the water, a heavy half circle in the net, the net dripping, unhooked him and slid him into the sack.

He spread the mouth of the sack and looked down in at the two big trout alive in the water.

Through the deepening water, Nick waded over to the hollow log. He took the sack off, over his head, the trout flopping as it came out of water, and hung it so the trout were deep in the water. Then he pulled himself up on the log and sat, the water from his trouser and boots running down into the stream. He laid his rod down, moved along to the shady end of the log and took the sandwiches out of his pocket. He dipped the sandwiches in the cold water. The current carried away the crumbs. He ate the sandwiches and dipped his hat full of water to drink, the water running out through his hat just ahead of his drinking.

It was cool in the shade, sitting on the log. He took a cigarette out and struck a match to light it. The match sunk into the gray wood, making a tiny furrow. Nick leaned over the side of the log, found a hard place and lit the match. He sat smoking and watching the river.

Ahead the river narrowed and went into a swamp. The river became smooth and deep and the swamp looked solid with cedar trees, their trunks close together, their branches solid. It would not be possible to walk through a swamp like that. The branches grew so low. You would have to keep almost level with the ground to move at all. You could not crash through the branches. That must be why the animals that lived in swamps were built the way they were, Nick thought.

He wished he had brought something to read. He felt like reading. He did not feel like going on into the swamp. He looked down the river. A big cedar slanted all the way across the stream. Beyond that the river went into the swamp.

Nick did not want to go in there now. He felt a reaction against deep wading with the water deepening up under his armpits, to hook big trout in places impossible to land them. In the swamp the banks were bare, the big cedars came together overhead, the sun did not come through, except in patches; in the fast deep water, in the half light, the fishing would be tragic. In the swamp fishing was a tragic adventure. Nick did not want it. He did not want to go down the stream any further today.

He took out his knife, opened it and stuck it in the log. Then he pulled up the sack, reached into it and brought out one of the trout. Holding him near the tail, hard to hold, alive, in his hand, he whacked him against the log. The trout quivered, rigid. Nick laid him on the log in the shade and broke the neck of the other fish the same way. He laid them side by side on the log. They were fine trout.

Nick cleaned them, slitting them from the vent to the tip of the jaw. All the insides and the gills and tongue came out in one piece. They were both males; long gray-white strips of milt, smooth and clean. All the insides clean and compact, coming out all together. Nick tossed the offal ashore for the minks to find.

He washed the trout in the stream. When he held them back up in the water they looked like live fish. Their color was not gone yet. He washed his hands and dried them on the log. Then he laid the trout on the sack spread out on the log, rolled them up in it, tied the bundle and put it in the landing net. His knife was still standing, blade stuck in the log. He cleaned it on the wood and put it in his pocket.

Nick stood up on the log, holding his rod, the landing

net hanging heavy, then stepped into the water and splashed ashore. He climbed the bank and cut up into the woods, toward the high ground. He was going back to camp. He looked back. The river just showed through the trees. There were plenty of days coming when he could fish the swamp.

E. M. FORSTER

THE ROAD FROM COLONUS

I

FOR NO VERY intelligible reason, Mr. Lucas had hurried ahead of his party. He was perhaps reaching the age at which independence becomes valuable, because it is so soon to be lost. Tired of attention and consideration, he liked breaking away from the younger members, to ride by himself and to dismount unassisted. Perhaps he also relished that more subtle pleasure of being kept waiting for lunch, and of telling the others on their arrival that it was of no consequence.

So, with childish impatience, he battered the animal's sides with his heels, and made the muleteer bang it with a thick stick and prick it with a sharp one, and jolted down the hillsides through clumps of flowering shrubs and stretches of anemones and asphodel, till he heard the sound of running water, and came in sight of the group of plane trees where they were to have their meal.

Even in England those trees would have been remarkable, so huge were they, so interlaced, so magnificently clothed in quivering green. And here in Greece they were unique, the one cool spot in that hard brilliant landscape, already scorched by the heat of an April sun. In their midst was hidden a tiny Khan or country inn, a frail mud building with a broad wooden balcony in which sat an old woman spinning, while a small brown pig, eating orange peel, stood beside her. On the wet earth below squatted two children, playing some primaeval game with their fingers; and their mother, none too clean either, was messing with some rice inside. As Mrs. Forman would have said, it was all very Greek, and the fastidious Mr. Lucas felt thankful that they were bringing their own food with them and should eat it in the open air.

Still, he was glad to be there – the muleteer had helped him off – and glad that Mrs. Forman was not there to forestall his opinions – glad even that he should not see Ethel for quite half an hour. Ethel was his youngest daughter, still unmarried. She was unselfish and affectionate, and it was generally understood that she was to devote her life to her father and be the comfort of his old age. Mrs. Forman always referred to her as Antigone, and Mr. Lucas tried to settle down to the role of Oedipus, which seemed the only one that public opinion allowed him.

He had this in common with Oedipus, that he was growing old. Even to himself it had become obvious. He had lost interest in other people's affairs, and seldom attended when they spoke to him. He was fond of talking himself but often forgot what he was going to say, and even when he succeeded, it seldom seemed worth the effort. His phrases and gestures had become stiff and set, his anecdotes, once so successful, fell flat, his silence was as meaningless as his speech. Yet he had led a healthy, active life, had worked steadily, made money, educated his children. There was nothing and no one to blame: he was simply growing old.

At the present moment, here he was in Greece, and one of the dreams of his life was realized. Forty years ago he had caught the fever of Hellenism, and all his life he had felt that could he but visit that land, he would not have lived in vain. But Athens had been dusty, Delphi wet, Thermopylae flat, and he had listened with amazement and cynicism to the rapturous exclamations of his companions. Greece was like

England: it was a man who was growing old, and it made no difference whether that man looked at the Thames or the Eurotas. It was his last hope of contradicting that logic of experience, and it was failing.

Yet Greece had done something for him, though he did not know it. It had made him discontented, and there are stirrings of life in discontent. He knew that he was not the victim of continual ill-luck. Something great was wrong, and he was pitted against no mediocre or accidental enemy. For the last month a strange desire had possessed him to die fighting.

"Greece is the land for young people," he said to himself as he stood under the plane trees, "but I will enter into it, I will possess it. Leaves shall be green again, water shall be sweet, the sky shall be blue. They were so forty years ago, and I will win them back. I do mind being old, and I will pretend no longer."

He took two steps forward, and immediately cold waters were gurgling over his ankle.

"Where does the water come from?" he asked himself. "I do not even know that." He remembered that all the hillsides were dry; yet here the road was suddenly covered with flowing streams.

He stopped still in amazement saying: "Water out of a tree – out of a hollow tree? I never saw nor thought of that before."

For the enormous plane that leant towards the Khan was hollow – it had been burnt out for charcoal – and from its living trunk there gushed an impetuous spring, coating the bark with fern and moss, and flowing over the mule track to create fertile meadows beyond. The simple country folk had paid to beauty and mystery such tribute as they could, for in the rind of the tree a shrine was cut, holding a lamp and a little picture of the Virgin, inheritor of the Naiad's and Dryad's joint abode.

"I never saw anything so marvellous before," said Mr. Lucas. "I could even step inside the trunk and see where the water comes from."

For a moment he hesitated to violate the shrine. Then he remembered with a smile his own thought – "the place shall be mine; I will enter it and possess it" – and leapt almost aggressively on to a stone within.

The water pressed up steadily and noiselessly from the hollow roots and hidden crevices of the plane, forming a wonderful amber pool ere it spilt over the lip of bark on to the earth outside. Mr. Lucas tasted it and it was sweet, and when he looked up the black funnel of the trunk he saw sky which was blue, and some leaves which were green; and he remembered, without smiling, another of his thoughts.

Others had been before him – indeed he had a curious sense of companionship. Little votive offerings to the presiding Power were fastened on to the bark – tiny arms and legs and eyes in tin, grotesque models of the brain or the heart – all tokens of some recovery of strength or wisdom or love. There was no such thing as the solitude of nature, for the sorrows and joys of humanity had pressed even into the bosom of a tree. He spread out his arms and steadied himself against the soft charred wood, and then slowly leant back, till his body was resting on the trunk behind. His eyes closed, and he had the strange feeling of one who is moving, yet at peace – the feeling of the swimmer, who, after long struggling with chopping seas, finds that after all the tide will sweep him to his goal.

So he lay motionless, conscious only of the stream below his feet, and that all things were a stream, in which he was moving.

He was aroused at last by a shock – the shock of an arrival perhaps, for when he opened his eyes, something unimagined, indefinable, had passed over all things, and made them intelligible and good.

There was meaning in the stoop of the old woman over her work, and in the quick motions of the little pig, and in her diminishing globe of wool. A young man came singing over the streams on a mule, and there was beauty in his pose and sincerity in his greeting. The sun made no accidental patterns upon the spreading roots of the trees, and there was intention in the nodding clumps of asphodel, and in the music of the water. To Mr. Lucas, who, in a brief space of time, had discovered not only Greece, but England and all the world and life, there seemed nothing ludicrous in the desire to hang within the tree another votive offering – a little model of an entire man.

"Why, here's papa, playing at being Merlin."

All unnoticed they had arrived – Ethel, Mrs. Forman, Mr. Graham, and the English-speaking dragoman. Mr. Lucas peered out at them suspiciously. They had suddenly become unfamiliar, and all that they did seemed strained and coarse.

"Allow me to give you a hand," said Mr. Graham, a young man who was always polite to his elders.

Mr. Lucas felt annoyed. "Thank you, I can manage, perfectly well by myself," he replied. His foot slipped as he stepped out of the tree, and went into the spring.

"Oh papa, my papa!" said Ethel, "what are you doing? Thank goodness I have got a change for you on the mule."

She tended him carefully, giving him clean socks and dry boots, and then sat him down on the rug beside the lunch basket, while she went with the others to explore the grove.

They came back in ecstasies, in which Mr. Lucas tried to join. But he found them intolerable. Their enthusiasm was superficial, commonplace, and spasmodic. They had no perception of the coherent beauty that was flowering around them. He tried at least to explain his feelings, and what he said was:

"I am altogether pleased with the appearance of this place. It impresses me very favourably. The trees are fine, remarkably fine for Greece, and there is something very poetic in the spring of clear running water. The people too seem kindly and civil. It is decidedly an attractive place."

Mrs. Forman upbraided him for his tepid praise.

"Oh, it is a place in a thousand!" she cried. "I could live and die here! I really would stop if I had not to be back at Athens! It reminds me of the Colonus of Sophocles."

"Well, *I* must stop," said Ethel. "I positively must."

"Yes, do! You and your father! Antigone and Oedipus. Of course you must stop at Colonus!"

Mr. Lucas was almost breathless with excitement. When he stood within the tree, he had believed that his happiness would be independent of locality. But these few minutes' conversation had undeceived him. He no longer trusted himself to journey through the world, for old thoughts, old wearinesses might be waiting to rejoin him as soon as he left the shade of the planes and the music of the virgin water. To sleep in the Khan with the gracious, kind-eyed country people, to watch the bats flit about within the globe of shade, and see the moon turn the golden patterns into silver – one such night would place him beyond relapse, and confirm him for ever in the kingdom he had regained. But all his lips could say was: "I should be willing to put in a night here."

"You mean a week, papa! It would be sacrilege to put in less."

"A week then, a week," said his lips, irritated at being corrected, while his heart was leaping with joy. All through lunch he spoke to them no more, but watched the place he should know so well, and the people who would so soon be his companions and friends. The inmates of the Khan only consisted of an old woman, a middle-aged woman, a young man and two children, and to none of them had he spoken, yet he loved them as he loved everything that moved or breathed or existed beneath the benedictory shade of the planes.

"*En route!*" said the shrill voice of Mrs. Forman. "Ethel! Mr. Graham! The best of things must end."

"To-night," thought Mr. Lucas, "they will light the little lamp by the shrine. And when we all sit together on the balcony, perhaps they will tell me which offerings they put up."

"I beg your pardon, Mr. Lucas," said Graham, "but they want to fold up the rug you are sitting on."

Mr. Lucas got up, saying to himself: "Ethel shall go to bed first, and then I will try to tell them about my offering too – for it is a thing I must do. I think they will understand if I am left with them alone."

Ethel touched him on the cheek. "Papa! I've called you three times. All the mules are here."

"Mules? What mules?"

"Our mules. We're all waiting. Oh, Mr. Graham, do help my father on."

"I don't know what you're talking about, Ethel."

"My dearest papa, we must start. You know we have to get to Olympia to-night."

Mr. Lucas in pompous, confident tones replied: "I always did wish, Ethel, that you had a better head for plans. You know perfectly well that we are putting in a week here. It is your own suggestion."

Ethel was startled into impoliteness. "What a perfectly

ridiculous idea. You must have known I was joking. Of course I meant I wished we could."

"Ah! if we could only do what we wished!" sighed Mrs. Forman, already seated on her mule.

"Surely," Ethel continued in calmer tones, "you didn't think I meant it."

"Most certainly I did. I have made all my plans on the supposition that we are stopping here, and it will be extremely inconvenient, indeed, impossible for me to start."

He delivered this remark with an air of great conviction, and Mrs. Forman and Mr. Graham had to turn away to hide their smiles.

"I am sorry I spoke so carelessly; it was wrong of me. But, you know, we can't break up our party, and even one night here would make us miss the boat at Patras."

Mrs. Forman, in an aside, called Mr. Graham's attention to the excellent way in which Ethel managed her father.

"I don't mind about the Patras boat. You said that we should stop here, and we are stopping."

It seemed as if the inhabitants of the Khan had divined in some mysterious way that the altercation touched them. The old woman stopped her spinning, while the young man and the two children stood behind Mr. Lucas, as if supporting him.

Neither arguments nor entreaties moved him. He said little, but he was absolutely determined, because for the first time he saw his daily life aright. What need had he to return to England? Who would miss him? His friends were dead or cold. Ethel loved him in a way, but, as was right, she had other interests. His other children he seldom saw. He had only one other relative, his sister Julia, whom he both feared and hated. It was no effort to struggle. He would be a fool as well as a coward if he stirred from the place which brought him happiness and peace.

At last Ethel, to humour him, and not disinclined to air her modern Greek, went into the Khan with the astonished dragoman to look at the rooms. The woman inside received them with loud welcomes, and the young man, when no one was looking, began to lead Mr. Lucas' mule to the stable.

"Drop it, you brigand!" shouted Graham, who always declared that foreigners could understand English if they chose. He was right, for the man obeyed, and they all stood waiting for Ethel's return.

She emerged at last, with close-gathered skirts, followed by the dragoman bearing the little pig, which he had bought at a bargain.

"My dear papa, I will do all I can for you, but stop in that Khan – no."

"Are there – fleas?" asked Mrs. Forman.

Ethel intimated that "fleas" was not the word.

"Well, I am afraid that settles it," said Mrs. Forman, "I know how particular Mr. Lucas is."

"It does not settle it," said Mr. Lucas. "Ethel, you go on. I do not want you. I don't know why I ever consulted you. I shall stop here alone."

"That is absolute nonsense," said Ethel, losing her temper. "How can you be left alone at your age? How would you get your meals or your bath? All your letters are waiting for you at Patras. You'll miss the boat. That means missing the London operas, and upsetting all your engagements for the month. And as if you could travel by yourself!"

"They might knife you," was Mr. Graham's contribution.

The Greeks said nothing; but whenever Mr. Lucas looked their way, they beckoned him towards the Khan. The children would even have drawn him by the coat, and the old woman on the balcony stopped her almost completed spinning, and fixed him with mysterious appealing eyes. As he fought, the issue assumed gigantic proportions, and he believed that he was not merely stopping because he had regained youth or seen beauty or found happiness, but because in that place and with those people a supreme event was awaiting him which would transfigure the face of the world. The moment was so tremendous that he abandoned words and arguments as useless, and rested on the strength of his mighty unrevealed allies: silent men, murmuring water, and whispering trees. For the whole place called with one voice, articulate to him, and his garrulous opponents became every minute more meaningless and absurd. Soon they would be tired and go chattering away into the sun, leaving him to the cool grove and the moonlight and the destiny he foresaw.

Mrs. Forman and the dragoman had indeed already started, amid the piercing screams of the little pig, and the struggle might have gone on indefinitely if Ethel had not called in Mr. Graham.

"Can you help me?" she whispered. "He is absolutely unmanageable."

"I'm no good at arguing – but if I could help you in any other way—" and he looked down complacently at his well-made figure.

Ethel hesitated. Then she said: "Help me in any way you can. After all, it is for his good that we do it."

"Then have his mule led up behind him."

So when Mr. Lucas thought he had gained the day, he suddenly felt himself lifted off the ground, and sat sideways on the saddle, and at the same time the mule started off at a trot. He said nothing, for he had nothing to say, and even his face showed little emotion as he felt the shade pass and heard the sound of the water cease. Mr. Graham was running at his side, hat in hand, apologizing.

"I know I had no business to do it, and I do beg your pardon awfully. But I do hope that some day you too will feel that I was – damn!"

A stone had caught him in the middle of the back. It was thrown by the little boy, who was pursuing them along the mule track. He was followed by his sister, also throwing stones.

Ethel screamed to the dragoman, who was some way ahead with Mrs. Forman, but before he could rejoin them, another adversary appeared. It was the young Greek, who had cut them off in front, and now dashed down at Mr. Lucas' bridle. Fortunately Graham was an expert boxer, and it did not take him a moment to beat down the youth's feeble defence, and to send him sprawling with a bleeding mouth into the asphodel. By this time the dragoman had arrived, the children, alarmed at the fate of their brother, had desisted, and the rescue party, if such it is to be considered, retired in disorder to the trees.

"Little devils!" said Graham, laughing with triumph. "That's the modern Greek all over. Your father meant money if he stopped, and they consider we were taking it out of their pocket."

"Oh, they are terrible – simple savages! I don't know how I shall ever thank you. You've saved my father."

"I only hope you didn't think me brutal."

"No," replied Ethel with a little sigh. "I admire strength."

Meanwhile the cavalcade re-formed, and Mr. Lucas, who, as Mrs. Forman said, bore his disappointment wonderfully well, was put comfortably on to his mule. They hurried up the opposite hillside, fearful of another attack, and it was not until they had left the eventful place far behind that

Ethel found an opportunity to speak to her father and ask his pardon for the way she had treated him.

"You seemed so different, dear father, and you quite frightened me. Now I feel that you are your old self again."

He did not answer, and she concluded that he was not unnaturally offended at her behaviour.

By one of those curious tricks of mountain scenery, the place they had left an hour before suddenly reappeared far below them. The Khan was hidden under the green dome, but in the open there still stood three figures, and through the pure air rose up a faint cry of defiance or farewell.

Mr. Lucas stopped irresolutely, and let the reins fall from his hand.

"Come, father dear," said Ethel gently.

He obeyed, and in another moment a spur of the hill hid the dangerous scene for ever.

II

IT WAS BREAKFAST time, but the gas was alight, owing to the fog. Mr. Lucas was in the middle of an account of a bad night he had spent. Ethel, who was to be married in a few weeks, had her arms on the table, listening.

"First the door bell rang, then you came back from the theatre. Then the dog started, and after the dog the cat. And at three in the morning a young hooligan passed by singing. Oh yes: then there was the water gurgling in the pipe above my head."

"I think that was only the bath water running away," said Ethel, looking rather worn.

"Well, there's nothing I dislike more than running water. It's perfectly impossible to sleep in the house. I shall give it up. I shall give notice next quarter. I shall tell the landlord plainly, 'The reason I am giving up the house is this: it is perfectly impossible to sleep in it.' If he says – says – well, what has he got to say?"

"Some more toast, father?"

"Thank you, my dear." He took it, and there was an interval of peace.

But he soon recommenced. "I'm not going to submit to the practising next door as tamely as they think. I wrote and told them so – didn't I?"

"Yes," said Ethel, who had taken care that the letter should not reach. "I have seen the governess, and she has promised to arrange it differently. And Aunt Julia hates noise. It will sure to be all right."

Her aunt, being the only unattached member of the family, was coming to keep house for her father when she left him. The reference was not a happy one, and Mr. Lucas commenced a series of half articulate sighs, which was only stopped by the arrival of the post.

"Oh, what a parcel!" cried Ethel. "For me! What can it be! Greek stamps. This is most exciting!"

It proved to be some asphodel bulbs, sent by Mrs. Forman from Athens for planting in the conservatory.

"Doesn't it bring it all back! You remember the asphodels, father. And all wrapped up in Greek newspapers. I wonder if I can read them still. I used to be able to, you know."

She rattled on, hoping to conceal the laughter of the children next door – a favourite source of querulousness at breakfast time.

"Listen to me! 'A rural disaster.' Oh, I've hit on something sad. But never mind. 'Last Tuesday at Plataniste, in the province of Messenia, a shocking tragedy occurred. A large tree' – aren't I getting on well? – 'blew down in the night and' – wait a minute – oh dear! 'crushed to death the five occupants of the little Khan there, who had apparently been sitting in the balcony. The bodies of Maria Rhomaides, the aged proprietress, and of her daughter, aged forty-six, were easily recognizable, whereas that of her grandson' – oh, the rest is really too horrid; I wish I had never tried it, and what's more I feel to have heard the name Plataniste before. We didn't stop there, did we, in the spring?"

"We had lunch," said Mr. Lucas, with a faint expression of trouble on his vacant face. "Perhaps it was where the dragoman bought the pig."

"Of course," said Ethel in a nervous voice. "Where the dragoman bought the little pig. How terrible!"

"Very terrible!" said her father, whose attention was wandering to the noisy children next door. Ethel suddenly started to her feet with genuine interest.

"Good gracious!" she exclaimed. "This is an old paper. It happened not lately but in April – the night of Tuesday the eighteenth – and we – we must have been there in the afternoon."

"So we were," said Mr. Lucas. She put her hand to her heart, scarcely able to speak.

"Father, dear father, I must say it: you wanted to stop there. All those people, those poor half savage people, tried to keep you, and they're dead. The whole place, it says, is in ruins, and even the stream has changed its course. Father dear, if it had not been for me, and if Arthur had not helped me, you must have been killed."

Mr. Lucas waved his hand irritably. "It is not a bit of good speaking to the governess, I shall write to the landlord and say, 'The reason I am giving up the house is this: the dog barks, the children next door are intolerable, and I cannot stand the noise of running water.' "

Ethel did not check his babbling. She was aghast at the narrowness of the escape, and for a long time kept silence. At last she said: "Such a marvellous deliverance does make one believe in Providence."

Mr. Lucas, who was still composing his letter to the landlord, did not reply.

ALICE MUNRO

THE FOUND BOAT

AT THE END of Bell Street, McKay Street, Mayo Street, there was the Flood. It was the Wawanash River, which every spring overflowed its banks. Some springs, say one in every five, it covered the roads on that side of town and washed over the fields, creating a shallow choppy lake. Light reflected off the water made everything bright and cold, as it is in a lakeside town, and woke or revived in people certain vague hopes of disaster. Mostly during the late afternoon and early evening, there were people straggling out to look at it, and discuss whether it was still rising, and whether this time it might invade the town. In general, those under fifteen and over sixty-five were most certain that it would.

Eva and Carol rode out on their bicycles. They left the road – it was the end of Mayo Street, past any houses – and rode right into a field, over a wire fence entirely flattened by the weight of the winter's snow. They coasted a little way before the long grass stopped them, then left their bicycles lying down and went to the water.

"We have to find a log and ride on it," Eva said.

"Jesus, we'll freeze our legs off."

"Jesus, we'll freeze our legs off!" said one of the boys who were there too at the water's edge. He spoke in a sour whine, the way boys imitated girls although it was nothing like the way girls talked. These boys – there were three of them were all in the same class as Eva and Carol at school and were known to them by name (their names being Frank,

Bud and Clayton), but Eva and Carol, who had seen and recognized them from the road, had not spoken to them or looked at them or, even yet, given any sign of knowing they were there. The boys seemed to be trying to make a raft, from lumber they had salvaged from the water.

Eva and Carol took off their shoes and socks and waded in. The water was so cold it sent pain up their legs, like blue electric sparks shooting through their veins, but they went on, pulling their skirts high, tight behind and bunched so they could hold them in front.

"Look at the fat-assed ducks in wading."

"Fat-assed fucks."

Eva and Carol, of course, gave no sign of hearing this. They laid hold of a log and climbed on, taking a couple of boards floating in the water for paddles. There were always things floating around in the Flood – branches, fence-rails, logs, road signs, old lumber; sometimes boilers, washtubs, pots and pans, or even a car seat or stuffed chair, as if somewhere the Flood had got into a dump.

They paddled away from shore, heading out into the cold lake. The water was perfectly clear, they could see the brown grass swimming along the bottom. Suppose it was the sea, thought Eva. She thought of drowned cities and countries. Atlantis. Suppose they were riding in a Viking boat – Viking boats on the Atlantic were more frail and narrow than this log on the Flood – and they had miles of clear sea beneath them, then a spired city, intact as a jewel irretrievable on the ocean floor.

"This is a Viking boat," she said. "I am the carving on the front." She stuck her chest out and stretched her neck, trying to make a curve, and she made a face, putting out her tongue. Then she turned and for the first time took notice of the boys.

“Hey, you sucks!” she yelled at them. “You’d be scared to come out here, this water is ten feet deep!”

“Liar,” they answered without interest, and she was.

They steered the log around a row of trees, avoiding floating barbed wire, and got into a little bay created by a natural hollow of the land. Where the bay was now, there would be a pond full of frogs later in the spring, and by the middle of summer there would be no water visible at all, just a low tangle of reeds and bushes, green, to show that mud was still wet around their roots. Larger bushes, willows, grew around the steep bank of this pond and were still partly out of the water. Eva and Carol let the log ride in. They saw a place where something was caught.

It was a boat, or part of one. An old rowboat with most of one side ripped out, the board that had been the seat just dangling. It was pushed up among the branches, lying on what would have been its side, if it had a side, the prow caught high.

Their idea came to them without consultation, at the same time:

“You guys! Hey, you guys!”

“We found you a boat!”

“Stop building your stupid raft and come and look at the boat!”

What surprised them in the first place was that the boys really did come, scrambling overland, half running, half sliding down the bank, wanting to see.

“Hey, where?”

“Where is it, I don’t see no boat.”

What surprised them in the second place was that when the boys did actually see what boat was meant, this old flood-smashed wreck held up in the branches, they did not understand that they had been fooled, that a joke had been played on them. They did not show a moment's disappointment, but seemed as pleased at the discovery as if the boat had been whole and new. They were already barefoot, because they had been wading in the water to get lumber, and they waded in here without a stop, surrounding the boat and appraising it and paying no attention even of an insulting kind to Eva and Carol who bobbed up and down on their log. Eva and Carol had to call to them.

"How do you think you're going to get it off?"

"It won't float anyway."

"What makes you think it will float?"

"It'll sink. Glub-blub-blub, you'll all be drownded."

The boys did not answer, because they were too busy walking around the boat, pulling at it in a testing way to see how it could be got off with the least possible damage. Frank, who was the most literate, talkative and inept of the three, began referring to the boat as *she*, an affectation which Eva and Carol acknowledged with fish-mouths of contempt.

"She's caught two places. You got to be careful not to tear a hole in her bottom. She's heavier than you'd think."

It was Clayton who climbed up and freed the boat, and Bud, a tall fat boy, who got the weight of it on his back to turn it into the water so that they could half float, half carry it to shore. All this took some time. Eva and Carol abandoned their log and waded out of the water. They walked overland to get their shoes and socks and bicycles. They did not need to come back this way but they came. They stood at the top of the hill, leaning on their bicycles. They did not go on home, but they did not sit down and frankly watch, either. They stood more or less facing each other, but glancing down at the water and at the boys struggling with the boat, as if they had just halted for a moment out of curiosity, and staying longer than they intended, to see what came of this unpromising project.

About nine o'clock, or when it was nearly dark – dark to people inside the houses, but not quite dark outside – they all returned to town, going along Mayo Street in a sort of procession. Frank and Bud and Clayton came carrying the boat, upside-down, and Eva and Carol walked behind, wheeling their bicycles. The boys' heads were almost hidden in the darkness of the overturned boat, with its smell of soaked wood, cold swampy water. The girls could look ahead and see the street lights in their tin reflectors, a necklace of lights climbing Mayo Street, reaching all the way up to the stand-pipe. They turned onto Burns Street heading for Clayton's house, the nearest house belonging to any of them. This was not the way home for Eva or for Carol either, but they followed along. The boys were perhaps too busy carrying the boat to tell them to go away. Some younger children were still out playing, playing hopscotch on the sidewalk though they could hardly see. At this time of year the bare sidewalk was still such a novelty and delight. These children cleared out of the way and watched the boat go by with unwilling respect; they shouted questions after it, wanting to know where it came from and what was going to be done with it. No one answered them. Eva and Carol as well as the boys refused to answer or even look at them.

The five of them entered Clayton's yard. The boys shifted weight, as if they were going to put the boat down.

"You better take it round to the back where nobody can see it," Carol said. That was the first thing any of them had said since they came into town.

The boys said nothing but went on, following a mud path between Clayton's house and a leaning board fence. They let the boat down in the back yard.

"It's a stolen boat, you know," said Eva, mainly for the effect. "It must've belonged to somebody. You stole it."

"You was the ones who stole it then," Bud said, short of breath. "It was you seen it first."

"It was you took it."

"It was all of us then. If one of us gets in trouble then all of us does."

"Are you going to tell anybody on them?" said Carol as she and Eva rode home, along the streets which were dark between the lights now and potholed from winter.

"It's up to you. I won't if you won't."

"I won't if you won't."

They rode in silence, relinquishing something, but not discontented.

The board fence in Clayton's back yard had every so often a post which supported it, or tried to, and it was on these posts that Eva and Carol spent several evenings sitting, jauntily but not very comfortably. Or else they just leaned against the fence while the boys worked on the boat. During the first couple of evenings neighborhood children attracted by the sound of hammering tried to get into the yard to see what was going on, but Eva and Carol blocked their way.

"Who said you could come in here?"

"Just us can come in this yard."

These evenings were getting longer, the air milder. Skipping was starting on the sidewalks. Further along the street there was a row of hard maples that had been tapped. Children drank the sap as fast as it could drip into the buckets. The old man and woman who owned the trees, and who hoped to make syrup, came running out of the house making noises as if they were trying to scare away crows. Finally, every spring, the old man would come out on his porch and fire his shotgun into the air, and then the thieving would stop.

None of those working on the boat bothered about stealing sap, though all had done so last year.

The lumber to repair the boat was picked up here and there, along back lanes. At this time of year things were lying around – old boards and branches, sodden mitts, spoons flung out with the dishwater, lids of pudding pots that had been set in the snow to cool, all the debris that can sift through and survive winter. The tools came from Clayton's cellar – left over, presumably, from the time when his father was alive – and though they had nobody to advise them the boys seemed to figure out more or less the manner in which boats are built, or rebuilt. Frank was the one who showed up with diagrams from books and *Popular Mechanics* magazines. Clayton looked at these diagrams and listened to Frank read the instructions and then went ahead and decided in his own way what was to be done. Bud was best at sawing. Eva and Carol watched everything from the fence and offered criticism and thought up names. The names for the boat that they thought of were: Water Lily, Sea Horse, Flood Queen, and Caro-Eve, after them because they had found it. The boys did not say which, if any, of these names they found satisfactory.

The boat had to be tarred. Clayton heated up a pot of tar on the kitchen stove and brought it out and painted slowly, his thorough way, sitting astride the overturned boat. The other boys were sawing a board to make a new seat. As Clayton worked, the tar cooled and thickened so that finally he could not move the brush any more. He turned to Eva and held out the pot and said, "You can go in and heat this on the stove."

Eva took the pot and went up the back steps. The kitchen

seemed black after outside, but it must be light enough to see in, because there was Clayton's mother standing at the ironing board, ironing. She did that for a living, took in wash and ironing.

"Please may I put the tar pot on the stove?" said Eva, who had been brought up to talk politely to parents, even wash-and-iron ladies, and who for some reason especially wanted to make a good impression on Clayton's mother.

"You'll have to poke up the fire then," said Clayton's mother, as if she doubted whether Eva would know how to do that. But Eva could see now, and she picked up the lid with the stove-lifter, and took the poker and poked up a flame. She stirred the tar as it softened. She felt privileged. Then and later. Before she went to sleep a picture of Clayton came to her mind; she saw him sitting astride the boat, tar-painting, with such concentration, delicacy, absorption. She thought of him speaking to her, out of his isolation, in such an ordinary peaceful taking-for-granted voice.

On the twenty-fourth of May, a school holiday in the middle of the week, the boat was carried out of town, a long way now, off the road over fields and fences that had been repaired, to where the river flowed between its normal banks. Eva and Carol, as well as the boys, took turns carrying it. It was launched in the water from a cow-trampled spot between willow bushes that were fresh out in leaf. The boys went first. They yelled with triumph when the boat did float, when it rode amazingly down the river current. The boat was painted black, and green inside, with yellow seats, and a strip of yellow all the way around the outside. There was no name on it, after all. The boys could not imagine that it needed any name to keep it separate from the other boats in the world.

Eva and Carol ran along the bank, carrying bags full of peanut butter-and-jam sandwiches, pickles, bananas, chocolate cake, potato chips, graham crackers stuck together with corn syrup and five bottles of pop to be cooled in the river water. The bottles bumped against their legs. They yelled for a turn.

"If they don't let us they're bastards," Carol said, and they yelled together, "We found it! We found it!"

The boys did not answer, but after a while they brought the boat in, and Carol and Eva came crashing, panting down the bank.

"Does it leak?"

"It don't leak yet."

"We forgot a bailing can," wailed Carol, but nevertheless she got in, with Eva, and Frank pushed them off, crying, "Here's to a Watery Grave!"

And the thing about being in a boat was that it was not solidly bobbing, like a log, but was cupped in the water, so that riding in it was not like being on something in the water, but like being in the water itself. Soon they were all going out in the boat in mixed-up turns, two boys and a girl, two girls and a boy, a girl and a boy, until things were so confused it was impossible to tell whose turn came next, and nobody cared anyway. They went down the river – those who weren't riding, running along the bank to keep up. They passed under two bridges, one iron, one cement. Once they saw a big carp just resting, it seemed to smile at them, in the bridge-shaded water. They did not know how far they had gone on the river, but things had changed – the water had got shallower, and the land flatter. Across an open field they saw a building that looked like a house, abandoned. They dragged the boat up on the bank and tied it and set out across the field.

"That's the old station," Frank said. "That's Pedder Station." The others had heard this name but he was the one who knew, because his father was the station agent in town. He said that this was a station on a branch line that had been torn up, and that there had been a sawmill here, but a long time ago.

Inside the station it was dark, cool. All the windows were broken. Glass lay in shards and in fairly big pieces on the floor. They walked around finding the larger pieces of glass and tramping on them, smashing them, it was like cracking ice on puddles. Some partitions were still in place, you could see where the ticket window had been. There was a bench lying on its side. People had been here, it looked as if people came here all the time, though it was so far from anywhere. Beer bottles and pop bottles were lying around, also cigarette packages, gum and candy wrappers, the paper from a loaf of bread. The walls were covered with dim and fresh pencil and chalk writings and carved with knives.

I LOVE RONNIE COLES
I WANT TO FUCK
KILROY WAS HERE
RONNIE COLES IS AN ASS-HOLE
WHAT ARE YOU DOING HERE?
WAITING FOR A TRAIN
DAWNA MARY-LOU BARBARA JOANNE

It was exciting to be inside this large, dark, empty place, with the loud noise of breaking glass and their voices ringing back from the underside of the roof. They tipped the old beer bottles against their mouths. That reminded them that they were hungry and thirsty and they cleared a place in the middle of the floor and sat down and ate the lunch. They drank the pop just as it was, lukewarm. They ate everything there was and licked the smears of peanut butter and jam off the bread-paper in which the sandwiches had been wrapped.

They played Truth or Dare.

"I dare you to write on the wall, I am a Stupid Ass, and sign your name."

"Tell the truth – what is the worst lie you ever told?"

"Did you ever wet the bed?"

"Did you ever dream you were walking down the street without any clothes on?"

"I dare you to go outside and pee on the railway sign."

It was Frank who had to do that. They could not see him, even his back, but they knew he did it, they heard the hissing sound of his pee. They all sat still, amazed, unable to think of what the next dare would be.

"I dare everybody," said Frank from the doorway, "I dare – Everybody."

"What?"

"Take off all our clothes."

Eva and Carol screamed.

"Anybody who won't do it has to walk – has to *crawl* – around this floor on their hands and knees."

They were all quiet, till Eva said, almost complacently, "What first?"

"Shoes and socks."

"Then we have to go outside, there's too much glass here."

They pulled off their shoes and socks in the doorway, in the sudden blinding sun. The field before them was bright as water. They ran across where the tracks used to go.

"That's enough, that's enough," said Carol. "Watch out for thistles!"

"Tops! Everybody take off their tops!"

"I won't! We won't, will we, Eva?"

But Eva was whirling round and round in the sun where the track used to be. "I don't care, I don't care! Truth or Dare! Truth or Dare!"

She unbuttoned her blouse as she whirled, as if she didn't know what her hand was doing, she flung it off.

Carol took off hers. "I wouldn't have done it, if you hadn't!"

"Bottoms!"

Nobody said a word this time, they all bent and stripped themselves. Eva, naked first, started running across the field, and then all the others ran, all five of them running bare through the knee-high hot grass, running towards the river. Not caring now about being caught but in fact leaping and yelling to call attention to themselves, if there was anybody to hear or see. They felt as if they were going to jump off a cliff and fly. They felt that something was happening to them different from anything that had happened before, and it had to do with the boat, the water, the sunlight, the dark ruined station, and each other. They thought of each other now hardly as names or people, but as echoing shrieks, reflections, all bold and white and loud and scandalous, and as fast as arrows. They went running without a break into the cold water and when it came almost to the tops of their legs they fell on it and swam. It stopped their noise. Silence, amazement, came over them in a rush. They dipped and floated and separated, sleek as mink.

Eva stood up in the water her hair dripping, water running down her face. She was waist deep. She stood on smooth stones, her feet fairly wide apart, water flowing between her legs. About a yard away from her Clayton also stood up, and they were blinking the water out of their eyes, looking at each other. Eva did not turn or try to hide; she was quivering from the cold of the water, but also with pride, shame, boldness, and exhilaration.

Clayton shook his head violently, as if he wanted to bang something out of it, then bent over and took a mouthful of river water. He stood up with his cheeks full and made a tight hole of his mouth and shot the water at her as if it was coming out of a hose, hitting her exactly, first one breast and then the other. Water from his mouth ran down her body. He hooted to see it, a loud self-conscious sound that nobody would have expected, from him. The others looked up from wherever they were in the water and closed in to see.

Eva crouched down and slid into the water, letting her head go right under. She swam, and when she let her head out, downstream, Carol was coming after her and the boys were already on the bank, already running into the grass, showing their skinny backs, their white, flat buttocks. They were laughing and saying things to each other but she couldn't hear, for the water in her ears.

"What did he do?" said Carol.

"Nothing."

They crept in to shore. "Let's stay in the bushes till they go," said Eva. "I hate them anyway. I really do. Don't you hate them?"

"Sure," said Carol, and they waited, not very long, until they heard the boys still noisy and excited coming down to the place a bit upriver where they had left the boat. They heard them jump in and start rowing.

"They've got all the hard part, going back," said Eva, hugging herself and shivering violently. "Who cares? Anyway. It never was our boat."

"What if they tell?" said Carol.

"We'll say it's all a lie."

Eva hadn't thought of this solution until she said it, but

as soon as she did she felt almost light-hearted again. The ease and scornfulness of it did make them both giggle, and slapping themselves and splashing out of the water they set about developing one of those fits of laughter in which, as soon as one showed signs of exhaustion, the other would snort and start up again, and they would make helpless – soon genuinely helpless – faces at each other and bend over and grab themselves as if they had the worst pain.

DRAMA AND DANGER

GUY DE MAUPASSANT

ON THE WATER

Translated by Chloë Hughes

LAST SUMMER I rented a country cottage on the banks of the Seine, several leagues from Paris, and every evening I'd go out there to sleep. After a few days, I made the acquaintance of one of my neighbors, a man between thirty or forty, who was quite the oddest fellow I'd ever seen. He was a veteran boatman and was still fanatical about the river – always near the water, on the water, or in the water. He must have been born in a boat and will surely end his days boating.

One evening, as we were strolling along the banks of the Seine, I asked him to share some stories of his life on the water. My companion instantly came alive, his expression changed, he became eloquent – almost poetic. He held in his heart a great passion, a devouring, irresistible passion: the river.

Ah, he told me, so many memories have I about this river that you see flowing there beside us! You street folk know nothing about the river. But listen to a fisherman utter the word. To him it is the mysterious, the deep, the unknown; the land of mirages and phantasmagoria where, by night, one sees things that aren't there, hears noises one knows not, shudders without knowing why; like walking through a cemetery. And it is, in fact, the most sinister of all cemeteries, in which one has no tomb.

Land feels confining to the boatman, but on dark nights, when there is no moon, the river is limitless. A sailor does not feel the same about the sea. True, she is often tough and troublesome, but she cries and howls. She is honest, the great sea; whereas the river is silent and treacherous. It does not grumble, it flows without making a sound, and this eternal flow of the water is more terrifying to me than the great ocean waves.

Dreamers claim that the sea hides vast bluish kingdoms within her folds, where the dead roam amidst big fishes, strange forests, and crystal caves. The river has but black depths where one rots in the mire. And yet it is beautiful when it gleams in the light of the rising sun and gently laps the bankside covered with whispering reeds.

As the poet said, referring to the ocean,

O waves, you know such tragic tales
—dreaded by praying mothers—
You recite them while riding the tides
—your desperate voices rolling in—
As day turns into night.

My word, the stories whispered by the slender reeds in such gentle little voices are far more sinister than the mournful tragedies relayed by the howling waves. But since you have asked me for some of my recollections, I will tell you about a singular event that befell me in these parts some ten years ago.

I was living as I am today, at Mother Lafon's house, and one of my closest friends, Louis Bernet – who incidentally has now given up boating, his boat shoes, not to mention his disheveled appearance to work at the Supreme Court – was residing in the village of C. . ., a couple of leagues downriver. We always dined together, sometimes at his house and sometimes at mine.

One evening, I wearily rowed back home alone in my

big boat, a twelve-footer that I always used at night; and I paused near the reeds about two hundred meters from the railway bridge to catch my breath. It was a sublime moment; the moon was resplendent, the river gleamed, and the air was calm and gentle. The tranquility tempted me. I thought how pleasant it would be to smoke a pipe in this spot and I impulsively seized the anchor, casting it into the river.

The boat floated downstream with the current until the end of the anchor chain stopped. I sat down at the back of the vessel on my sheepskin, making myself as comfortable as possible. Not a single sound could be heard, only sometimes I sensed an almost imperceptible lapping at the water's edge and noticed taller clumps of reeds that assumed surprising shapes and appeared to move at times.

The water was perfectly still, but I was disturbed by the remarkable silence that encircled me. All the creatures, frogs and toads, the nocturnal serenaders of the marsh, were quiet. Suddenly, a frog croaked close by on my right. I shuddered, it stopped. I heard nothing more and decided to smoke a little in order to distract myself. Though I was known as a seasoned pipe smoker, I could not smoke. As soon as I took the second puff, my heart started racing and I gave up. I began to sing. The sound of my voice troubled me. So, I stretched out on the bottom boards and looked up at the heavens. For a short while I was at peace but, momentarily, the gentle sway of the water disturbed me; it seemed as though the vessel were lurching violently between the banks of the river striking one side then the other. At that point I thought an invisible being or force was enticing it out of the water and raising it up only to let it fall again. I was thrown around as if I were in a foul storm. Noises surrounded me. I leaped up.

The water glimmered and all was calm.

I realized that my nerves were a little shaken and resolved to set off. I pulled on the anchor chain. The boat started to move, then I felt a resistance. I pulled harder. Still the anchor would not come up. It was snagged on something at the bottom of the river and I could not free it. I began pulling again but it was useless. I used my oars to make the boat turn toward the current with the intention of shifting the position of the anchor. But it was in vain, it held fast. I lost my temper and shook the chain furiously. Nothing budged. Despondent, I sat down and reflected upon my situation. I could not fathom how to break this chain or detach it for it was enormous and riveted to a piece of wood as thick as my arm at the bow of the boat. But since the fine weather continued, I thought that it surely would not be long before some fisherman would come to my aid. My mishap had calmed me. I sat and could finally smoke my pipe. I had a bottle of rum, drank two or three glasses and was able to laugh at the situation. It was very warm, so, if need be, I could spend the night under the lovely stars with no harm done.

All of a sudden there was faint knock on the hull of the boat. I was startled and broke out in a cold sweat from head to toe. Indubitably, this noise was caused by some piece of wood carried in the current, but that was enough. Once again, I was gripped by a peculiar nervous agitation. I seized the chain, tensed my muscles and put forth a desperate effort. The anchor held firm. Exhausted, I sat down again.

Be that as it may, the waterway had gradually become enveloped by a thick white fog laying very close to the surface. When standing up I could no longer see the river, my feet or my boat. I could only make out the tips of the reeds, the land beyond which lay all pale in the moonlight, and the big black stains rising up in the sky that were cast by thickets of Italian poplars. I was buried to the waist in a remarkable white cotton blanket and visited by wild vagaries of the mind. I imagined that someone was trying to climb into my vessel that I could no longer discern, and that the river, hidden by the dense fog, was full of strange beings who were swimming all around me. I was experiencing horrible discomfort. A band was tightening around my temples, my heart was beating to the point of suffocation and, losing my wits, I thought of swimming to safety. But then again, the very idea made me shiver in terror. I saw myself lost, wandering aimlessly in this thick fog, struggling amidst grasses and reeds that I could not evade, groaning with fear, neither seeing the bank, nor retrieving my boat; and I had the feeling that I would be dragged by the feet to the very depths of this black water.

Indeed, I would have had to go upstream at least five hundred meters to find a spot free of bushes and rushes where I could set foot, and there was a nine out of ten chance that I wouldn't be able to find my way in this fog and would drown, no matter how well I could swim.

I tried to reason with myself. My will not to be afraid was strong, but there was something else within me besides my will, and that something else was scared. I asked myself what could be making me fearful. The brave *me* taunted the cowardly *me*. Never have I been as gripped by the rival personalities that exist within us as I was that day. One was willing and the other was resisting, each taking turns winning the battle.

The ridiculous, inexplicable fear grew and grew, turning itself into terror. I remained frozen, my eyes wide open, my ears tense with anticipation. Why? I did not know but I felt it must be terrible. Were a fish to have jumped out of the water, as oft they do, I am certain that's all it would have taken to send me overboard, stiff and unconscious.

Nonetheless, through intense effort I just about managed to come to my senses again. I took up my bottle of rum and took several large gulps. Then an idea came to mind and, with all my might, I started to scream in all directions successively. Once my throat had become absolutely paralyzed, I listened. A dog was howling far off in the distance.

I took another swig and stretched out at the bottom of my boat. I stayed like that for an hour, maybe two, without sleeping, my eyes wide open, surrounded by nightmares. I dared not get up and yet I desperately wanted to. I kept putting it off, minute by minute. I told myself, "Come on, get up!" and was too afraid to make a move. I finally pulled myself up with infinite caution – as though my life depended on the slightest noise that I might make, and I looked over the gunwale. I was dazzled by the most marvelous, the most astonishing spectacle one could ever see. It was phantasmagorical, from the land of the fairies – one of those visions described by travelers returning from distant lands whom we listen to without believing.

The fog that two hours earlier was floating on the water, gradually dissipated and had amassed on the embankment, leaving the river absolutely clear. On each side of the water an uninterrupted column of some six or seven meters formed and glistened in the moonlight with the superb intensity of snow, so much so that one saw nothing else but the river shimmering between these two white mountains, and high above my head, a great illuminating full moon drifted across the bluish, milky sky.

All the creatures in the water had awakened. The frogs croaked furiously and every few moments, sometimes to my right, sometimes to my left, I heard the toads summon the stars in their metallic and melancholic monotones. Strangely enough, I was no longer afraid; I was in the thick of a landscape so extraordinary that the most remarkable things could not have surprised me.

How long this all lasted, I know not, for I eventually dozed off. When I opened my eyes, the moon had set and the sky was full of clouds. The water lapped mournfully and a biting wind blew in the deep darkness. I drained the rum bottle, then I listened, shivering, to the rustling reeds and the sinister sound of the river. I tried to see, but could not distinguish my boat, nor even my hands as I held them up to my eyes.

Little by little, however, the blackness became less impenetrable. All of a sudden, I thought that I perceived a shadow gliding by quite close to me. I cried out, a voice answered; it was a fisherman. I called him; he approached and I told him of my misadventure. He drew up alongside my craft, and we both tugged at the anchor chain. The anchor did not budge. Day was breaking – bleak, gray, wet and bitterly cold – one of those days that brings sorrow and ill-fortune. I caught sight of another vessel. We hailed it. The man on board joined his efforts to ours and then, very gradually, the anchor gave way. It rose, but slowly, slowly, freighted with considerable weight. At last, our eyes rested on a black mass, and we hauled it on board. It was the corpse of an old woman with a large stone that hung round her neck.

TRADITIONAL MEXICAN

LA LLORONA

Translated and adapted by Jaime Marroquín Arredondo

MANY YEARS AGO, in a humble plateau village beside a wide river, there lived a beautiful girl named María. She had long black hair and smooth almond skin; her dark eyes shone like the night sky. Some villagers said that her beauty might have gone to her head and spoiled her. Others said she was spoiled by people because she was beautiful. Villagers often stopped, bending down to admire her and give her small gifts. As a little girl, she was confident and proud when she walked through the town square or down to the river to help her mother wash clothes and gather water. "*Qué niña tan hermosa*," people declared. *Such a lovely girl.*

As María grew into a young woman, her beauty deepened, but so did her vanity. Relatives and friends of the family gave her colorfully dyed blouses, skirts, and shawls. A doting aunt presented her with silver earrings and a necklace studded with polished turquoise and red jasper. "This will help you catch the eye of a nice young man," her aunt said with a smile.

"I don't need jewels to catch a man," María replied.

Her aunt laughed. "I saw Julio talking with you after church."

María made a sour face. "He is from a poor family. A cactus picker. I would never marry him."

María's mother suggested that Diego, a hardworking young man with kind eyes, might be a good match. But María rejected the idea: "He is not handsome enough."

Later, gazing at her reflection in a quiet pool at the river's edge, María said to herself, "I will marry the richest, most handsome man in the land." She refused the *cortejo* of all of the young *galanes* of the village.

One day, a dashing young ranchero rode into town on a large stallion, finely bridled and saddled. The man wore a tailored blue velvet jacket accented by a red silk sash and tie. His hair and mustache were perfectly groomed and he spoke with the grace of a true *heredero*. The villagers learned that he was the son of wealthy family with a grand hacienda near Durango.

The handsome young man stayed at the local inn. After dinner he stepped into the courtyard where people gathered around to hear him play guitar. He strummed and sang beautifully, and he looked directly at María as she stood by her mother's side. María averted her eyes, but the man stared even more intently. After finishing his song, the ranchero approached María and her mother, bowed, and introduced himself as Fernando Mota-Ramirez. Much to his surprise, María turned away. But the gentleman kept his composure and asked the embarrassed mother for permission to court her daughter.

The next night, Fernando visited María's home, but she would not see him. He left an expensive silk scarf and a gold pendant for her, but she would not accept his gifts.

"What are you doing?" her exasperated mother asked. "Isn't he good enough for you?"

"Don't be a fool," her father admonished her. "A chance like this will never come again."

María was very attracted to the man, but she wanted to be sure he was the right one.

The following night was very hot, and María walked down to the river to cool her feet. While she splashed in the shallows, Fernando approached and, so as not to alarm her, spoke softly from several feet away. "Dear María, how beautiful you look in the light of the moon."

María blushed and turned to face him.

"You are the most beautiful woman I've ever beheld," he continued. "No one is lovelier and more gracious. I will make you the happiest woman in the world."

These were the words María wanted to hear.

They were married that summer, and a year later she bore their first child, a son. María learned that her husband had fallen out with his family and that they must set up their own farm outside her village, raising corn and a few horses and cattle. Soon there was another child, a daughter. The young family seemed happy, strolling along the river in the evening when the work was done.

Whether it was the long, dry seasons or some longing in the man's untamed heart, Fernando spent more and more time away from his farm and family. He claimed to be doing business, reconnecting with wealthy cousins, securing assets for the future. But he would be gone for many weeks, arriving home with nothing but increasing indifference toward María. It was only the children he cared for. María still loved Fernando, and reached for him in their bedroom when the candles went out, but he rolled over and would not touch her. He wouldn't even smile at her in the morning when she made his coffee.

María's heart was breaking, her pride was seared, and her resentment grew. When she challenged Fernando, he said he would leave her and marry Valentina, a rich woman-friend of his cousin. When he spent time with his children, María would sometimes hear him say, "Your mother is a peasant," or "She can't read and doesn't know about the world." This made María furious.

One afternoon after Fernando had been drinking, he said, "I will leave with the children on Monday. They will meet my new friend." María knew this must be the other woman he spoke of, and she rushed at Fernando, screaming, "No! No! You leave those children in their rightful home." Fernando smacked María across the face and pushed her out of the way.

One of the only ways María could calm herself was to walk along the river. She gazed at the moving water, the stately herons, the deer drinking quietly. "Not everything goes the way you want it to," her mother tried to soothe her one afternoon as they followed the riverbank path. Ancient cypress trees towered overhead and they heard the calls of the cuckoo. "But a woman must keep going, like the river," her mother went on. "She cannot stop, even if she wants to." María listened, but her mother's words offered little comfort.

Fernando went away for two months, leaving the farm work to María and two hired men who felt sorry for the abandoned wife, but kept their distance and spoke only of farm matters. On a rainy October day, Fernando rode in on his horse. He dismounted, hugged his son and daughter, and waved to the workmen, but he did not greet María. She watched him spend the afternoon playing with his children. Finally, when the children went out to feed the chickens, he looked at María and said, "I am marrying Valentina. Someone worthy of my name and new estate."

María's heart froze inside her chest. Pain and anger seized her. But she said nothing. "I will stay in town tonight," Fernando continued. "In the morning I will speak to the judge." He put on his coat, said goodnight to his children, and galloped off through the rain.

No one knows what fury rose in María's mind and heart, but as darkness fell and the rising water swept along the muddy banks, she gathered her son and daughter and led them to the river.

"Why are we going out tonight?" her son asked.

María's red eyes began to tear, and she said, "To find justice." The boy did not understand, but he obeyed his mother.

"We're getting wet, Mami," her daughter said.

"Yes," María replied. "We must cool the fires."

The children were confused and scared. Standing over the steepest bank at the bend of the roiling river, María muttered something and pushed her children over the edge. It was dark but she could see them splash into the water. She heard their cries, "*¡Ayúdanos, mamá!, ¡Ayúdanos!*" *Help, Mama! Help!*

In a moment of blazing clarity, María realized what she'd done and called out to them. Their screams echoed back. She ran down the bank and waded into the swift water toward their bobbing heads. She could not reach them. Splashing up the bank, she ran farther downstream, but bushes and trees blocked her way. She jumped into the river again and tried to swim toward the last glimpses of their little heads, their fading cries. She flailed in the raging torrent, and her body became weak and heavy.

The next morning the rain had stopped and an old man was looking along the river for a lost goat. The river crested at midnight and was now receding. Bits of straw and debris were snagged in the bushes and something colorful caught his attention. The old man came hobbling into town, sweating and breathless, calling out to all who would listen. "A beautiful woman lies dead on the river bank. Come quick." Many people ran down to the place he described and found

María tangled in a willow, her arms stretched out, maybe in some last attempt to grasp her drowning children.

The children were never found. The whole village grieved. It is said that when Fernando was told, he screamed and wept, and rode off to the north, never to be seen or heard of again. María was prepared for burial in a white gown. The priest struggled with his words. The sobs of friends and family faded into the night.

When complete darkness settled on the plateau and the moonless sky erased the line between land and water, an eerie sound drifted up to the village. People wondered if it were a coyote or a strange bird. But soon it rang clear as the cries of a woman. People stepped from their doors and heard the wailing, and then the words: "*¡Ay, mis hijos! ¿Dónde están mis hijos?*" *My children, my children! Where are my children?*"

Julio and Diego, who now worked together and had families of their own, were returning late and saw what they could hardly believe: a white-robed woman floating over the water. At first people thought them crazy, but then others saw the apparition. The workmen at Fernando and María's deserted farm described a woman dressed in white burial clothes with long flowing hair flying over the water, weeping and crying out, "My children. Where are my children?" They all knew it was María, but they no longer spoke her name, only *La Llorona*, the weeping woman.

They say La Llorona is still looking for her children.

AMBROSE BIERCE

AN OCCURRENCE AT OWL CREEK BRIDGE

I

A MAN STOOD upon a railroad bridge in northern Alabama, looking down into the swift water twenty feet below. The man's hands were behind his back, the wrists bound with a cord. A rope closely encircled his neck. It was attached to a stout cross-timber above his head and the slack fell to the level of his knees. Some loose boards laid upon the sleepers supporting the metals of the railway supplied a footing for him and his executioners – two private soldiers of the Federal army, directed by a sergeant who in civil life may have been a deputy sheriff. At a short remove upon the same temporary platform was an officer in the uniform of his rank, armed. He was a captain. A sentinel at each end of the bridge stood with his rifle in the position known as "support," that is to say, vertical in front of the left shoulder, the hammer resting on the forearm thrown straight across the chest – a formal and unnatural position, enforcing an erect carriage of the body. It did not appear to be the duty of these two men to know what was occurring at the centre of the bridge, they merely blockaded the two ends of the foot planking that traversed it.

Beyond one of the sentinels nobody was in sight; the railroad ran straight away into a forest for a hundred yards, then, curving, was lost to view. Doubtless there was an outpost farther along. The other bank of the stream was open ground – a gentle acclivity topped with a stockade of vertical tree trunks, loopholed for rifles, with a single embrasure through which protruded the muzzle of a brass cannon commanding the bridge. Midway of the slope between bridge and fort were the spectators – a single company of infantry in line, at "parade rest," the butts of the rifles on the ground, the barrels inclining slightly backward against the right shoulder, the hands crossed upon the stock. A lieutenant stood at the right of the line, the point of his sword upon the ground, his left hand resting upon his right. Excepting the group of four at the centre of the bridge, not a man moved. The company faced the bridge, staring stonily, motionless. The sentinels, facing the banks of the stream, might have been statues to adorn the bridge. The captain stood with folded arms, silent, observing the work of his subordinates, but making no sign. Death is a dignitary who when he comes announced is to be received with formal manifestations of respect, even by those most familiar with him. In the code of military etiquette silence and fixity are forms of deference.

The man who was engaged in being hanged was apparently about thirty-five years of age. He was a civilian, if one might judge from his habit, which was that of a planter. His features were good – a straight nose, firm mouth, broad forehead, from which his long, dark hair was combed straight back, falling behind his ears to the collar of his well-fitting frock-coat. He wore a mustache and pointed beard, but no whiskers; his eyes were large and dark gray, and had a kindly expression which one would hardly have expected in one whose neck was in the hemp. Evidently this was no vulgar assassin. The liberal military code makes provision for hanging many kinds of persons, and gentlemen are not excluded.

The preparations being complete, the two private soldiers stepped aside and each drew away the plank upon which he had been standing. The sergeant turned to the captain, saluted and placed himself immediately behind that officer, who in turn moved apart one pace. These movements left the condemned man and the sergeant standing on the two ends of the same plank, which spanned three of the cross-ties of the bridge. The end upon which the civilian stood almost, but not quite, reached a fourth. This plank had been held in place by the weight of the captain; it was now held by that of the sergeant. At a signal from the former the latter would step aside, the plank would tilt and the condemned man go down between two ties. The arrangement commended itself to his judgment as simple and effective. His face had not been covered nor his eyes bandaged. He looked a moment at his "unsteadfast footing," then let his gaze wander to the swirling water of the stream racing madly beneath his feet. A piece of dancing driftwood caught his attention and his eyes followed it down the current. How slowly it appeared to move! What a sluggish stream!

He closed his eyes in order to fix his last thoughts upon his wife and children. The water, touched to gold by the early sun, the brooding mists under the banks at some distance down the stream, the fort, the soldiers, the piece of drift – all had distracted him. And now he became conscious of a new disturbance. Striking through the thought of his dear ones was a sound which he could neither ignore nor understand, a sharp, distinct, metallic percussion like the stroke of a blacksmith's hammer upon the anvil; it had the same ringing quality. He wondered what it was, and whether immeasurably distant or near by – it seemed both. Its recurrence was regular, but as slow as the tolling of a death knell. He awaited each stroke with impatience and – he knew not why – apprehension. The intervals of silence grew progressively longer; the delays became maddening. With their greater infrequency the sounds increased in strength and sharpness. They hurt his ear like the thrust of a knife;

he feared he would shriek. What he heard was the ticking of his watch.

He unclosed his eyes and saw again the water below him. "If I could free my hands," he thought, "I might throw off the noose and spring into the stream. By diving I could evade the bullets and, swimming vigorously, reach the bank, take to the woods and get away home. My home, thank God, is as yet outside their lines; my wife and little ones are still beyond the invader's farthest advance."

As these thoughts, which have here to be set down in words, were flashed into the doomed man's brain rather than evolved from it the captain nodded to the sergeant. The sergeant stepped aside.

II

PEYTON FARQUHAR WAS a well-to-do planter, of an old and highly respected Alabama family. Being a slave owner and like other slave owners a politician he was naturally an original secessionist and ardently devoted to the Southern cause. Circumstances of an imperious nature, which it is unnecessary to relate here, had prevented him from taking service with the gallant army that had fought the disastrous campaigns ending with the fall of Corinth, and he chafed under the inglorious restraint, longing for the release of his energies, the larger life of the soldier, the opportunity for distinction. That opportunity, he felt, would come, as it comes to all in war time. Meanwhile he did what he could. No service was too humble for him to perform in aid of the South, no adventure too perilous for him to undertake if consistent with the character of a civilian who was at heart a soldier, and who in good faith and without too much qualification assented to at least a part of the frankly villainous dictum that all is fair in love and war.

One evening while Farquhar and his wife were sitting on a rustic bench near the entrance to his grounds, a gray-clad soldier rode up to the gate and asked for a drink of water. Mrs. Farquhar was only too happy to serve him with her own white hands. While she was fetching the water her husband approached the dusty horseman and inquired eagerly for news from the front.

"The Yanks are repairing the railroads," said the man, "and are getting ready for another advance. They have reached the Owl Creek bridge, put it in order and built a stockade on the north bank. The commandant has issued an order, which is posted everywhere, declaring that any civilian caught interfering with the railroad, its bridges, tunnels or trains will be summarily hanged. I saw the order."

"How far is it to the Owl Creek bridge?" Farquhar asked.

"About thirty miles."

"Is there no force on this side the creek?"

"Only a picket post half a mile out, on the railroad, and a single sentinel at this end of the bridge."

"Suppose a man – a civilian and student of hanging – should elude the picket post and perhaps get the better of the sentinel," said Farquhar, smiling, "what could he accomplish?"

The soldier reflected. "I was there a month ago," he replied. "I observed that the flood of last winter had lodged a great quantity of driftwood against the wooden pier at this end of the bridge. It is now dry and would burn like tow."

The lady had now brought the water, which the soldier drank. He thanked her ceremoniously, bowed to her husband and rode away. An hour later, after nightfall, he repassed the plantation, going northward in the direction from which he had come. He was a Federal scout.

III

AS PEYTON FARQUHAR fell straight downward through the bridge he lost consciousness and was as one already dead. From this state he was awakened – ages later, it seemed to him – by the pain of a sharp pressure upon his throat, followed by a sense of suffocation. Keen, poignant agonies seemed to shoot from his neck downward through every fibre of his body and limbs. These pains appeared to flash along well-defined lines of ramification and to beat with an inconceivably rapid periodicity. They seemed like streams of pulsating fire heating him to an intolerable temperature. As to his head, he was conscious of nothing but a feeling of fulness – of congestion. These sensations were unaccompanied by thought. The intellectual part of his nature was already effaced; he had power only to feel, and feeling was torment. He was conscious of motion. Encompassed in a luminous cloud, of which he was now merely the fiery heart, without material substance, he swung through unthinkable arcs of oscillation, like a vast pendulum. Then all at once, with terrible suddenness, the light about him shot upward with the noise of a loud plash; a frightful roaring was in his ears, and all was cold and dark. The power of thought was restored; he knew that the rope had broken and he had fallen into the stream. There was no additional strangulation; the noose about his neck was already suffocating him and kept the water from his lungs. To die of hanging at the bottom of a river! – the idea seemed to him ludicrous. He opened his eyes in the darkness and saw above him a gleam of light, but how distant, how inaccessible! He was still sinking, for the light became fainter and fainter until it was a mere glimmer. Then it began to grow, and brighten, and he knew that he was rising toward the surface – knew it with reluctance, for he was now very comfortable. "To be hanged and drowned," he thought, "that is not so bad; but I do not wish to be shot. No; I will not be shot; that is not fair."

He was not conscious of an effort, but a sharp pain in his wrist apprised him that he was trying to free his hands. He gave the struggle his attention, as an idler might observe the feat of a juggler, without interest in the outcome. What splendid effort! – what magnificent, what superhuman strength! Ah, that was a fine endeavor! Bravo! The cord fell away; his arms parted and floated upward, the hands dimly seen on each side in the growing light. He watched them with a new interest as first one and then the other pounced upon the noose at his neck. They tore it away and thrust it fiercely aside, its undulations resembling those of a water-snake. "Put it back, put it back!" He thought he shouted these words to his hands, for the undoing of the noose had been succeeded by the direst pang that he had yet experienced. His neck ached horribly; his brain was on fire; his heart, which had been fluttering faintly, gave a great leap, trying to force itself out at his mouth. His whole body was racked and wrenched with an insupportable anguish! But his disobedient hands gave no heed to the command. They beat the water vigorously with quick, downward strokes, forcing him to the surface. He felt his head emerge; his eyes were blinded by the sunlight; his chest expanded convulsively, and with a supreme and crowning agony his lungs engulfed a great draught of air, which instantly he expelled in a shriek!

He was now in full possession of his physical senses. They

were, indeed, preternaturally keen and alert. Something in the awful disturbance of his organic system had so exalted and refined them that they made record of things never before perceived. He felt the ripples upon his face and heard their separate sounds as they struck. He looked at the forest on the bank of the stream, saw the individual trees, the leaves and the veining of each leaf – saw the very insects upon them: the locusts, the brilliant-bodied flies, the gray spiders stretching their webs from twig to twig. He noted the prismatic colors in all the dewdrops upon a million blades of grass. The humming of the gnats that danced above the eddies of the stream, the beating of the dragonflies' wings, the strokes of the water-spiders' legs, like oars which had lifted their boat – all these made audible music. A fish slid along beneath his eyes and he heard the rush of its body parting the water.

He had come to the surface facing down the stream; in a moment the visible world seemed to wheel slowly round, himself the pivotal point, and he saw the bridge, the fort, the soldiers upon the bridge, the captain, the sergeant, the two privates, his executioners. They were in silhouette against the blue sky. They shouted and gesticulated, pointing at him. The captain had drawn his pistol, but did not fire; the others were unarmed. Their movements were grotesque and horrible, their forms gigantic.

Suddenly he heard a sharp report and something struck the water smartly within a few inches of his head, spattering his face with spray. He heard a second report, and saw one of the sentinels with his rifle at his shoulder, a light cloud of blue smoke rising from the muzzle. The man in the water saw the eye of the man on the bridge gazing into his own through the sights of the rifle. He observed that it was a gray eye and remembered having read that gray eyes were keenest, and that all famous marksmen had them. Nevertheless, this one had missed.

A counter-swirl had caught Farquhar and turned him half round; he was again looking into the forest on the bank opposite the fort. The sound of a clear, high voice in a monotonous singsong now rang out behind him and came across the water with a distinctness that pierced and subdued all other sounds, even the beating of the ripples in his ears. Although no soldier, he had frequented camps enough to know the dread significance of that deliberate, drawling, aspirated chant; the lieutenant on shore was taking a part in the morning's work. How coldly and pitilessly – with what an even, calm intonation, presaging, and enforcing tranquillity in the men – with what accurately measured intervals fell those cruel words:

"Attention, company! . . . Shoulder arms! . . . Ready! . . . Aim! . . . Fire!"

Farquhar dived – dived as deeply as he could. The water roared in his ears like the voice of Niagara, yet he heard the dulled thunder of the volley and, rising again toward the surface, met shining bits of metal, singularly flattened, oscillating slowly downward. Some of them touched him on the face and hands, then fell away, continuing their descent. One lodged between his collar and neck; it was uncomfortably warm and he snatched it out.

As he rose to the surface, gasping for breath, he saw that he had been a long time under water; he was perceptibly farther down stream – nearer to safety. The soldiers had almost finished reloading; the metal ramrods flashed all at once in the sunshine as they were drawn from the barrels, turned in the air, and thrust into their sockets. The two sentinels fired again, independently and ineffectually.

The hunted man saw all this over his shoulder; he was

now swimming vigorously with the current. His brain was as energetic as his arms and legs; he thought with the rapidity of lightning.

"The officer," he reasoned, "will not make that martinet's error a second time. It is as easy to dodge a volley as a single shot. He has probably already given the command to fire at will. God help me, I cannot dodge them all!"

An appalling plash within two yards of him was followed by a loud, rushing sound, *diminuendo*, which seemed to travel back through the air to the fort and died in an explosion which stirred the very river to its deeps! A rising sheet of water curved over him, fell down upon him, blinded him, strangled him! The cannon had taken a hand in the game. As he shook his head free from the commotion of the smitten water he heard the deflected shot humming through the air ahead, and in an instant it was cracking and smashing the branches in the forest beyond.

"They will not do that again," he thought; "the next time they will use a charge of grape. I must keep my eye upon the gun; the smoke will apprise me – the report arrives too late; it lags behind the missile. That is a good gun."

Suddenly he felt himself whirled round and round – spinning like a top. The water, the banks, the forests, the now distant bridge, fort and men – all were commingled and blurred. Objects were represented by their colors only; circular horizontal streaks of color – that was all he saw. He had been caught in a vortex and was being whirled on with a velocity of advance and gyration that made him giddy and sick. In a few moments he was flung upon the gravel at the foot of the left bank of the stream – the southern bank – and behind a projecting point which concealed him from his enemies. The sudden arrest of his motion, the abrasion of one of his hands on the gravel, restored him, and he wept with delight. He dug his fingers into the sand, threw it over himself in handfuls and audibly blessed it. It looked like diamonds, rubies, emeralds; he could think of nothing beautiful which it did not resemble. The trees upon the bank were giant garden plants; he noted a definite order in their arrangement, inhaled the fragrance of their blooms. A strange, roseate light shone through the spaces among their trunks and the wind made in their branches the music of aeolian harps. He had no wish to perfect his escape – was content to remain in that enchanting spot until retaken.

A whiz and rattle of grapeshot among the branches high above his head roused him from his dream. The baffled cannoneer had fired him a random farewell. He sprang to his feet, rushed up the sloping bank, and plunged into the forest.

All that day he traveled, laying his course by the rounding sun. The forest seemed interminable; nowhere did he discover a break in it, not even a woodman's road. He had not known that he lived in so wild a region. There was something uncanny in the revelation.

By nightfall he was fatigued, footsore, famishing. The thought of his wife and children urged him on. At last he found a road which led him in what he knew to be the right direction. It was as wide and straight as a city street, yet it seemed untraveled. No fields bordered it, no dwelling anywhere. Not so much as the barking of a dog suggested human habitation. The black bodies of the trees formed a straight wall on both sides, terminating on the horizon in a point, like a diagram in a lesson in perspective. Overhead, as he looked up through this rift in the wood, shone great golden stars looking unfamiliar and grouped in strange constellations. He was sure they were arranged in some order which had a secret and malign significance. The wood on either side was full of singular noises, among which – once, twice, and again – he distinctly heard whispers in an unknown tongue.

His neck was in pain and lifting his hand to it he found it horribly swollen. He knew that it had a circle of black where the rope had bruised it. His eyes felt congested; he could no longer close them. His tongue was swollen with thirst; he relieved its fever by thrusting it forward from between his teeth into the cold air. How softly the turf had carpeted the untraveled avenue – he could no longer feel the roadway beneath his feet!

Doubtless, despite his suffering, he had fallen asleep while walking, for now he sees another scene – perhaps he has merely recovered from a delirium. He stands at the gate of his own home. All is as he left it, and all bright and beautiful in the morning sunshine. He must have traveled the entire night. As he pushes open the gate and passes up the wide white walk, he sees a flutter of female garments; his wife, looking fresh and cool and sweet, steps down from the veranda to meet him. At the bottom of the steps she stands waiting, with a smile of ineffable joy, an attitude of matchless grace and dignity. Ah, how beautiful she is! He springs forward with extended arms. As he is about to clasp her he feels a stunning blow upon the back of the neck; a blinding white light blazes all about him with a sound like the shock of a cannon – then all is darkness and silence!

Peyton Farquhar was dead; his body, with a broken neck, swung gently from side to side beneath the timbers of the Owl Creek bridge.

ELIZABETH JANE HOWARD

THREE MILES UP

THERE WAS ABSOLUTELY nothing like it.

An unoriginal conclusion, and one that he had drawn a hundred times during the last fortnight. Clifford would make some subtle and intelligent comparison, but he, John, could only continue to repeat that it was quite unlike anything else. It had been Clifford's idea, which, considering Clifford, was surprising. When you looked at him, you would not suppose him capable of it. However, John reflected, he had been ill, some sort of breakdown these clever people went in for, and that might account for his uncharacteristic idea of hiring a boat and travelling on canals. On the whole, John had to admit, it was a good idea. He had never been on a canal in his life, although he had been in almost every kind of boat, and thought he knew a good deal about them; so much indeed, that he had embarked on the venture in a light-hearted, almost a patronising manner. But it was not nearly as simple as he had imagined. Clifford, of course, knew nothing about boats; but he had admitted that almost everything had gone wrong with a kind of devilish versatility which had almost frightened him. However, that was all over, and John, who had learned painfully all about the boat and her engine, felt that the former at least had run her gamut of disaster. They had run out of food, out of petrol, and out of water; had dropped their windlass into the deepest lock, and, more humiliating, their boathook into a side-pond. The head had come off the hammer. They had been disturbed for one whole night by a curious rustling in the cabin, like a rat in a paper bag, when there was no paper, and, so far as they knew, no rat. The battery had failed and had had to be recharged. Clifford had put his elbow through an already cracked window in the cabin. A large piece of rope had wound itself round the propeller with a malignant intensity which required three men and half a morning to unravel. And so on, until now there was really nothing left to go wrong, unless one of them drowned, and surely it was impossible to drown in a canal.

"I suppose one might easily drown in a lock?" he asked aloud.

"We must be careful not to fall into one," Clifford replied.

"What?" John steered with fierce concentration, and never heard anything people said to him for the first time, almost on principle.

"I said we must be careful not to fall *into* a lock."

"Oh. Well there aren't any more now until after the Junction. Anyway, we haven't yet, so there's really no reason why we should start now. I only wanted to know whether we'd drown if we did."

"Sharon might."

"What?"

"Sharon might."

"Better warn her then. She seems agile enough." His concentrated frown returned, and he settled down again to the wheel. John didn't mind where they went, or what happened, so long as he handled the boat, and all things considered, he handled her remarkably well. Clifford planned and John steered: and until two days ago they had both quarrelled and argued over a smoking and unusually temperamental primus. Which reminded Clifford of Sharon. Her advent and the weather were really their two unadulterated strokes of good fortune. There had been no rain, and Sharon had, as it were, dropped from the blue on to the boat, where she speedily restored domestic order, stimulated evening conversation, and touched the whole venture with her attractive being: the requisite number of miles each day were achieved, the boat behaved herself, and admirable meals were steadily and regularly prepared. She had, in fact, identified herself with the journey, without making the slightest effort to control it: a talent which many women were supposed in theory to possess, when, in fact, Clifford reflected gloomily, most of them were bored with the whole thing, or tried to dominate it.

Her advent was a remarkable, almost a miraculous piece of luck. He had, after a particularly ill-fed day, and their failure to dine at a small hotel, desperately telephoned all the women he knew who seemed in the least suitable (and they were surprisingly few), with no success. They had spent a miserable evening, John determined to argue about everything, and he, Clifford, refusing to speak; until, both in a fine state of emotional tension, they had turned in for the night. While John snored, Clifford had lain distraught, his resentment and despair circling round John and then touching his own smallest and most random thoughts; until his mind found no refuge and he was left, divided from it, hostile and afraid, watching it in terror racing on in the dark like some malignant machine utterly out of his control.

The next day things had proved no better between them, and they had continued throughout the morning in a silence which was only occasionally and elaborately broken. They had tied up for lunch beside a wood, which hung heavy and magnificent over the canal. There was a small clearing beside which John then proposed to moor, but Clifford failed to achieve the considerable leap necessary to stop the boat; and they had drifted helplessly past it. John flung him a line, but it was not until the boat was secured, and they were safely in the cabin, that the storm had broken. John, in attempting to light the primus, spilt a quantity of paraffin on Clifford's bunk. Instantly all his despair of the previous evening had contracted. He hated John so much that he could have murdered him. They both lost their tempers, and for the ensuing hour and a half had conducted a blazing quarrel, which, even at the time, secretly horrified them both in its intensity.

It had finally ended with John striding out of the cabin, there being no more to say. He had returned almost at once, however.

"I say, Clifford. Come and look at this."

"At what?"

"Outside, on the bank."

For some unknown reason Clifford did get up and did look. Lying face downwards quite still on the ground, with her arms clasping the trunk of a large tree, was a girl.

"How long has she been there?"

"She's asleep."

"She can't have been asleep all the time. She must have heard some of what we said."

"Anyway, who is she? What is she doing here?"

Clifford looked at her again. She was wearing a dark twill shirt and dark trousers, and her hair hung over her face, so that it was almost invisible. "I don't know. I suppose she's alive?"

John jumped cautiously ashore. "Yes, she's alive all right. Funny way to lie."

"Well, it's none of our business anyway. Anyone can lie on a bank if they want to."

"Yes, but she must have come in the middle of our row, and it does seem queer to stay, and then go to sleep."

"Extraordinary," said Clifford wearily. Nothing was really extraordinary, he felt, nothing. "Are we moving on?"

"Let's eat first. I'll do it."

"Oh, I'll do it."

The girl stirred, unclasped her arms, and sat up. They had all stared at each other for a moment, the girl slowly pushing the hair from her forehead. Then she had said: "If you will give me a meal, I'll cook it." Afterwards they had left her to wash up, and walked about the wood, while Clifford suggested to John that they ask the girl to join them. "I'm sure she'd come," he said. "She didn't seem at all clear about what she was doing."

"We can't just pick somebody up out of a wood," said John, scandalised.

"Where do you suggest we pick them up? If we don't have someone, this holiday will be a failure."

"We don't know anything about her."

"I can't see that that matters very much. She seems to cook well. We can at least ask her."

"All right. Ask her then. She won't come."

When they returned to the boat, she had finished the washing up, and was sitting on the floor of the cockpit, with her arms stretched behind her head. Clifford asked her; and she accepted as though she had known them a long time and they were simply inviting her to tea.

"Well, but look here," said John, thoroughly taken aback. "What about your things?"

"My things?" she looked inquiringly and a little defensively from one to the other.

"Clothes and so on. Or haven't you got any? Are you a gipsy or something? Where do you come from?"

"I am not a gipsy," she began patiently; when Clifford, thoroughly embarrassed and ashamed, interrupted her.

"Really, it's none of our business who you are, and there is absolutely no need for us to ask you anything. I'm very glad you will come with us, although I feel we should warn you that we are new to this life, and anything might happen."

"No need to warn me," she said and smiled gratefully at him.

After that, they both felt bound to ask her nothing; John because he was afraid of being made to look foolish by Clifford, and Clifford because he had stopped John.

"Good Lord, we shall never get rid of her; and she'll fuss about condensation," John had muttered aggressively as he started the engine. But she was very young, and did not fuss about anything. She had told them her name, and settled down, immediately and easily: gentle, assured and unselfconscious to a degree remarkable in one so young. They were never sure how much she had overheard them, for she gave no sign of having heard anything. A friendly but uncommunicative creature.

The map on the engine box started to flap, and immediately John asked, "Where are we?"

"I haven't been watching, I'm afraid. Wait a minute."

"We just passed under a railway bridge," John said helpfully.

"Right. Yes. About four miles from the Junction, I think. What is the time?"

"Five-thirty."

"Which way are we going when we get to the Junction?"

"We haven't time for the big loop. I must be back in London by the 15th."

"The alternative is to go up as far as the basin, and then simply turn round and come back, and who wants to do that?"

"Well, we'll know the route then. It'll be much easier coming back."

Clifford did not reply. He was not attracted by the route being easier, and he wanted to complete his original plan.

"Let us wait till we get there." Sharon appeared with tea and marmalade sandwiches.

"All right, let's wait." Clifford was relieved.

"It will be almost dark by six-thirty. I think we ought to have a plan," John said. "Thank you, Sharon."

"Have tea first." She curled herself on to the floor with her back to the cabin doors and a mug in her hands.

They were passing rows of little houses with gardens that backed on to the canal. They were long narrow strips, streaked with cinder paths, and crowded with vegetables and chicken huts, fruit trees and perambulators; sometimes ending with fat white ducks, and sometimes in a tiny patch of grass with a bench on it.

"Would you rather keep ducks or sit on a bench?" asked Clifford.

"Keep ducks," said John promptly. "More useful. Sharon wouldn't mind which she did. Would you, Sharon?" He liked saying her name, Clifford noticed. "You could be happy anywhere, couldn't you?" He seemed to be presenting her with the widest possible choice.

"I might *be* anywhere," she answered after a moment's thought.

"Well you happen to be on a canal, and very nice for us."

"In a wood, and then on a canal," she replied contentedly, bending her smooth dark head over her mug.

"Going to be fine tomorrow," said John. He was always a little embarrassed at any mention of how they found her and his subsequent rudeness.

"Yes. I like it when the whole sky is so red and burning and it begins to be cold."

"*Are* you cold?" said John, wanting to worry about it: but she tucked her dark shirt into her trousers and answered composedly:

"Oh no. I am never cold."

They drank their tea in a comfortable silence. Clifford started to read his map, and then said they were almost on to another sheet. "New country," he said with satisfaction. "I've never been here before."

"You make it sound like an exploration; doesn't he, Sharon?" said John.

"Is that a bad thing?" She collected the mugs. "I am going to put these away. You will call me if I am wanted for anything." And she went into the cabin again.

There was a second's pause, a minute tribute to her departure; and, lighting cigarettes, they settled down to stare at the long silent stretch of water ahead.

John thought about Sharon. He thought rather desperately that really they still knew nothing about her, and that when they went back to London, they would, in all probability, never see her again. Perhaps Clifford would fall in love with her, and she would naturally reciprocate, because she was so young and Clifford was reputed to be so fascinating and intelligent, and because women were always foolish and loved the wrong man. He thought all these things with equal intensity, glanced cautiously at Clifford, and supposed he was thinking about her; then wondered what she would be like in London, clad in anything else but her dark trousers and shirt. The engine coughed; and he turned to it in relief.

Clifford was making frantic calculations of time and distance; stretching their time, and diminishing the distance, and groaning that with the utmost optimism they could not be made to fit. He was interrupted by John swearing at the engine, and then for no particular reason he remembered Sharon, and reflected with pleasure how easily she left the mind when she was not present, how she neither obsessed nor possessed one in her absence, but was charming to see.

The sun had almost set when they reached the Junction, and John slowed down to neutral while they made up their minds. To the left was the straight cut which involved the longer journey originally planned; and curving away to the right was the short arm which John advocated. The canal was fringed with rushes, and there was one small cottage with no light in it. Clifford went into the cabin to tell Sharon where they were, and then, as they drifted slowly in the middle of the Junction, John suddenly shouted: "Clifford! What's the third turning?"

"There are only two." Clifford reappeared. "Sharon is busy with dinner."

"No, look. Surely that is another cut."

Clifford stared ahead. "Can't see it."

"Just to the right of the cottage. Look. It's not so dark as all that."

Then Clifford saw it very plainly. It seemed to wind away from the cottage on a fairly steep curve, and the rushes shrouding it from anything but the closest view were taller than the rest.

"Have another look at the map. I'll reverse for a bit."

"Found it. It's just another arm. Probably been abandoned," said Clifford eventually.

The boat had swung round; and now they could see the continuance of the curve dully gleaming ahead, and banked by reeds.

"Well, what shall we do?"

"Getting dark. Let's go up a little way, and moor. Nice quiet mooring."

"With some nice quiet mudbanks," said John grimly. "Nobody uses that."

"How do you know?"

"Well, look at it. All those rushes, and it's sure to be thick with weed."

"Don't go up it then. But we shall go aground if we drift about like this."

"*I* don't mind going up it," said John doggedly. "What about Sharon?"

"What about her?"

"Tell her about it."

"We've found a third turning," Clifford called above the noise of the primus through the cabin door.

"One you had not expected?"

"Yes. It looks very wild. We were thinking of going up it."

"Didn't you say you wanted to explore?" she smiled at him.

"You are quite ready to try it? I warn you we shall probably run hard aground. Look out for bumps with the primus."

"I am quite ready, and I am quite sure we shan't run aground," she answered with charming confidence in their skill.

They moved slowly forward in the dusk. Why they did not run aground, Clifford could not imagine: John really was damned good at it. The canal wound and wound, and the reeds grew not only thick on each bank, but in clumps across the canal. The light drained out of the sky into the water and slowly drowned there; the trees and the banks became heavy and black.

Clifford began to clear things away from the heavy dew which had begun to rise. After two journeys he remained in the cabin, while John crawled on, alone. Once, on a bend, John thought he saw a range of hills ahead with lights on them, but when he was round the curve, and had time to look again he could see no hills: only a dark indeterminate waste of country stretched ahead.

He was beginning to consider the necessity of mooring, when they came to a bridge; and shortly after, he saw a dark mass which he took to be houses. When the boat had crawled for another fifty yards or so, he stopped the engine, and drifted in absolute silence to the bank. The houses, about half a dozen of them, were much nearer than he had at first imagined, but there were no lights to be seen. Distance is always deceptive in the dark, he thought, and jumped ashore with a bow line. When, a few minutes later, he took a sounding with the boathook, the water proved unexpectedly deep; and he concluded that they had by incredible good fortune moored at the village wharf. He made everything fast, and joined the others in the cabin with mixed feelings of pride and resentment; that he should have achieved so much under such difficult conditions, and that they (by "they" he meant Clifford), should have contributed so little towards the achievement. He found Clifford reading Bradshaw's *Guide to the Canals and Navigable Rivers* in one corner, and Sharon, with her hair pushed back behind her ears, bending over the primus with a knife. Her ears are pale, exactly the colour of her face, he thought; wanted to touch them; then felt horribly ashamed, and hated Clifford.

"Let's have a look at Bradshaw," he said, as though he had not noticed Clifford reading it.

But Clifford handed him the book in the most friendly manner, remarking that he couldn't see where they were. "In fact you have surpassed yourself with your brilliant navigation. We seem to be miles from anywhere."

"What about your famous ordnance?"

"It's not on any sheet I have. The new one I thought we should use only covers the loop we planned. There is precisely three quarters of a mile of this canal shown on the present sheet and then we run off the map. I suppose there must once have been trade here, but I cannot imagine what, or where."

"I expect things change," said Sharon. "Here is the meal."

"How can you see to cook?" asked John, eyeing his plate ravenously.

"There is a candle."

"Yes, but we've selfishly appropriated that."

"Should I need more light?" she asked, and looked troubled.

"There's no should about it. I just don't know how you do it, that's all. Chips exactly the right colour, and you never drop anything. It's marvellous."

She smiled a little uncertainly at him and lit another candle. "Luck, probably," she said, and set it on the table.

They ate their meal, and John told them about the mooring. "Some sort of village. I think we're moored at the wharf. I couldn't find any rings without the torch, so I've used the anchor." This small shaft was intended for Clifford, who had dropped the spare torch-battery in the washing-up bowl, and forgotten to buy another. But it was only a small shaft, and immediately afterwards John felt much better. His aggression slowly left him, and he felt nothing but a peaceful and well-fed affection for the other two.

"Extraordinary cut off this is," he remarked over coffee.

"It is very pleasant in here. Warm, and extremely full of us."

"Yes. I know. A quiet village, though, you must admit."

"I shall believe in your village when I see it."

"Then you would believe it?"

"No he wouldn't, Sharon. Not if he didn't want to, and couldn't find it on the map. That map!"

The conversation turned again to their remoteness, and to how cut off one liked to be and at what point it ceased to be desirable; to boats, telephones, and, finally, canals: which, Clifford maintained, possessed the perfect proportions of urbanity and solitude.

Hours later, when they had turned in for the night, Clifford reviewed the conversation, together with others they had had, and remembered with surprise how little Sharon had actually said. She listened to everything and occasionally, when they appealed to her, made some small composed remark which was oddly at variance with their passionate interest. "She has an elusive quality of freshness about her," he thought, "which is neither naïve nor stupid nor dull, and she invokes no responsibility. She does not want us to know what she was, or why we found her as we did, and curiously, I, at least, do not want to know. She is what women ought to be," he concluded with sudden pleasure; and slept.

He woke the next morning to find it very late, and stretched out his hand to wake John.

"We've all overslept. Look at the time."

"Good Lord! Better wake Sharon."

Sharon lay between them on the floor, which they had ceded her because, oddly enough, it was the widest and most comfortable bed. She seemed profoundly asleep, but at the mention of her name sat up immediately, and rose, almost as though she had not been asleep at all.

The morning routine which, involving the clothing of three people and shaving of two of them, was necessarily a long and complicated business, began. Sharon boiled water, and Clifford, grumbling gently, hoisted himself out of his bunk and repaired with a steaming jug to the cockpit. He put the jug on a seat, lifted the canvas awning, and leaned out. It was absolutely grey and still; a little white mist hung over the canal, and the country stretched out desolate and unkempt on every side with no sign of a living creature. The village, he thought suddenly: John's village: and was possessed of a perilous uncertainty and fear. I am getting worse, he thought, this holiday is doing me no good. I am mad. I imagined that he said we moored by a village wharf. For several seconds he stood gripping the gunwale, and searching desperately for anything, huts, a clump of trees, which could in the darkness have been mistaken for a village. But there was nothing near the boat except tall rank rushes which did not move at all. Then, when his suspense was becoming unbearable, John joined him with another steaming jug of water.

"We shan't get anywhere at this rate," he began; and then . . . "Hullo! Where's my village?"

"I was wondering that," said Clifford. He could almost have wept with relief, and quickly began to shave, deeply ashamed of his private panic.

"Can't understand it," John was saying. It was no joke, Clifford decided, as he listened to his hearty puzzled ruminations.

At breakfast John continued to speculate upon what he had or had not seen, and Sharon listened intently while she filled the coffee pot and cut bread. Once or twice she met Clifford's eye with a glance of discreet amusement.

"I must be mad, or else the whole place is haunted," finished John comfortably. These two possibilities seemed to relieve him of any further anxiety in the matter, as he ate a huge breakfast and set about greasing the engine.

"Well," said Clifford, when he was alone with Sharon. "What do you make of that?"

"It is easy to be deceived in such matters," she answered perfunctorily.

"Evidently. Still, John is an unlikely candidate you must admit. Here, I'll help you dry."

"Oh no. It is what I am here for."

"Not entirely, I hope."

"Not entirely." She smiled and relinquished the cloth. John eventually announced that they were ready to start. Clifford, who had assumed that they were to recover their journey, was surprised, and a little alarmed, to find John intent upon continuing it. He seemed undeterred by the state of the canal, which, as Clifford immediately pointed out, rendered navigation both arduous and unrewarding. He announced that the harder it was, the more he liked it, adding very firmly that "anyway we must see what happens."

"We shan't have time to do anything else."

"Thought you wanted to explore."

"I do, but . . . what do you think, Sharon?"

"I think John will have to be a very good navigator to manage that." She indicated the rush and weed-ridden reach before them. "Do you think it's possible?"

"Of course it's possible. I'll probably need some help though."

"I'll help you," she said.

So on they went.

They made incredibly slow progress. John enjoys showing off his powers to her, thought Clifford, half amused, half exasperated, as he struggled for the fourth time in an hour to scrape weeds off the propeller.

Sharon eventually retired to cook lunch.

"Surprising amount of water here," John said suddenly.

"Oh?"

"Well, I mean, with all this weed and stuff, you'd expect the canal to have silted up. I'm sure nobody uses it."

"The whole thing is extraordinary."

"Is it too late in the year for birds?" asked Clifford later.

"No, I don't think so. Why?"

"I haven't heard one, have you?"

"Haven't noticed, I'm afraid. There's someone anyway. First sign of life."

An old man stood near the bank watching them. He was dressed in corduroy and wore a straw hat.

"Good morning," shouted John, as they drew nearer.

He made no reply, but inclined his head slightly. He seemed very old. He was leaning on a scythe, and as they drew almost level with him, he turned away and began slowly cutting rushes. A pile of them lay neatly stacked beside him.

"Where does this canal go? Is there a village further on?" Clifford and John asked simultaneously. He seemed not to hear, and as they chugged steadily past, Clifford was about to suggest that they stop and ask again, when he called after them: "Three miles up you'll find the village. Three miles up that is," and turned away to his rushes again.

"Well, now we know something, anyway," said John.

"We don't even know what the village is called."

"Soon find out. Only three miles."

"Three miles!" said Clifford darkly. "That might mean anything."

"Do you want to turn back?"

"Oh no, not now. I want to see this village now. My curiosity is thoroughly aroused."

"Shouldn't think there'll be anything to see. Never been in such a wild spot. Look at it."

Clifford looked at it. Half wilderness, half marsh, dank and grey and still, with single trees bare of their leaves;

clumps of hawthorn that might once have been hedge, sparse and sharp with berries; and, in the distance, hills and an occasional wood: these were all one could see, beyond the lines of rushes which edged the canal winding ahead.

They stopped for a lengthy meal, which Sharon described as lunch and tea together, it being so late; and then, appalled at how little daylight was left, continued.

"We've hardly been any distance at all," said John forlornly. "Good thing there were no locks. I shouldn't think they'd have worked if there were."

"*Much* more than three miles," he said, about two hours later. Darkness was descending and it was becoming very cold.

"Better stop," said Clifford.

"Not yet. I'm determined to reach that village."

"Dinner is ready," said Sharon sadly. "It will be cold."

"Let's stop."

"You have your meal. I'll call if I want you."

Sharon looked at them, and Clifford shrugged his shoulders. "Come on. I will. I'm tired of this."

They shut the cabin doors. John could hear the pleasant clatter of their meal, and just as he was coming to the end of the decent interval which he felt must elapse before he gave in, they passed under a bridge, the first of the day, and, clutching at any straw, he immediately assumed that it prefaced the village. "I think we're nearly there," he called.

Clifford opened the door. "The village?"

"No, a bridge. Can't be far now."

"You're mad, John. It's pitch dark."

"You can see the bridge though."

"Yes. Why not moor under it?"

"Too late. Can't turn round in this light, and she's not

good at reversing. Must be nearly there. You go back, I don't need you."

Clifford shut the door again. He was beginning to feel irritated with John behaving in this childish manner and showing off to impress Sharon. It was amusing in the morning, but really he was carrying it a bit far. Let him manage the thing himself then. When, a few minutes later, John shouted that they had reached the sought after village, Clifford merely pulled back the little curtain over a cabin window, rubbed the condensation, and remarked that he could see nothing. "No light at least."

"He is happy anyhow," said Sharon peaceably.

"Going to have a look round," said John, slamming the cabin doors and blowing his nose.

"Surely you'll eat first?"

"If you've left anything. My God it's cold! It's *unnaturally* cold."

"We won't be held responsible if he dies of exposure will we?" said Clifford.

She looked at him, hesitated a moment, but did not reply, and placed a steaming plate in front of John. She doesn't want us to quarrel, Clifford thought, and with an effort of friendliness he asked: "What does tonight's village look like?"

"Much the same. Only one or two houses you know. But the old man called it a village." He seemed uncommunicative; Clifford thought he was sulking. But after eating the meal, he suddenly announced, almost apologetically, "I don't think I shall walk round. I'm absolutely worn out. You go if you like. I shall start turning in."

"All right. I'll have a look. You've had a hard day."

Clifford pulled on a coat and went outside. It was, as John said, incredibly cold and almost overwhelmingly silent. The clouds hung very low over the boat, and mist was rising everywhere from the ground, but he could dimly discern the black huddle of cottages lying on a little slope above the bank against which the boat was moored. He did actually set foot on shore, but his shoe sank immediately into a marshy hole. He withdrew it, and changed his mind. The prospect of groping round those dark and silent houses became suddenly distasteful, and he joined the others with the excuse that it was too cold and that he also was tired.

A little later, he lay half conscious in a kind of restless trance, with John sleeping heavily opposite him. His mind seemed full of foreboding, fear of something unknown and intangible: he thought of them lying in warmth on the cold secret canal with desolate miles of water behind and probably beyond; the old man and the silent houses; John, cut off and asleep, and Sharon, who lay on the floor beside him. Immediately he was filled with a sudden and most violent desire for her, even to touch her, for her to know that he was awake.

"Sharon," he whispered; "Sharon, Sharon," and stretched down his fingers to her in the dark.

Instantly her hand was in his, each smooth and separate finger warmly clasped. She did not move or speak, but his relief was indescribable and for a long while he lay in an ecstasy of delight and peace, until his mind slipped imperceptibly with her fingers into oblivion.

When he woke he found John absent and Sharon standing over the primus. "He's outside," she said.

"Have I overslept again?"

"It is late. I am boiling water for you now."

"We'd better try and get some supplies this morning."

"There is no village," she said, in a matter of fact tone.

"What?"

"John says not. But we have enough food, if you don't mind this queer milk from a tin."

"No, I don't mind," he replied, watching her affectionately. "It doesn't really surprise me," he added after a moment.

"The village?"

"No village. Yesterday I should have minded awfully. Is that you, do you think?"

"Perhaps."

"It doesn't surprise you about the village at all, does it? Do you love me?"

She glanced at him quickly, a little shocked, and said quietly: "Don't you know?" then added: "It doesn't surprise me."

John seemed very disturbed. "I don't like it," he kept saying as they shaved. "Can't understand it at all. I could have sworn there were houses last night. You saw them didn't you?"

"Yes."

"Well, don't you think it's very odd?"

"I do."

"Everything looks the same as yesterday morning. I don't like it."

"It's an adventure you must admit."

"Yes, but I've had enough of it. I suggest we turn back."

Sharon suddenly appeared, and, seeing her, Clifford knew that he did not want to go back. He remembered her saying: "Didn't you say you wanted to explore?" She would think him weak-hearted if they turned back all those dreary miles with nothing to show for it. At breakfast, he exerted himself in persuading John to the same opinion. John finally agreed to one more day, but, in turn, extracted a promise that they would then go back whatever happened. Clifford agreed to this, and Sharon for some inexplicable reason laughed at them both. So that eventually they prepared to set off in an atmosphere of general good humour.

Sharon began to fill the water tank with their four-gallon can. It seemed too heavy for her, and John dropped the starter and leapt to her assistance.

She let him take the can and held the funnel for him. Together they watched the rich even stream of water disappear.

"You shouldn't try to do that," he said. "You'll hurt yourself."

"Gipsies do it," she said.

"I'm awfully sorry about that. You know I am."

"I should not have minded if you had thought I was a gipsy."

"I do like you," he said, not looking at her. "I do like you. You won't disappear altogether when this is over, will you?"

"You probably won't find I'll disappear for good," she replied comfortingly.

"Come on," shouted Clifford.

It's all right for *him* to talk to her, John thought, as he struggled to swing the starter. He just doesn't like me doing it; and he wished, as he had begun often to do, that Clifford was not there.

They had spasmodic engine trouble in the morning, which slowed them down; and the consequent halts, with the difficulty they experienced of mooring anywhere (the banks seemed nothing but marsh), were depressing and cold. Their good spirits evaporated: by lunchtime John was plainly irritable and frightened, and Clifford had begun to hate the grey silent land on either side, with the woods and hills which remained so consistently distant. They both wanted to give it up by then, but John felt bound to stick to his promise, and Clifford was secretly sure that Sharon wished to continue.

While she was preparing another late lunch, they saw a small boy who stood on what once had been the towpath watching them. He was bare-headed, wore corduroy, and had no shoes. He held a long reed, the end of which he chewed as he stared at them.

"Ask him where we are," said John; and Clifford asked.

He took the reed out of his mouth, but did not reply.

"Where do you live then?" asked Clifford as they drew almost level with him.

"I told you. Three miles up," he said; and then he gave a sudden little shriek of fear, dropped the reed, and turned to run down the bank the way they had come. Once he looked back, stumbled and fell, picked himself up sobbing, and ran faster. Sharon had appeared with lunch a moment before, and together they listened to his gasping cries growing fainter and fainter, until he had run himself out of their sight.

"What on earth frightened him?" said Clifford.

"I don't know. Unless it was Sharon popping out of the cabin like that."

"Nonsense. But he was a very frightened little boy. And, I say, do you realise . . ."

"He was a very foolish little boy," Sharon interrupted. She was angry, Clifford noticed with surprise, really angry, white and trembling, and with a curious expression which he did not like.

"We might have got something out of him," said John sadly.

"Too late now," Sharon said, She had quite recovered herself.

They saw no one else. They journeyed on throughout the afternoon; it grew colder, and at the same time more and more airless and still. When the light began to fail, Sharon disappeared as usual to the cabin. The canal became more tortuous, and John asked Clifford to help him with the turns. Clifford complied unwillingly: he did not want to leave Sharon, but as it had been he who had insisted on their continuing, he could hardly refuse. The turns were nerve-racking, as the canal was very narrow and the light grew worse and worse.

"All right if we stop soon?" asked John eventually.

"Stop now if you like."

"Well, we'll try and find a tree to tie up to. This swamp is awful. Can't think how that child ran."

"That child . . ." began Clifford anxiously; but John, who had been equally unnerved by the incident, and did not want to think about it, interrupted. "Is there a tree ahead anywhere?"

"Can't see one. There's a hell of a bend coming though. Almost back on itself. Better slow a bit more."

"Can't. We're right down as it is."

They crawled round, clinging to the outside bank, which seemed always to approach them, its rushes to rub against their bows, although the wheel was hard over. John grunted with relief; and they both stared ahead for the next turn.

They were presented with the most terrible spectacle. The canal immediately broadened, until no longer a canal but a sheet, an infinity, of water stretched ahead; oily, silent, and still, as far as the eye could see, with no country edging it, nothing but water to the low grey sky above it. John had almost immediately cut out the engine, and now he tried desperately to start it again, in order to turn round. Clifford instinctively glanced behind them. He saw no canal at all, no inlet, but grasping and close to the stern of the boat, the reeds and rushes of a marshy waste closing in behind them.

He stumbled to the cabin doors and pulled them open. It was very neat and tidy in there, but empty. Only one stern door of the cabin was free of its catch, and it flapped irregularly backwards and forwards with their movements in the boat.

There was no sign of Sharon at all.

CORMAC McCARTHY

THE DARK WATERS

HER FIRST HIGH yelp was thin and clear as the air itself, its tenuous and diminishing echoes sounding out the coves and hollows, trebling to a high ring like the last fading note of a chime glass. He could hear the boy breathing in the darkness at his elbow, trying to breathe quietly, listening too hard. She sounded again, and he stood and touched the boy's shoulder lightly. Let's go, he said.

The strung-out ringing yelps came like riflefire. The boy was on his feet. Has she treed yet? he asked.

No. She's jest hit it now. Then he added: She's close though, hot. He started down the steep hummock on which they had been resting, through a maze of small pines whose polished needles thick on the ground made the descent a series of precarious slides from trunk to trunk, until they got to the gully at the bottom, a black slash in the earth beyond which he could see nothing although he knew there was a field there, pitched sharply down to the creek some hundred yards farther on. He dropped into the gully, heard the beaded rush of sliding dirt as the boy followed, came up the other side, and started out through the field at a jog-trot, the heavy weeds popping and his corduroy setting up a rhythmic zip-zip as he ran.

The cottonwoods at the creek loomed up stark and pale out of the darkness; he crossed a low wreck of barbed wire, heard again the resonant creak of the rusty staples in the checked and split cedar post as the boy crossed behind him. They were in the woods above the creek then, rattling through the stiff frosted leaves.

Lady's sharp trail-call still broke excitedly off to their right. They moved out under the dark trees, through a stand of young cedars gathered in a clearing, vespertine figures, rotund and druidical in their black solemnity. When the man reached the far side, the woods again, he stopped, and the boy caught up with him.

Which way is she going? He was trying not to sound winded.

The man paused for just a moment more. Then he said, Same way he is – motioning loosely with his hand. His back melted into the darkness again. The boy moved after him, keeping his feet high, following the sound of the brittle leaves. Their path angled down toward the creek, and he could hear at intervals the rush of water, high now after the rain, like the rumble of a distant freight passing.

Watch a log, the man called back to him. He jumped just in time, half stumbled over the windfall trunk, lost his balance, ricocheted off a sapling, went on, holding his head low, straining to see. Trees appeared, slid past with slow gravity before folding again into the murk beyond. They were climbing now, a long rise, and when he came over the crest he caught a glimpse of the figure ahead of him, framed darkly for an instant against the glaucous drop of sky. Below him he could make out the course of the creek. They dipped into a low saddle in the ridge, rose again, and the man was no longer there. He stopped and listened. Lady's clear voice was joined by another, lower and less insistent. She was much closer now, quartering down, coming closer. He could follow her progress, listening between the explosions of his breath. Then she stopped.

There was a moment of silence; then the other dog yapped

once. Sounds of brush crashing. Two wild yelps just off to his right and then a concussion of water. A low voice at his side said: He's got her in the creek, come on. The man started down the side of the hill, the boy behind him, and out onto a small flat set in the final slope to the creek and dominated by a thick beech tree. Something was coming down from the ridge above them, and they halted. A long shadow swept past in a skitter of leaves and on toward the creek bank. There was one short chopped bark and then a splash. They followed, sidling down the slope and out along the bank where the water gathered a thin membranous light by which they could see, directed by frantic surging sounds and low intermittent growls, some suggestion of figures struggling there, and the new dog striking out in the water to join them. The fight moved down, out in deep water and under the shadow of the far bank. The snarls stopped, and there was only the desperate rending of water.

A light blinked through the trees to their right, went out, appeared again, bobbing, unattached and eerie in the blackness. They could hear the dry frosted crack of sticks and brush, muted voices. The light darted out, peered again suddenly down upon them, sweeping an arc along the edge of the creek.

Howdy, a voice said.

Cas?

Yeah . . . that you, Marion?

Bring that light; they're in the creek.

They came down the slope, four dismembered legs hobbling in the swatch of light as they descended.

Throw your light, Sylder said.

They came alongside, dispensing an aura of pipe-smoke and dog-hair. The shorter one was working the beam slowly over the creek.

Whereabouts? he said.

Down some. Howdy, Bill.

Howdy, the other said. In the glare emanating from the flashlight their breath was smoke-white, curling, clinging about their heads in a vaporous canopy. The oval of the flashbeam scudded down the glides against the far bank, passed, backed, came to rest on the combatants clinching in the icy water, the coon's eyes glowing red pin points, his fur wetly bedraggled and his tail swaying in crestfallen buoyancy on the current. The big dog was circling him warily, trudging the water with wearying paws and failing enthusiasm. They could see Lady's ear sticking out from under the coon's front leg, and then her hindquarters bobbed up, surging through the face of the creek with a wild flash of tail and sinking back in a soundless swirl.

Cas swung the beam to shore, scrabbled up a handful of rock and handed the light to the other man. Hold it on him, he said. He scaled a rock at the coon. It cut a slow arc in the beam and pitched from sight with a muffled slurp. The big hound started for shore, and Lady's tail had made another desperate appearance when the second rock, a flitting shadow, curving, flashed water under the coon's face.

He turned loose and struck out downstream, stroking with the current. The big dog, on the other bank now, had set up a pitiful moaning sound, pacing, the man with the light calling to him in a hoarse and urgent voice, Hunt im up, boy, hunt im up. He turned to the men. He's skeered of rocks, he explained.

Hush a minute, Sylder said, taking the light from him. Lady was already some thirty yards below them. When the light hit her, she turned her head back, and her eyes came pale orange, ears fanned out and floating, treading the water down before her with a tired and grim determination. She had her mouth turned up at the corners in a macabre and ludicrous grin as if to keep out the water.

Ho, gal, Sylder called. Ho, gal. They were moving down the creek too, raking through the brush. She's fixin to drownd herself, someone said.

Ho, gal, Ho. . . .

He never even felt the water. He couldn't hear them any more, hadn't heard them call since he left them somewhere back up the creek, when he hit the bullbriers full tilt, not feeling them either, aware only of them pulling at his coat and legs like small hands trying to hold him. Then he was over the bank, feet reaching for something and finally skewing on the slick mud, catapulting him in a stifflegged parabola down and out into the water, arms flailing, but not falling yet, not until he had already stopped, teetering thigh-deep, and took a first step out into the current where he collapsed forward like a shot heron.

But he didn't even feel it. When he came up again, he was in water past his waist, the soft creek floor squirming away beneath his feet as if he were walking the bodies of a colony of underwater creatures clustered there. He could see a little better now. There was no light on the bank, and he thought: I come down too far. And no voices, only the sounds of the creek chattering and running past all around him. Then he went in again, over his head this time, and came up treading water and with something pushing against his chest. He got his arms under it and Lady's head came up, and her eyes rolled at him dumbly. He reached and got hold of her collar, the creek bottom coming up and sliding off under his feet, falling backwards now with the dog rolling over him and beginning to struggle, until his leg hit a rock, and he reached for it and steadied himself and rose again and began to flounder shoreward with the dog in tow.

They came with the light and Sylder looked at him huddled in the willows, still holding the dog. He didn't say anything, just disappeared into the woods, returning in a few minutes with a pile of brush and dead limbs.

One of the men was kneeling with him and stroking then examining her. She looks all right, he said, don't she, son? He couldn't get his mouth open, so he just nodded. He was beyond cold now, paralyzed.

The other man said: Son, you goin to take your death. We better get you home fore you freeze settin right there.

He nodded again. He wanted to get up, but he couldn't bear the rub of his clothes where he moved.

Sylder had the fire going by then, a great crackling sound as the dry brush took, orange light leaping among the trees. He could see him in silhouette moving about, feeding the flames.

Then he came back. He gathered the quivering hound up in one arm and motioned for the boy to follow. You come here, he said. And get them clothes off.

He got up then and labored stiffly after them.

Sylder put the hound by the fire and turned to the boy. Lemme have that coat, he said.

The boy peeled off the leaden mackinaw and handed it over to him. He passed it around the trunk of a sapling, gathered the ends up in his hands, and twisted what looked to be a gallon of water out of the loose wool. Then he hung it over a bush. When he looked back the boy was still standing there.

Get em off, he said.

He started pulling his clothes off, the man taking from him in turn shirt and trousers, socks and drawers, wringing them and hanging them over a pole propped on forks before the fire. When he was finished, he stood naked, white as a slug in the cup of firelight. Sylder took off his coat and threw it to him.

Put it on, he said. And get your ass over here in front of the fire.

The two men were behind him in the woods; he could hear them crashing about, see the wink of their light. One of them came back toting a huge log and dropped it on the fire. A flurry of sparks ascended, flared, lost in the smoke pulling at the bare limbs overhead, returned, tracing their slow fall redly through the dark trees downwind.

He sat in a trampled matting of vines, the long coat just covering his buttocks. Sylder made a final adjustment to the pole and came over. He lit a cigarette and stood regarding him.

Kind of cool, ain't it? he said.

The boy looked up at him. Cool enough, he said.

The clothes had begun to steam, looking like some esoteric game quartered and smoking on the spit.

Then he said, What'd you do with the coon?

Coon?

Yeah. The coon.

Goddamn, the boy said, I never saw the coon.

Oh, Sylder said. But his voice was giving him away. Hell, I figured you'd of got the coon too.

Shoo, the boy said. Over his teeth the firelight rippled and danced.

The two men were warming their hands at the fire, the shorter one grinning good-naturedly at the boy. The other hound had appeared, hovering suddenly at the rim of light and snuffling at the steaming wool and then slouching past them with nervous indifference, the slack hound grace, to where Lady lay quietly, peering across her paws into the fire. He nosed at her, and she raised her head to look at him with her sad red eyes. He stood so for a minute, looking past her, then stepped neatly over her and melted silently into the black wickerwork of the brush. The other man moved over to her and reached down to pat her head. One ear was mangled and crusting with blood.

Coon's hard on a Walker, he said. Walker's got too much heart. Old Redbone like that – he motioned toward the blackness that encircled them – he'll quit if it gets too rough. Little old Walker though – he addressed the dog now – she jest got too much heart, ain't she?

When Sylder let him out of the car, his clothes were still wet. You better scoot in there fast, he told him. Your maw raise hell with you?

Naw, he said, she'll be asleep.

Well, Sylder said. We'll go again. You got to stay out of the creek, though. Here, I got to get on. My old lady'll be standin straight up.

All right, we'll see ye. He let the door fall.

Night, Sylder said. The car pulled away, trailing ropy plumes of smoke, the one red taillight bobbing. He turned toward the house, lightless and archaic among the crumbling oaks, crossed the frosted yard. His shadow swept upward to the lean-to roof, dangled from a limb, upward again, laced with branches, stood suddenly upon the roof. He slid downward over the eaves and disappeared in the black square of the gable window.

OLEKSANDER DOVZHENKO

EASTER FLOOD

Translated from the Ukrainian by
Dzvinia Orlowsky and Ali Kinsella

from *Enchanted Desna*

ONCE WE LIVED in harmony with nature. In winter, we froze; in summer, we baked in the sun. In fall, we plodded through thick mud. In spring, water flooded us. Whoever has never experienced this has never really lived. Spring flowed freely from the Desna. Back then, no one gave much thought to taming nature and the water flowed as it wished. At times, the Desna stretched so far across the land, not only did it swallow our woods and meadows, but entire villages as well. People called out from their homes to be saved, and this, precisely, brought us glory.

One could write an entire book about how Grandfather, Father, and I saved our neighbors and their cows and horses. Today, such heroics would have won me a holiday at Artek, the Young Pioneer camp. But back then, we knew no Arteks. Remember, all this happened a long time ago. I've forgotten exactly which year on Easter Eve the flood grew so big no one – not even Grandfather or Grandmother – had ever seen anything like it.

A storm had broken out, just around dusk. Water rose with tremendous speed. In one day, it filled the forests, hayfields, and gardens. The Desna wailed all night. Bells tolled. People shouted in the dark for help; dogs howled. The storm continued. No one slept. In the morning, streets overflowed, but still the water came. What could we do?

As if in answer to this question, the police superintendent sent the big officer Makar to pay Father a visit.

"You gotta go save the people in Zahrebellia. Haven't you heard? They're drowning," he ordered Father in a hoarse voice. "You're the only one around with a boat. Besides, you're a sailor."

Overhearing this, Mother burst into tears, "But it's Holy Easter!"

Father shushed her, then said to Makar, "Look, I'd like to save them, but I'm afraid of committing a sin. At daybreak it'll be Easter Sunday. I must eat a crust of holy Easter bread and have a drink. I haven't had a drink for two months. I can't scorn Easter."

"You'll rot in a prison cell," snapped Makar, pausing for a moment to sniff our roasted suckling pig. "Instead of being honored for saving people and cattle, you'll be fighting off fleas in jail."

"Okay," Father gave up. "Damn it, you scoundrel. I'm coming."

Mother, who always got anxious before Easter, continued to despair, "Where do you think you're going? It's Easter!"

"We'll have to eat it unblessed. If we sin, we sin. Makar, sit down. Christ is Risen! Pour another round. Here's to spring, the Easter willow, to the flood and its disasters!"

Having broken fast we gradually fell asleep, one by one, and slept through mass. It was only at dawn and with great difficulty that we began rowing to the flooded village of Zahrebellia. The whole congregation was perched on the thatched roofs, clutching their unblessed Easter breads. This was an especially unusual scene to see at sunrise – as if we were all in a dream or fairy tale. As the sun rose before us, our eyes opened onto a new world. Everything was different – but somehow more commanding, and festive. The water, clouds, the current – everything was drifting, restlessly surging ahead, foaming and glistening in the sunlight.

Such a beautiful spring!

With full strength we rowed under Father's shrewd direction. We were hot from rowing hard, but happy in our work. Father sat with an oar at the stern, happy and strong. He felt like a savior, a hero delivered to the drowning, a Vasco da Gama. And though life had offered him puddles instead of oceans, his soul was as vast as a sea. That's precisely why our Vasco da Gama could never come to terms with this incongruity and chose to sink his ships at the tavern. They say that to a drunkard the sea is only knee deep. It took me a long time to understand that this was a lie. Father sank his ships in dirty taverns so that the small puddles of his life could, at least for a short while, become the immeasurable, endless sea.

The water rose and raged. Barely had the villagers comprehended how they'd come to be on an island, than that island also began to disappear under the water.

"Save us!"

Water poured foaming into the streets and meadows, hissed under the cottage foundations and doors, flooding stables, sheepfolds, and barns. Then it rose three and a half feet more and rushed into the houses through doors and windows.

"For God's sake, save us!"

Houses shook under the current. An eerie cry was heard from the pens. Terrified horses tied to posts stood up to their necks in water. Pigs had already drowned. Bloated, drowned oxen were being carried in the flood from villages higher up along the Desna. Water had reached the church and was climbing the very iconostasis. The entire village was flooded. Only Yarema Bobyr, a relative of ours on Grandfather's side, escaped the disaster. He somehow knew all the forewarnings of such natural occurrences and especially put his faith in mice. Bobyr knew about the flood as early as winter. On the feast of the Epiphany, when he saw mice scurrying out of the barns and pantries across the snow, our cunning uncle knew a disaster would strike in spring. Despite the foolish, impudent neighbors teasing him, he stripped the thatch over the entrance hall, built a small animal pen on the roof with a stairway leading to it, and filled the whole attic with a good supply of hay and grain. So now, when the village was hollering in despair, "Save us," instead of "Christ is Risen," the entire Bobyr family was happily breaking the fast on their rooftop manger surrounded by cows, horses, sheep, hens, and doves just like the scene in an old painting that once hung in our church.

"Save us! Our house is being swept away!" someone shouted from below.

"Christ is Risen!" Bobyr shouted back.

At this point, Christ got to hear curses hollered back and forth across the water that would've put a blush on even the most case-hardened judge. Someone started the rumor that during Lent the priest's wife had eaten to her heart's content butter and eggs she'd stolen from his private stock. There was a great outcry. On second thought, however, this talk was not anti-religious or blasphemous. Sitting on their roofs holding their unsanctified Easter breads among the drowned cattle, all that the believers probably wanted was for God to show a little more concern for the world he'd created. Put simply, they thought God, Mother Mary, and the saints could do better than these oppressive and untimely sorrows.

"What the devil kind of Easter bread is this," someone yelled, "when, God forgive us, we have to eat it unblessed? The whole parish crowded on our roofs, while catfish swim freely inside our houses!"

"Christ is Risen, you drowned ducks!" Father exulted as

his boat skimmed over the wattle fence into the yard and bumped its nose into the roof.

"Damn it all!" elderly Lev Kyianytsia shouted from his thatch. He then handed Father a shot of *horilka*. "Indeed He is risen. Save us, Petro, and try not to laugh. Our house'll be swept under any minute. See, it's already moving."

"Save us! Have mercy!" the women screamed.

"May we be enlightened this day of resurrection, good people! The Easter of our Lord, Easter from death to life, from earth to heaven . . ." three voices sang out in the distance.

"Help! We're drowning!"

Suddenly a small boat bobbed out from behind the houses bearing the pastor Kyrylo, the deacon Yakym, and the sacristan Luka at the helm. The clergymen had been busy rowing from house to house, blessing the Easter breads, hoping to lift the religious morale of their parishioners.

"Father Kyrylo, come here quick! The children are crying for a piece of Easter bread!"

"Patience, Christians!" Father Kyrylo shouted back. "The Almighty savior has sent us a sign in His waters, which are blessed tidings of a good harvest of cereals and grasses. Where are you steering, damn it! To the roof or I'll fall out of the boat!"

Somehow the sacristan docked the boat along the thatch. The servants of the sect sprinkled the Easter bread and *pysanky* with the blessed water of spring. And little by little each had a drink to ward off the cold and started to forget what song was best for the occasion.

"Father Kyrylo, perhaps instead of 'May we be enlightened,' 'Down the Mother Volga' would be apter," Father joked.

"That's not funny!" the priest replied angrily. He hated my

father for being handsome and for his irreverence. "Even on a holy day, you blast God, you immoral infidel."

"All of you, let's get this confession of the faith thing straight once and for all. I'm not against God," Father said merrily as he hauled in a half-drowned heifer with a lasso. "Sashko, grab her by the horns. Hold on, don't be afraid."

He continued, "I'll run the rope under her belly now. I'm not against God or Easter or even against Lent. I'm not against His ox or His ass or any of His beasts. If, at times, I'm angry with His all-powerful, all-wise, all-seeing eye, that doesn't mean I don't believe in Him – or in some other God!"

"You'll burn in hell for such words!" intervened the deacon on the Lord's behalf.

"Don't care," said Father, and, balancing the heifer on a pole, he managed to deftly haul it into the boat.

"Where else should a sinner such as I burn? Of course, God in the sky knows better than we what's what when it comes to letting loose fires and floods on his people, or mice or a drought, or evil men in power, or a war. My own interests and common sense might not be that great, although I am one of God's creations. But I am neither wicked nor foolish. Why should I praise my Lord for sending us such a flood – especially on Easter? What's God planning with all this water? Personally, I don't see any good in it."

"God works in mysterious ways." Father Kyrylo reprimanded him.

"Of course," Father agreed, surveying the flooded landscape. "There must have been some great divine purpose in such a gift of water. But at this moment, the only thing I can count on is that my pants are getting wet and my head's not getting any drier."

"Shut up, you blasphemer!" blared Father Kyrylo. Just then came a sudden turn of events. The priest suddenly lost his balance. Thrashing about in the air with his hands, he fell headfirst into the water. This made the boat sway in the opposite direction, and only ripples indicated the place where the deacon and sacristan had disappeared.

Roars of laughter came from the thatched roofs of the flooded village. Both the young and old laughed until they couldn't catch their breath. Can you imagine? Laughter at the blessed bread and at themselves, at the whole world on Easter – on thatched roofs amid horses and cows, the heads and horns barely showing above the cold water. The Zahrebellia villagers didn't quite grasp the patterns and meaning of natural disasters. Instead, they welcomed the opportunity to make fun of everything, even Holy Easter. My father, that great and kind man, could not suppress a smile as he looked around at these people. "What a parish!" he said. "Every spring for over a thousand years these folks have been getting drenched. And yet, even the devil can't drown or drive them out."

Father hooked an oar handle through Kyrylo's gold chain, pulled him out of the water like a catfish and into our ark with its cows and horses. Then we hauled out the deacon, but we were laughing so hard that we forgot about the sacristan Luka. Perhaps, in the end, he was eaten by crawfish.

LOVE AND LOSS

ZORA NEALE HURSTON

MAGNOLIA FLOWER

THE BROOK LAUGHED and sang. When it encountered hard places in its bed, it hurled its water in sparkling dance figures up into the moonlight.

It sang louder, louder; danced faster, faster, with a coquettish splash! at the vegetation on its banks.

At last it danced boisterously into the bosom of the St. John's, upsetting the whispering hyacinths who shivered and blushed, drunk with the delight of moon kisses.

The Mighty One turned peevishly in his bed and washed the feet of the Palmetto palms so violently that they awoke and began again the gossip they had left off when the Wind went to bed. A palm cannot speak without wind. The river had startled it also, for the winds sleep on the bosom of waters.

The palms murmured noisily of seasons and centuries, mating and birth and the transplanting of life. Nature knows nothing of death.

The river spoke to the brook.

"Why, O Young Water, do you hurry and hurl yourself so riotously about with your chatter and song? You disturb my sleep."

"Because, O Venerable One," replied the brook, "I am young. The flowers bloom, the trees and wind say beautiful things to me: there are lovers beneath the orange trees on my banks, – but most of all because the moon shines upon me with a full face."

"That is not sufficient reason for you to disturb my sleep," the river retorted. "I have cut down mountains and moved whole valleys into the sea, and I am not so noisy as *you* are."

The river slapped its banks angrily.

"But," added the brook diffidently, "I passed numbers of lovers as I came on. There was also a sweet-voiced night-bird."

"No matter, no matter!" scolded the river. "I have seen millions of lovers, child. I have borne them up and down, listened to those things that are uttered more with the breath than with the lips, gathered infinite tears, and some lovers have even flung themselves upon the soft couch I keep in my bosom, and slept."

"Tell me about some of them!" eagerly begged the brook.

"Oh, well," the river muttered, "I am wide awake now, and I suppose brooks must be humored."

THE RIVER'S STORY

"Long ago, as men count years, men who were pale of skin held a dark race of men in a bondage. The dark ones cried out in sorrow and travail, – not here in my country, but farther north. Many rivers carried their tears to the sea and the tide would bring some of them to me. The Wind brought cries without end.

"But there were some among the slaves who did not weep, but fled in the night to safety, – some to the far north, some to the far south, for here the red man, the panther, and the bear alone were to be feared. One of them from the banks of the Savannah came here. He was large and black and strong. His heart was strong and thudded with an iron sound in his breast. The forest made way for him, the beasts were afraid of him, and he built a house. He gathered stones and bits of metal, yellow and white – such as men love and for which they die – and grew wealthy. How? I do not know. Rivers take no notice of such things. We sweep men, stones, metal – all, ALL to the sea. All are as grass; all must to the sea in the end.

"He married Swift Deer, a Cherokee Maiden, and five years – as men love to clip Time into bits – passed.

"They had now a daughter, Magnolia Flower they called her, for she came at the time of their opening.

"When they had been married five years, she was four years old.

"Then the tide brought trouble rumors to me of hate, strife and destruction, – war, war, war.

"The blood of those born in the North flowed to sea, mingled with that of the southern-born. Bitter Waters, Troubled Winds. Rains that washed the dust from Heaven but could not beat back the wails of anguish, the thirst for blood and glory; the prayers for that which God gives not into the hands of man – Vengeance, – fires of hate to sear and scorch the ground: wells of acid tears to blight the leaf.

"Then all men walked free in the land, and Wind and Water again grew sweet.

"The man-made time notches flew by, and Magnolia Flower was in full-bloom. Her large eyes burned so brightly in her dark-brown face that the Negroes trembled when she looked angrily upon them. 'She curses with her eyes,' they said. 'Some evil surely will follow.'

"Black men came and went now as they pleased and the father had many to serve him, for now he had built a house such as white men owned when he was in bondage.

"His heart, of the ex-slave Bentley, was iron to all but Magnolia Flower. Swift Deer was no longer swift. Too many kicks and blows, too many grim chokings had slowed her feet and heart.

"He had done violence to workmen. There was little law in this jungle, and that was his, – 'Do as I bid you or suffer my punishment.'

"He was hated, but feared more.

"He hated anything that bore the slightest resemblance to his former oppressors. His servants must be black, very black or Cherokee.

"The flower was seventeen and beautiful. Bentley thought often of a mate for her now, but one that would not offend him either in spirit or flesh. He must be full of humility, and black.

"One day, as the sun gave me a good-night kiss and the stars began their revels, I bore a young Negro yet not a Negro, for his skin was the color of freshly barked cypress, golden with the curly black hair of the white man.

"There were many Negroes in Bentley's Village and he wished to build a school that would teach them useful things.

"Bentley hated him at once; but ordered a school-house to be built, for he wished Magnolia to read and write.

"But before two weeks had passed, the teacher had taught the Flower to read strange marvels with her dark eyes, and she had taught the teacher to sing with his eyes, his hands, his whole body in her presence or whenever he thought of her, – not in her father's house, but beneath that clump of palms, those three that bathe their toes eternally and talk.

"They busied themselves with dreams of creation, while Bentley swore the foundation of the school-room into place.

" 'Nothing remains for me to do, now that I have your consent, but to ask your father for your sweet self. I know I am poor, but I have a great Vision, a high purpose, and he shall not be ashamed of me!'

"She clung fearfully to him.

" 'No, don't, John, don't. He'll say "Naw!" and cuss. He – he don't like you at all. Youse too white.'

" 'I'll get him out of that, just trust me, precious. Then I can just *own* you – just let me talk to him!'

"She wept and pleaded with him – told him of Bentley's terrible anger and his violence, begged him to take her away and send her father word; but he refused to hear her, and walked up to her house and seated himself upon the broad verandah to wait for the father of Magnolia Flower.

"She flew to Swift Deer and begged her to persuade her lover not to brave Bentley's anger. The older woman crept out and tearfully implored him to go. He stayed.

"At dusk Bentley came swearing in. It had been a hot day; the men had cut several poor pieces of timber and seemed all bent on driving him to the crazy-house, he complained.

"Swift Deer slunk into the house at his approach, dragging her daughter after her.

"What followed was too violent for words to tell, – strength against strength, steel against steel. Threats bellowed from Bentley's bull throat seemed no more than little puffs of air to the lover. Of course, he would leave Bentley's house; but he would stay in the vicinity until he was told to leave by the Flower, – his Flower of sweetness and purity – and he would marry her unless hell froze over.

" 'Better eat up dem words an' git out whilst ah letcher,' the old man growled.

"Bentley drew up his lips in a great roll glare.

" 'No!' John shouted, giving him glare for his rage boiling and tumbling out from behind these ramparts, as it were. His eye reddened, a vessel in the center of his forehead stood out, gorged with blood, and his great hands twitched. For good or evil, Bentley was a strong man, mind and body.

"Swift Deer could no longer restrain her daughter. Magnolia Flower burst triumphantly upon the verandah.

" 'Well, papa, you don't say that I haven't picked a man. No one else in forty miles round would stand up to you like John!'

" 'Ham! Jim! Israel!' Bentley howled, on the verge of apoplexy. The men appeared. 'Take dis here yaller skunk an' lock him in dat back-room. I'm a gonna hang 'im high as Hamon come sun up, law uh no law.'

"A short struggle, and John was tied hand and foot.

" 'Stop!' cried Magnolia Flower, fighting, clawing, biting, kicking like a brown fiend for her lover. One brawny worker held her until John was helplessly bound.

"But when she looked at all three of the men with her eye of fire, they shook in superstitious fear.

" 'Oh, Moh Gawd!' breathed Ham, terrified. 'She's cussing us, she's cussing us all wid her eyes. Sump'm sho gwine happen.'

"Her eye was indeed something to affright the timid and even give the strong heart pause. A woman robbed of her love is more terrible than an army with banners.

" 'Oh, I wish I could!' she uttered in a voice flat with intensity. 'You'd all drop dead on the spot.'

"Swift Deer had crept out and stood beside the child. She screamed and clasped her hands over her daughter's lips.

" 'Say not such words, Magnolia,' she pleaded. 'Take them back into your bosom unsaid.'

" 'Leave her be,' Bentley laughed acidly. 'Ah got a dose uh mah medicine ready for her too. Befo' ah hangs dis yaller pole-cat ahm gwinter marry her to crazy Joe, an' John kin look on; den ah'll hang *him*, and she kin look on. Magnolia and Joe oughter have fine black chillen. Ha! Ha!'

"The girl never uttered a sound. She smiled with her lips

but her eyes burned every bit of courage to cinders in those who saw her.

"John was locked in the stout back-room. The windows were guarded and Ham sat with a loaded gun at the door.

"Magnolia was locked in the parlor where she ran up and down, tearing her heavy black hair. She beat helplessly upon the doors, she hammered the windows, making little mewing noises in her throat like a cat deprived of her litter.

"The house grew grimly still. Bentley had forced his wife to accompany him to their bedroom. She lay fearfully awake but he slept peacefully, if noisily.

" 'Magnolia Flower!' Ham called softly as he turned the key stealthily in the lock of her prison. 'Come on out. Ah caint stan' dis here weekedness uh yo pappy!'

" 'No thank you, Ham. I'll stay right here and make him kill me long with John, if you don't let him out too.'

" 'Lawd a mussy knows ah wisht ah could, but de ole man's got de key in his britches.'

" 'I'm going and get it, Ham,' she announced as she stepped over the threshold to freedom.

" 'Lawd! He'll kill me sho's you born.'

"Her feet were already on the stairs.

" 'I'll have that key or die. Ham, you put some victuals in that rowboat.'

"Half for love, half for fear, Ham obeyed.

"No one but Magnolia Flower would have entered Bentley's bed-room as she did, under the circumstances but to her the circumstances were her reasons for going. The big horse pistol under his pillow, the rack of guns in the hall, and her father's giant hands – none of these stopped her. She knew three lives, – her own, her lover's, and Ham's – hung on her success; but she went and returned with that key.

"One minute more and they flew down the path to the three leaning palms into the boat away northward.

"The morning came. Bentley ate hugely. The new rope hung ominously from the arm of the giant oak in the yard. Preacher Ike had eaten his breakfast with Bentley and the idiot, Crazy Joe, had forced himself into a pair of clean hickory pants.

"Bentley turned the key and flung open the door, stood still a moment in a grey rage and stalked to the back-room door, feeling for the key meanwhile.

"When he had fully convinced himself that the key was gone, he did not bother to open the door.

" 'Ham, it 'pears dat Magnolia an' dat yaller dog aint heah dis mawnin', so you an' Swift Deer will hafta do, being ez y'all let 'em git away.' He said this calmly and stalked toward the gun rack; but his anger was too large to be contained in one human heart. His arteries corded his face, his eyes popped, and he fell senseless as he stretched his hand for the gun. Rage had burst his heart at being outwitted by a girl.

"This all happened more than forty years ago, as men reckon time. Soon Swift Deer died, and the house built by strong Bentley fell to decay. White men came and built a town and Magnolia Flower and her eyes passed from the hearts of people who had known her."

The brook had listened, tensely thrilled to its very bottom at times. The river flowed calmly on, shimmering under the moon as it moved ceaselessly to the sea.

An old couple picked their way down to the water's edge. He had once been tall – he still bore himself well. The little old woman clung lovingly to his arm.

"It's been forty-seven years, John," she said sweetly, her voice full of fear. "Do you think we can find the place?"

"Why yes, Magnolia, my Flower, unless they have cut down our trees; but if they are standing, we'll know 'em – couldn't help it."

"Yes, sweetheart, there they are. Hurry and let's sit on the roots like we used to and trail our fingers in the water. Love is wonderful, isn't it, dear?"

They hugged the trunks of the three clustering palms lovingly; then hugged each other and sat down shyly upon the heaped up roots.

"You never have regretted, Magnolia?"

"Of course not! But, John, listen, did you ever hear a river make such a sound? Why it seems almost as if it were talking – that murmuring noise, you know."

"Maybe, it's welcoming us back. I always felt that it loved you and me, somehow."

RABINDRANATH TAGORE

THE RIVER STAIRS

Translated by Jadunath Sarker

IF YOU WISH to hear of days gone by, sit on this step of mine, and lend your ears to the murmur of the rippling water.

The month of *Ashwin*, September, was about to begin. The river was in full flood. Only four of my steps peeped above the surface. The water had crept up to the low-lying parts of the bank, where the *kachu* plant grew dense beneath the branches of the mango grove. At that bend of the river, three old brick-heaps towered above the water around them. The fishing-boats, moored to the trunks of the *bābla* trees on the bank, rocked on the heaving flow-tide at dawn. The path of tall grasses on the sandbank had caught the newly risen sun; they had just begun to flower, and were not yet in full bloom.

The little boats puffed out their tiny sails on the sunlit river. The Brahmin priest had come to bathe with his ritual vessels. The women arrived in twos and threes to draw water. I knew this was the time of Kusum's coming to the bathing-stairs.

But that morning I missed her. Bhuban and Swarno mourned at the *ghāt*, the bathing place. They said that their friend had been led away to her husband's house, which was a place far away from the river, with strange people, strange houses, and strange roads.

In time she almost faded out of my mind. A year passed. The women at the *ghāt* now rarely talked of Kusum. But one evening I was startled by the touch of the long familiar feet. Ah, yes, but those feet were now without anklets, they had lost their old music.

Kusum had become a widow. They said that her husband had worked in some far-off place, and that she had met him only once or twice. A letter brought her the news of his death. A widow at eight years old, she had rubbed out the wife's red mark from her forehead, stripped off her bangles, and come back to her old home by the Ganges. But she found few of her old playmates there. Of them, Bhuban, Swarno, and Amala were married, and gone away; only Sarat remained, and she too, they said, would be wed in December next.

As the Ganges rapidly grows to fulness with the coming of the rains, even so did Kusum day by day grow to the fulness of beauty and youth. But her dull-coloured robe, her pensive face, and quiet manners drew a veil over her youth, and hid it from men's eyes as in a mist. Ten years slipped away, and none seemed to have noticed that Kusum had grown up.

One morning such as this, at the far end of a far-off September, a tall, young, fair-skinned Sanyasi, coming I know not whence, took shelter in the Shiva temple in front of me. His arrival was announced abroad in the village. The women left their pitchers behind, and crowded into the temple to bow to the holy man.

The crowd increased day by day. The Sanyasi's fame rapidly spread among the womenkind. One day he would recite the *Bhágbat*, another day he would expound the *Gita*, or hold forth upon a holy book in the temple. Some sought him for counsel, some for spells, some for medicines.

So, months passed away. In April, at the time of the solar eclipse, vast crowds came here to bathe in the Ganges. A fair was held under the *bābla* tree. Many of the pilgrims went to visit the Sanyasi, and among them were a party of women from the village where Kusum had been married.

It was morning. The Sanyasi was counting his beads on my steps, when all of a sudden one of the women pilgrims nudged another, and said: "Why! He is our Kusum's husband!" Another parted her veil a little in the middle with two fingers and cried out: "Oh dear me! So it is! He is the younger son of the Chattergu family of our village!" Said a third, who made little parade of her veil: "Ah! he has got exactly the same brow, nose, and eyes!" Yet another woman, without turning to the Sanyasi, stirred the water with her pitcher, and sighed: "Alas! That young man is no more; he will not come back. Bad luck to Kusum!"

But, objected one, "He had not such a big beard"; and another, "He was not so thin"; or "He was most probably not so tall." That settled the question for the time, and the matter spread no further.

One evening, as the full moon arose, Kusum came and sat upon my last step above the water, and cast her shadow upon me.

There was no other at the *ghāt* just then. The crickets were chirping about me. The din of brass gongs and bells had ceased in the temple – the last wave of sound grew fainter and fainter, until it merged like the shade of a sound in the dim groves of the farther bank. On the dark water of the Ganges lay a line of glistening moonlight. On the bank above, in bush and hedge, under the porch of the temple, in the base of ruined houses, by the side of the tank, in the palm grove, gathered shadows of fantastic shape. The bats swung from the *chhatim* boughs. Near the houses the loud clamour of the jackals rose and sank into silence.

Slowly the Sanyasi came out of the temple. Descending a few steps of the *ghāt* he saw a woman sitting alone, and was about to go back, when suddenly Kusum raised her head, and looked behind her. The veil slipped away from her. The moonlight fell upon her face, as she looked up.

The owl flew away hooting over their heads. Starting at the sound, Kusum came to herself and put the veil back on her head. Then she bowed low at the Sanyasi's feet.

He gave her a blessing and asked: "Who are you?"

She replied: "I am called Kusum."

No other word was spoken that night. Kusum went slowly back to her house which was hard by. But the Sanyasi remained sitting on my steps for long hours that night. At last when the moon passed from the east to the west, and the Sanyasi's shadow, shifting from behind, fell in front of him, he rose up and entered the temple.

Henceforth I saw Kusum come daily to bow at his feet. When he expounded the holy books, she stood in a corner listening to him. After finishing his morning service, he used to call her to himself and speak on religion. She could not have understood it all; but, listening attentively in silence, she tried. As he directed her, so she acted implicitly. She daily served at the temple – ever alert in the god's worship – gathering flowers for the *puja*, and drawing water from the Ganges to wash the temple floor.

The winter was drawing to its close. We had cold winds. But now and then in the evening the warm spring breeze would blow unexpectedly from the south; the sky would lose its chilly aspect; pipes would sound, and music was heard in the village after a long silence. The boatmen would set their crafts drifting down the current, stop rowing, and begin to sing the songs of Krishna. This was the season.

Just then I began to miss Kusum. For some time she had given up visiting the temple, the *ghāt*, or the Sanyasi.

What happened next, I do not know, but after a while the two met together on my steps one evening.

With downcast looks, Kusum asked: "Master, did you send for me?"

"Yes, why do I not see you? Why have you grown neglectful of late in serving the gods?"

She kept silent.

"Tell me your thoughts without reserve."

Half averting her face, she replied: "I am a sinner, Master, and hence I have failed in the worship."

The Sanyasi said: "Kusum, I know there is unrest in your heart."

She gave a slight start, and, drawing the end of her sári over her face, she sat down on the step at the Sanyasi's feet, and wept.

He moved a little away, and said: "Tell me what you have in your heart, and I shall show you the way to peace."

She replied in a tone of unshaken faith, stopping now and then for words: "If you bid me, I must speak out. But, then, I cannot explain it clearly. You, Master, must have guessed it all. I adored one as a god, I worshipped him, and the bliss of that devotion filled my heart to fulness. But one night I dreamt that the lord of my heart was sitting in a garden somewhere, clasping my right hand in his left, and whispering to me of love. The whole scene did not appear to me at all strange. The dream vanished, but its hold on me remained. Next day when I beheld him he appeared in another light than before. That dream-picture continued to haunt my mind. I fled far from him in fear, and the picture clung to me. Thenceforth my heart has known no peace – all has grown dark within me!"

While she was wiping her tears and telling this tale, I felt that the Sanyasi was firmly pressing my stone surface with his right foot.

Her speech done, the Sanyasi said:

"You must tell me whom you saw in your dream."

With folded hands, she entreated: "I cannot."

He insisted: "You must tell me who he was."

Wringing her hands she asked: "Must I tell it?"

He replied: "Yes, you must."

Then crying, "You are he, Master!" she fell on her face on my stony bosom, and sobbed.

When she came to herself, and sat up, the Sanyasi said slowly: "I am leaving this place to-night that you may not see me again. Know that I am a Sanyasi, not belonging to this world. *You* must forget me."

Kusum replied in a low voice: "It will be so, Master."

The Sanyasi said: "I take my leave."

Without a word more Kusum bowed to him, and placed the dust of his feet on her head. He left the place.

The moon set; the night grew dark. I heard a splash in the water. The wind raved in the darkness, as if it wanted to blow out all the stars of the sky.

ERSKINE CALDWELL

WARM RIVER

THE DRIVER STOPPED at the suspended footbridge and pointed out to me the house across the river. I paid him the quarter fare for the ride from the station two miles away and stepped from the car. After he had gone I was alone with the chill night and the star-pointed lights twinkling in the valley and the broad green river flowing warm below me. All around me the mountains rose like black clouds in the night, and only by looking straight heavenward could I see anything of the dim afterglow of sunset.

The creaking footbridge swayed with the rhythm of my stride and the momentum of its swing soon overcame my pace. Only by walking faster and faster could I cling to the pendulum as it swung in its wide arc over the river. When at last I could see the other side, where the mountain came down abruptly and slid under the warm water, I gripped my handbag tighter and ran with all my might.

Even then, even after my feet had crunched upon the gravel path, I was afraid. I knew that by day I might walk the bridge without fear; but at night, in a strange country, with dark mountains towering all around me and a broad green river flowing beneath me, I could not keep my hands from trembling and my heart from pounding against my chest.

I found the house easily, and laughed at myself for having run from the river. The house was the first one to come upon after leaving the footbridge, and even if I should have missed it, Gretchen would have called me. She was there on the steps of the porch waiting for me. When I heard her familiar voice calling my name, I was ashamed of myself for having been frightened by the mountains and the broad river flowing below.

She ran down the gravel path to meet me.

"Did the footbridge frighten you, Richard?" she asked excitedly, holding my arm with both of her hands and guiding me up the path to the house.

"I think it did, Gretchen," I said; "but I hope I outran it."

"Everyone tries to do that at first, but after going over it once, it's like walking a tightrope. I used to walk tightropes when I was small – didn't you do that, too, Richard? We had a rope stretched across the floor of our barn to practice on."

"I did, too, but it's been so long ago I've forgotten how to do it now."

We reached the steps and went up to the porch. Gretchen took me to the door. Someone inside the house was bringing a lamp into the hall, and with the coming of the light I saw Gretchen's two sisters standing just inside the open door.

"This is my little sister, Anne," Gretchen said. "And this is Mary."

I spoke to them in the semidarkness, and we went on into the hall. Gretchen's father was standing beside a table holding the lamp a little to one side so that he could see my face. I had not met him before.

"This is my father," Gretchen said. "He was afraid you wouldn't be able to find our house in the dark."

"I wanted to bring a light down to the bridge and meet you, but Gretchen said you would get here without any trouble. Did you get lost? I could have brought a lantern down with no trouble at all."

I shook hands with him and told him how easily I had found the place.

"The hack driver pointed out to me the house from the other side of the river, and I never once took my eyes from the light. If I had lost sight of the light, I'd probably be stumbling around somewhere now in the dark down there getting ready to fall into the water."

He laughed at me for being afraid of the river.

"You wouldn't have minded it. The river is warm. Even in winter, when there is ice and snow underfoot, the river is as warm as a comfortable room. All of us here love the water down there."

"No, Richard, you wouldn't have fallen in," Gretchen said, laying her hand in mine. "I saw you the moment you got out of the hack, and if you had gone a step in the wrong direction, I was ready to run to you."

I wished to thank Gretchen for saying that, but already she was going to the stairs to the floor above, and calling me. I went with her, lifting my handbag in front of me. There was a shaded lamp, lighted but turned low, on the table at the end of the upper hall, and she picked it up and went ahead into one of the front rooms.

We stood for a moment looking at each other, and silent.

"There is fresh water in the pitcher, Richard. If there is anything else you would like to have, please tell me. I tried not to overlook anything."

"Don't worry, Gretchen," I told her. "I couldn't wish for anything more. It's enough just to be here with you, anyway. There's nothing else I care for."

She looked at me quickly, and then she lowered her eyes. We stood silently for several minutes, while neither of us could think of anything to say. I wanted to tell her how glad I was to be with her, even if it was only for one night, but I knew I could say that to her later. Gretchen knew why I had come.

"I'll leave the lamp for you, Richard, and I'll wait downstairs for you on the porch. Come as soon as you are ready."

She had left before I could offer to carry the light to the stairhead for her to see the way down. By the time I had picked up the lamp, she was out of sight down the stairs.

I walked back into the room and closed the door and bathed my face and hands, scrubbing the train dust with brush and soap. There was a row of hand-embroidered towels on the rack, and I took one and dried my face and hands. After that I combed my hair, and found a fresh handkerchief in the handbag. Then I opened the door and went downstairs to find Gretchen.

Her father was on the porch with her. When I walked through the doorway, he got up and gave me a chair between them. Gretchen pulled her chair closer to mine, touching my arm with her hand.

"Is this the first time you have been up here in the mountains, Richard?" her father asked me, turning in his chair towards me.

"I've never been within a hundred miles of here before, sir. It's a different country up here, but I suppose you would think the same about the coast, wouldn't you?"

"Oh, but Father used to live in Norfolk," Gretchen said. "Didn't you, Father?"

"I lived there for nearly three years."

There was something else he would say, and both of us waited for him to continue.

"Father is a master mechanic," Gretchen whispered to me. "He works in the railroad shops."

"Yes," he said after a while, "I've lived in many places, but here is where I wish to stay."

My first thought was to ask him why he preferred the mountains to other sections, but suddenly I was aware that both he and Gretchen were strangely silent. Between them, I sat wondering about it.

After a while he spoke again, not to me and not to Gretchen, but as though he were speaking to someone else on the porch, a fourth person whom I had failed to see in the darkness. I waited, tense and excited, for him to continue.

Gretchen moved her chair a few inches closer to mine, her motions gentle and without sound. The warmth of the river came up and covered us like a blanket on a chill night.

"After Gretchen and the other two girls lost their mother," he said, almost inaudibly, bending forward over his knees and gazing out across the broad green river, "after we lost their mother, I came back to the mountains to live. I couldn't stay in Norfolk, and I couldn't stand it in Baltimore. This was the only place on earth where I could find peace. Gretchen remembers her mother, but neither of you can yet understand how it is with me. Her mother and I were born here in the mountains, and we lived here together for almost twenty years. Then after she left us, I moved away, foolishly believing that I could forget. But I was wrong. Of course I was wrong. A man can't forget the mother of his children, even though he knows he will never see her again."

Gretchen leaned closer to me, and I could not keep my eyes from her darkly framed profile beside me. The river below us made no sound; but the warmth of its vapor would not let me forget that it was still there.

Her father had bent farther forward in his chair until his arms were resting on his knees, and he seemed to be trying to see someone on the other side of the river, high on the mountain top above it. His eyes strained, and the shaft of light that came through the open doorway fell upon them and glistened there. Tears fell from his face like fragments of stars, burning into his quivering hands until they were out of sight.

Presently, still in silence, he got up and moved through the doorway. His huge shadow fell upon Gretchen and me as he stood there momentarily before going inside. I turned and looked towards him but, even though he was passing from sight, I could not keep my eyes upon him.

Gretchen leaned closer against me, squeezing her fingers into the hollow of my hand and touching my shoulder with her cheeks as though she were trying to wipe something from them. Her father's footsteps grew fainter, and at last we could no longer hear him.

Somewhere below us, along the bank of the river, an express train crashed down the valley, creaking and screaming through the night. Occasionally its lights flashed through the openings in the darkness, dancing on the broad green river like polar lights in the north, and the metallic echo of its steel rumbled against the high walls of the mountains.

Gretchen clasped her hands tightly over my hand, trembling to her fingertips.

"Richard, why did you come to see me?"

Her voice was mingled with the screaming metallic echo of the train that now seemed far off.

I had expected to find her looking up into my face, but when I turned to her, I saw that she was gazing far down into the valley, down into the warm waters of the river. She knew why I had come, but she did not wish to hear me say why I had.

I do not know why I had come to see her, now. I had liked Gretchen, and I had desired her above anyone else I knew. But I could not tell her that I loved her, after having heard her father speak of love. I was sorry I had come, now after having heard him speak of Gretchen's mother as he did. I knew Gretchen would give herself to me, because she loved me; but I had nothing to give her in return. She was beautiful, very beautiful, and I had desired her. That was before. Now, I knew that I could never again think of her as I had come prepared.

"Why did you come, Richard?"

"Why?"

"Yes, Richard; why?"

My eyes closed, and what I felt was the memory of the star-pointed lights twinkling down in the valley and the warmth of the river flowing below and the caress of her fingers as she touched my arm.

"Richard, please tell me why you came."

"I don't know why I came, Gretchen."

"If you only loved me as I love you, Richard, you would know why."

Her fingers trembled in my hand. I knew she loved me. There had been no doubt in my mind from the first. Gretchen loved me.

"Perhaps I should not have come," I said. "I made a mistake, Gretchen. I should have stayed away."

"But you will be here only for tonight, Richard. You are leaving early in the morning. You aren't sorry that you came for just this short time, are you, Richard?"

"I'm not sorry that I am here, Gretchen, but I should not have come. I didn't know what I was doing. I haven't any right to come here. People who love each other are the only ones—"

"But you do love me just a little, don't you, Richard? You couldn't possibly love me nearly so much as I love you, but can't you tell me that you do love me just a little? I'll feel much happier after you have gone, Richard."

"I don't know," I said, trembling.

"Richard, please—"

With her hands in mine I held her tightly. Suddenly I felt something coming over me, a thing that stabbed my body with its quickness. It was as if the words her father had uttered were becoming clear to me. I had not realized before that there was such a love as he had spoken of. I had believed that men never loved women in the same way that a woman loved a man, but now I knew there could be no difference.

We sat silently, holding each other's hands for a long time. It was long past midnight, because the lights in the valley below were being turned out; but time did not matter.

Gretchen clung softly to me, looking up into my face and laying her cheek against my shoulder. She was as much mine as a woman ever belongs to a man, but I knew then that I could never force myself to take advantage of her love, and to go away knowing that I had not loved her as she loved me. I had not believed any such thing when I came. I had traveled all that distance to hold her in my arms for a few hours, and then to forget her, perhaps forever.

When it was time for us to go into the house, I got up and put my arms around her. She trembled when I touched her, but she clung to me as tightly as I held her, and the hammering of her heart drove into me, stroke after stroke, like an expanding wedge, the spears of her breasts.

"Richard, kiss me before you go," she said.

She ran to the door, holding it open for me. She picked up the lamp from the table and walked ahead up the stairs to the floor above.

At my door she waited until I could light her lamp, and then she handed me mine.

"Good night, Gretchen," I said.

"Good night, Richard."

I turned down the wick of her lamp to keep it from smoking, and then she went across the hall towards her room.

"I'll call you in the morning in time for you to catch your train, Richard."

"All right, Gretchen. Don't let me oversleep, because it leaves the station at seven-thirty."

"I'll wake you in plenty of time, Richard," she said.

The door was closed after her, and I turned and went into my room. I shut the door and slowly began to undress. After I had blown out the lamp and had got into bed, I lay tensely awake. I knew I could never go to sleep, and I sat up in bed and smoked cigarette after cigarette, blowing the smoke through the screen at the window. The house was quiet. Occasionally, I thought I heard the sounds of muffled movements in Gretchen's room across the hall, but I was not certain.

I could not determine how long a time I had sat there on the edge of the bed, stiff and erect, thinking of Gretchen, when suddenly I found myself jumping to my feet. I opened the door and ran across the hall. Gretchen's door was closed, but I knew it would not be locked, and I turned the knob noiselessly. A slender shaft of light broke through the opening I had made. It was not necessary to open the door wider, because I saw Gretchen only a few steps away, almost within arm's reach of me. I closed my eyes tightly for a moment, thinking of her as I had all during the day's ride up from the coast.

Gretchen had not heard me open her door, and she did not know I was there. Her lamp was burning brightly on the table.

I had not expected to find her awake, and I had thought surely she would be in bed. She knelt on the rug beside her bed, her head bowed over her arms and her body shaken with sobs.

Gretchen's hair was lying over her shoulders, tied over the top of her head with a pale blue ribbon. Her nightgown was white silk, hemmed with a delicate lace, and around her neck the collar of lace was thrown open.

I knew how beautiful she was when I saw her then, even though I had always thought her lovely. I had never seen a girl so beautiful as Gretchen.

She had not heard me at her door, and she still did not know I was there. She knelt beside her bed, her hands clenched before her, crying.

When I had first opened the door, I did not know what I was about to do; but now that I had seen her in her room, kneeling in prayer beside her bed, unaware that I was looking upon her and hearing her words and sobs, I was certain that I could never care for anyone else as I did for her. I had not known until then, but in the revelation of a few seconds I knew that I did love her.

I closed the door softly and went back to my room. There I found a chair and placed it beside the window to wait for the coming of day. At the window I sat and looked down into the bottom of the valley where the warm river lay. As my eyes grew more accustomed to the darkness, I felt as if I were coming closer and closer to it, so close that I might have reached out and touched the warm water with my hands.

Later in the night, towards morning, I thought I heard someone in Gretchen's room moving softly over the floor as one who would go from window to window. Once I was certain I heard someone in the hall, close to my door.

When the sun rose over the top of the mountain, I got up and dressed. Later, I heard Gretchen leave her room and go downstairs. I knew she was hurrying to prepare breakfast for me before I left to get on the train. I waited awhile, and after a quarter of an hour I heard her coming back up the stairs. She knocked softly on my door, calling my name several times.

I jerked open the door and faced her. She was so surprised at seeing me there, when she had expected to find me still asleep, that she could not say anything for a moment.

"Gretchen," I said, grasping her hands, "don't hurry to get me off – I'm not going back this morning – I don't know what was the matter with me last night – I know now that I love you—"

"But, Richard – last night you said—"

"I did say last night that I was going back early this morning, Gretchen, but I didn't know what I was talking about. I'm not going back now until you go with me. I'll tell you what I mean as soon as breakfast is over. But first of all I wish you would show me how to get down to the river. I have got to go down there right away and feel the water with my hands."

HUYNH QUANG NHUONG

SO CLOSE

MY GRANDMOTHER WAS very fond of cookies made of banana, egg, and coconut, so my mother and I always stopped at Mrs. Hong's house to buy these cookies for her on our way back from the marketplace. My mother also liked to see Mrs. Hong because they had been very good friends since grade-school days. While my mother talked with her friend, I talked with Mrs. Hong's daughter, Lan. Most of the time Lan asked me about my older sister, who was married to a teacher and lived in a nearby town. Lan, too, was going to get married – to a young man living next door, Trung.

Trung and Lan had been inseparable playmates until the day tradition did not allow them to be alone together anymore. Besides, I think they felt a little shy with each other after realizing that they were man and woman.

Lan was a lively, pretty girl who attracted the attention of all the young men of our hamlet. Trung was a skillful fisherman who successfully plied his trade on the river in front of their houses. Whenever Lan's mother found a big fish on the kitchen windowsill she would smile to herself. Finally she decided that Trung was a fine young man and would make a good husband for her daughter.

Trung's mother did not like the idea of her son giving good fish away, but she liked the cookies Lan brought her from time to time. Besides, the girl was very helpful; whenever she was not busy at her house Lan would come over in the evening and help Trung's mother repair her son's fishing net.

Trung was happiest when Lan was helping his mother. They did not talk to each other, but they could look at each other when his mother was busy with her work. Each time Lan went home Trung looked at the chair Lan had just left and secretly wished that nobody would move it.

One day when Trung's mother heard her son call Lan's name in his sleep, she decided it was time to speak to the girl's mother about marriage. Lan's mother agreed they should be married and even waived the custom whereby the bridegroom had to give the bride's family a fat hog, six chickens, six ducks, three bottles of wine, and thirty kilos of fine rice, for the two families had known each other for a long time and were good neighbors.

The two widowed mothers quickly set the dates for the engagement announcement and for the wedding ceremony. Since their decision was immediately made known to relatives and friends, Trung and Lan could now see each other often.

One day as Trung helped Lan to plant a mango tree behind her house, he asked her: "Have you ever looked at those dainty town boys who pass by your house all the time?" Instead of answering Trung, Lan poked a hard finger at his ribs and laughed. Then she said: "You are not bad looking at all; so don't bother about them. Besides, my mother said that in darkness everything, everybody looks the same!" To a shy young man like Trung the remark was quite bold, but he was very pleased and happy.

At last it was the day of their wedding. Friends and relatives arrived early in the morning to help them celebrate. They brought gifts of ducks, chickens, baskets filled with fruits, rice wine, and colorful fabrics. Even though the two houses were next to each other, the two mothers observed all the proper wedding day traditions.

First Trung and his friends and relatives came to Lan's house. Lan and he prayed at her ancestors' altars and asked for their blessing. Then they joined everyone for a luncheon.

After lunch there was a farewell ceremony for the bride. Lan stepped out of her house and joined the greeting party that was to accompany her to Trung's home. Tradition called for her to cry and to express her sorrow at leaving her parents behind and forever becoming the daughter of her husband's family. In some villages the bride was even supposed to cling so tightly to her mother that it would take several friends to pull her away from her home. But instead of crying, Lan smiled. She asked herself, why should she cry? The two houses were separated by only a garden; she could run home and see her mother anytime she wanted to. So Lan willingly followed Trung and prayed at his ancestors' altars before joining everyone in the big welcome dinner at Trung's house that ended the day's celebrations.

Later in the evening of the wedding night Lan went to the river to take a bath. Because crocodiles infested the river, people of our hamlet who lived along the riverbank chopped down trees and put them in the river to form barriers and protect places where they washed their clothes, did their dishes, or took a bath. This evening, a wily crocodile had avoided the barrier by crawling up the riverbank and sneaked up behind Lan. The crocodile grabbed her and went back to the river by the same route that it had come.

Trung became worried when Lan did not return. He went to the place where she was supposed to bathe, only to find that her clothes were there but she had disappeared. Panic-stricken, he yelled for his relatives. They all rushed to the riverbank with lighted torches. In the flickering light they found traces of water and crocodile claw prints on the wet soil. Now they knew that a crocodile had grabbed the young bride and dragged her into the river.

Since no one could do anything for the girl, all of Trung's relatives returned to the house, urging the bridegroom to do the same. But the young man refused to leave the place, he just stood there, crying and staring at the clothes of his bride.

Suddenly the wind brought him the sound of Lan calling his name. He was very frightened, for according to an old belief a crocodile's victim must lure a new victim to his master; if not, the first victim's soul must stay with the beast forever.

Trung rushed back to the house and woke all his relatives. Nobody doubted he thought he had heard her call, but they all believed that he was the victim of a hallucination. Everyone pleaded with him and tried to convince him that nobody could survive when snapped up by a crocodile and dragged into the river to be drowned and eaten by the animal.

The young man brushed aside all their arguments and rushed back to the river. Once again, he heard the voice of his bride in the wind, calling his name. Again he rushed back and woke his relatives. Again they tried to persuade him that it was a hallucination, although some of the old folks suggested that maybe the ghost of the young girl was having to dance and sing to placate the angry crocodile because she failed to bring it a new victim.

No one could persuade Trung to stay inside. His friends wanted to go back to the river with him, but he said no. He resented them for not believing him that there were desperate cries in the wind.

Trung stood in front of the deep river alone in the darkness. He listened to the sound of the wind and clutched the clothes Lan had left behind. The wind became stronger and stronger and often changed direction as the night progressed, but he did not hear any more calls. Still he had no doubt that the voice he had heard earlier was absolutely real. Then at dawn, when the wind died down, he again heard, very clearly, Lan call him for help.

Her voice came from an island about six hundred meters away. Trung wept and prayed: "You were a good girl when you were still alive, now be a good soul. Please protect me so that I can find a way to kill the beast in order to free you from its spell and avenge your tragic death." Suddenly, while wiping away his tears, he saw a little tree moving on the island. The tree was jumping up and down. He squinted to see better. The tree had two hands that were waving at him. And it was calling his name.

Trung became hysterical and yelled for help. He woke all his relatives and they all rushed to his side again. At first they thought that Trung had become stark mad. They tried to lead him back to his house, but he fiercely resisted their attempt. He talked to them incoherently and pointed his finger at the strange tree on the island. Finally his relatives saw the waving tree. They quickly put a small boat into the river and Trung got into the boat along with two other men. They paddled to the island and discovered that the moving tree was, in fact, Lan. She had covered herself with leaves because she had no clothes on.

At first nobody knew what had really happened because Lan clung to Trung and cried and cried. Finally, when Lan could talk they pieced together her story.

Lan had fainted when the crocodile snapped her up. Had she not fainted, the crocodile surely would have drowned her before carrying her off to the island. Lan did not know how many times the crocodile had tossed her in the air and smashed her against the ground, but at one point, while being tossed in the air and falling back onto the crocodile's jaw, she regained consciousness. The crocodile smashed her against the ground a few more times, but Lan played dead. Luckily the crocodile became thirsty and returned to the river to drink. At that moment Lan got up and ran to a nearby tree and climbed up it. The tree was very small. Lan stayed very still for fear that the snorting, angry crocodile, roaming around trying to catch her again, would find her and shake her out of the tree. Lan stayed in this frozen position for a long time until the crocodile gave up searching for her and went back to the river. Then she started calling Trung to come rescue her.

Lan's body was covered with bruises, for crocodiles soften up big prey before swallowing it. They will smash it against the ground or against a tree, or keep tossing it into the air. But fortunately Lan had no broken bones or serious cuts. It was possible that this crocodile was very old and had lost most of its teeth. Nevertheless, the older the crocodile, the more intelligent it usually was. That was how it knew to avoid the log barrier in the river and to snap up the girl from behind.

Trung carried his exhausted bride into the boat and paddled home. Lan slept for hours and hours. At times she would sit up with a start and cry out for help, but within three days she was almost completely recovered.

Lan's mother and Trung's mother decided to celebrate their children's wedding a second time, because Lan had come back from the dead. All their friends came and sang to the happy couple. At midnight, at the end of the last serenade, "The Wedding Night," the bride and bridegroom were supposed to open the windows of their room to thank the minstrels. But Lan and Trung kept the window closed. Perhaps they were too tired or too busy to open it. The serenade party left good-humoredly, saying one could do well only one thing at a time!

SALWA ELHAMAMSY

BY THE NILE

ACCORDING TO AN ancient Egyptian legend, there were angry times when the Nile River flooded, and other times when he bestowed gentle blessings to irrigate the fields and provide a bounty of fish. The legend said that the pharaoh's minister suggested that every year before the flood season a beautiful girl be prepared as a sacrifice to the Nile. The pharaoh agreed on the idea of a Nile Bride, and it is said that the sacrifice was accompanied by a lavish ceremony attended by thousands of people.

She arrives early and chooses the same place for all these meetings, same café, and nearly the same table facing the Nile River at sunset. She lets her eyes travel over the water and into the distance, through the creamy clouds.

She never wanted to accept the legend of the Nile Bride, she never believed in sacrificing her life to make other people happier, as her mother keeps urging, pushing her to do – even blaming her when she fails.

Forty years old and still unmarried. "Unacceptable," her mother admonishes.

Her friend was the connection, she suggested Laila. The man is divorced, the father of three children who are staying with their mother. He is well off. "He is a nice person," her friend told her.

"Would you like anything to drink, madam?"

Madam! Who said that? she asked herself. She is still a single girl! *I feel young,* she thought. But yes, at forty she looks old enough to be called "madam."

"A lemon juice, please, with ice," she answered the waiter.

Looking deeply at the combined colours reflected on the page of the Nile, she admired golden ripples and the tall old palms along the banks. She studied the white sails of boats tacking upriver, then took a deep breath and relaxed back into her seat.

"Here you are, madam. Lemon juice with ice."

Laila took a sip of the juice. She always resorts to the river. A great sense of comfort fills her when she sits by the Nile. So many memories she shared with the Nile. He witnessed her happy years with her parents who used to take her and her brothers on boating excursions. They would point to stately egrets feeding along the shore and wonder over the splash of a big fish. The river also witnessed her sadness after her father passed away, when she came several times trying to find some sort of solace in the endless swirling currents. When Laila travelled to the UK to study, she had a walk by the Thames River where images of the Nile continued to flood her mind.

At 6 p.m., the appointed time, she saw her friend entering from the café gate with a tall man. The friend waved to Laila and led the man towards her seat.

Her friend introduced the prospective groom. Laila smiled and invited them to sit down.

It always happens like this. Laila did not remember how many prospective grooms she's met in the past twenty-two years, since she turned eighteen. These were not occasions she remembered fondly.

Laila, just try to be a nice, beautiful, charming, smiling bride, her mother's words rang in her mind.

She started chatting with her friend to give the king, the prospective groom, a chance to have a good look at his possible prize. It's like window-shopping a woman, Laila thought.

Traditional Egyptian families often spoke of a girl's marriage from the time she was a child, they pray for her to be a beautiful bride, to find a good man, as if it were the only reason for her existence. If she doesn't find a husband, she might be socially isolated. She noticed that she received fewer and fewer invitations from friends, most of whom were now married and having children.

As her mother advised, after some small talk with her friend, giving the man a few minutes to take her in, she asked him a question and smiled. She should not show too much personality at first, her mother also coached. She should let him lead the conversation. She should answer his inquiries simply and with a warm smile. After the meeting, she should go home and wait for the results.

This always happens in the same place by the Nile, the great river who witnessed all the times her heart was strained by the failure of these staged meetings. Laila has not found her love yet, but at the same time, she did not like this way of prospecting for marriage. But what to do with the insistence of her old mother? "You should get married before I die," her words haunted Laila. How many times had Laila tried to comfort her mother by agreeing to these awkward meetings?

The same words washed over her again and again. For how long should she endure this muddy whirlpool? At the same time, she wanted to rest her mother's broken heart. Her mother worries that when she dies her daughter will be left alone.

Laila looked at the man who was talking to her. He was

handsome – tall, slim, with a smoothly shaved face. And as a banker, he kept discussing the serious situation of the Egyptian pound currency in front of the dollar, and what is expected in the next fiscal quarter. Laila pretended to be listening while she looked past him at a boat sailing downriver carrying brightly dressed passengers. Another ship was tying up at the dock.

The man kept talking about himself and his future career. An hour passed. The sun was setting.

Laila felt some shaking. Waves rolled into the pier, wakes caused by the crossing back and forth of large boats. Some vessels on the Nile started their trips just before sunset, other boats returned at dusk to drop off passengers. "Everyone has their own schedule," Laila suddenly said aloud.

"Excuse me? What do you mean?" asked the man.

"I mean, myself. I have many things to do." Laila picked up her handbag and set down enough money to cover the bill. "Sorry, I have to go."

Laila walked off, leaving them astonished.

What is she going to tell her old mother? As she walked, the river caressed her with his waves, showing his love, urging her forward. Laila rejected the old legend of the Nile Bride. *It never happened*, she thought. This river would never allow that to happen.

LESLEY NNEKA ARIMAH

WHAT IS A VOLCANO?

THE GOD OF ants and the goddess of rivers were feuding. Their feud was in the early stages, more a cause for rolled eyes and snickers than alarm. River had divided one of her streams, and the new current washed away a small anthill of no real consequence, except Ant had grown especially fond of this fledgling colony. He complained first to the goddess of hearts, legendary for her sympathy. Then to the god of vengeance, known for his, well, vengeance. Ant approached many other deities, trying to talk them onto his side of things, but those who did not smite him simply laughed, for Ant was the most minor of the gods, hardly more than a spirit, and who even knew there was a god of ants, did you?

So Ant began to exact his revenge in little ways, dumping mounds of dirt into small waters so that they sludged and ran slow. River retaliated by overflowing the banks Ant scouted for his colonies, rendering the once-dry shores too wet to build anything of use. Ant then had his minions shred the reeds that stemmed the tide in a small village, so that the waters ran into the crops and the angry farmers cursed the river.

They backed and forthed for five human centuries, and if anyone asked River what she thought of Ant, she responded with an affectionate laugh peppered with annoyance. Such a small man with small concerns, but a fun diversion for such a woman as she. No one asked Ant what he thought of River, but someone should have known that you do not take small things from small men. Ant loathed River. He hated the condescending laugh she gave when his name was mentioned. He hated that she seemed to take pleasure in finding the tiny colonies he'd squirreled by a lake or stream. One day, he came upon the washed-out remains of one such colony, the queen mired in mud, undignified, laid bare for anyone to see. So mighty was River, so respected and loved and worshipped. What were ants to her? He decided to show River what it felt like to lose.

The mightiest river, from which all rivers flowed, was the source of River's power. Ant sent one ant with one stone into the stillest, deepest part. Then he sent another. And another. At first, the stones just added a nice pebbled finish to the bed of the river. But over a thousand years, the stones began to amass.

River's new twins distracted her or she would have noticed the change in current sooner. But for now, they were delightful girls whose eyes followed her and her alone. So rare was the birth of god-twins that they drew a steady stream of visitors bearing tribute and admiration. Two firstborn, how marvelous. They would become the most powerful river goddesses the world had ever seen. When the flow of guests finally abated, River noticed the waning of her power, too much to be the result of the birth, from which she had long since recovered. Leaving her daughters in the care of her sister, she walked the bank. When she got to the site of Ant's not-quite-finished dam, she pushed a wave at it, not knowing its cause or the resentment that cemented it. The stone wall repelled the wave, so powerfully that it knocked her over. Ant, who had been in the process of adding more stones, laughed and laughed, but silently, so he did not give away his hiding place. See River, knocked to the ground by the forces she controlled!

The problem with those who don't know real power is that they do not know real power. River pushed again with all her rage, and this time the wall gave, the force of the water so great that it burst over the dam and flooded half the world. And in this half of the world was the largest ant colony you can imagine, a maze created over generations, a honeycomb of earth piled into a mountain so high that even the god of mountains was forced to respect it. But River's fury washed it away.

Seeing this, Ant lost all reason. He ran to River's house and, while her sister slept, slipped through an open window and snatched the children. He hid one girl in a colony of army ants, ordering them to guard the child from anyone who would take her, and the other he hid in a location where River would never think to look.

Unaware that her daughters had been taken, River dealt instead with the other gods and goddesses whose dwelling places were flooded. The god of birds had lost a quarter of his flock when they tired with no place to land. She begged forgiveness and they gave it easily, because was this not our River, so known to us, and had she not just birthed the next generation of gods?

The wail alerted her. So much anguish in that wail. River rushed back to her house, hoping the familiar voice or its anguish was simply a trick in her ear. But there was her sister, ripping her hair out by the roots, and there was the empty crib, barely cooled of the warmth of her girls. River released a tsunami of sound, and every god that could walk or fly, every spirit that haunted every place, came to her. Who, she wanted to know, and where? No one could think of anyone who would wish River such harm. Even Death shrugged his innocence, he who had taken something from everyone present. River's sister hadn't seen or heard anything, lost as she had been in the sweetest of sleeps. No one said it, but they all thought, *This is what you get for asking a godling to do the work of a god.* None of them, not even Love, kept in contact with their half-divine siblings, lest they discover that by putting the most powerful of their bloodline to rest, they might graduate to godhood themselves. Poor River, so indulgent, so generous, and look how she had been repaid.

The other gods prepared to smite her sister, and River was scared by the emptiness inside her where loyalty should lie. Then a field spirit stepped forward, terrified but determined, and held up a fragment of the dam for everyone to see. Ants. It was ants that held the wall together, and resentment that gave them the power.

River didn't want to believe it. Ant was responsible? The little god with whom she'd traded pranks for millennia? Rage replaced disbelief, and River went hunting.

If Ant had stuck around when he'd dropped the first girl with the army ants, he could have prevented the scene to which he returned. If he'd stuck around, he would have noticed that the loss of the ancestral ant colony lessened his ant-controlling powers. He would have seen the ants swarm the child the moment he turned away, so eager for the taste of god-flesh. What many don't know, a secret god-mothers have kept for eternity, is that god-children are just that, children. And just as a human child must learn to talk and to walk and to join the world of their parents, so must a god-child learn to become a deity. But unlike human children, god-children must even learn to grow, guided by their mothers from one stage to the next until they attain godhood. River's child was too young to know she was divine and could not be eaten, and so she was. Ant returned to shards of bone picked clean of marrow. He heard his name being screamed across the world and he knew River could never, ever know. She would drown the universe.

Ant ground the girl's bones to dust and compacted it with panic and regret into a small blue stone. Into the stone he whispered the location of the dead girl's sister, then deleted it from his memory. Such knowledge was too dangerous to have in these times. Then he went into hiding among the humans, trying to live as one of them. He married human women who bore children he suffocated as they slept, lest they leave a divine trail that led to his end. When the women grew suspicious, he abandoned them, and they would go mad or move on with their lives, slowly forgetting him as one does a god who answers no prayers.

River searched the world for her girls. She dug up every anthill she could find. The army ants were too frightened to tell her what they'd done, but they did tell her that the ant god had gone to live among the humans. River searched for Ant. She dug through entire lineages trying to find him. When, after three hundred years, the sky god dared to mention the neglected waters of the world, she dried up entire countries out of spite. This is our River, one god reminded the other, our sweet River. Let us help, not hinder. And so they sent emissaries from every spirit realm, second daughters and minor spirits of similar powers, godlings all, promising their aid for a hundred years. But River's grief was so deep it consumed them, and her grief became their own. They forgot their mothers and their brothers and the lovers they'd promised to return to; they forgot that they'd had a past before this grief removed everything from inside of them. How, they wondered, can a body feel full to bursting with grief but also hollow? These godlings of land and air and memory resisted this loss of themselves, but River's sorrow drowned them. Their husbands, their children, their homes became like reflections in a rough stream, fractured beyond recognition.

They tore the world apart. Unprecedented rains. Earthquakes that ravaged every region. One godling who had come from the house of flames set an entire city on fire trying to find River's girls. It was a dark century for humankind and godkind alike. Then the female godlings got craftier in their search. They made themselves visible to human eyes, tempting men and women, threatening men and women, building a network of spies across the globe who lit candles and prayed to them and passed this new religion on to their children. Every new convert was a new set of eyes in the world, a new set of ears to catch whispers of men who didn't seem to fit in, or men who rose to ungodly success but never seemed to pray. Many a good man was lost to angry godlings who peeled his skin away, searching for the god that might be hidden inside.

But after seven hundred fruitless years and countless human believers in her service, it dawned on River that she might never see her twins again. She collapsed where she stood, and every emissary lay down as well. Dust settled on them, then grime and so much debris that they became part of the earth, hills of hips and buttocks and woe.

All but one. The only one who felt the rage of River, multiplied by that most powerful feeling that won't let a person rest: guilt. River's sister, not quite goddess. The guilt turned in her belly like a ship in a storm. She'd slept while her sister's children were taken. Blame, so like a god itself, shadowed her, occupied her bed like a lover, whispered to her like a dearest friend. Her name was eventually forgotten. Soon all called her She Who Betrayed River, a name that over the years degenerated to Betrayed River, then Bereaver, which stuck, and eventually even Bereaver forgot she had ever been anyone else. Guilt crushed every milestone in her life to dust so that she knew only Before and After. And Before seemed like the unfathomable dream of a foolish woman.

Long after River and her women collapsed, Bereaver searched alone, turning every crust of earth to find Ant and her nieces. Whenever a kind wind caught a whisper and blew Ant's name into her ear, she would follow it to the city, town, village to which he had run and pluck the man, woman, child who had seen him last. She pulled every secret from them, things they didn't even know they knew, and afterward she'd pull out their eyes, tongue, heart, so they'd never know a thing again. Sometimes she just missed him. Other times, the trail was so stale it crumbled to nothing when she walked it, the people who had known the human Ant long dead.

Ant tried to live quiet lives, but eventually someone would sense something about him, be it his wickedness or his divinity, and he would be run out of town – or become so highly acclaimed he feared catching the attention of a god who would recognize him. Much as it galled him, he knew he would have to set his godhood aside if he wanted to keep his life. He would also have to separate himself from the stone that held his secrets.

So into the stone Ant whispered everything he'd ever been and sealed it with the human name he'd taken for this earth. He kept only his immortality, so that he could one day live to be restored, no longer hunted. He tried to bury the stone, but animals circled the spot and began to dig. He gave it to a boy, but the boy ran to show his friends, so Ant snatched it back and buried the boy instead. In his despair, he carved a cave into a hill and thought to hide there for eternity. He pulled in a large rock and made it his bed, as penance. But a hundred years went by and he became bored with piety and regret. Poking his head out of the cave, he saw a girl hauling a pail of water. The water wasn't hers, he was sure, and yet she bore it on her head with grace and little complaint. He watched her for days, carrying water back and forth, back and forth, but for whom? To do what? Boys sometimes danced around her, trying to distract her from her task, but on she went, day after day. It dawned on Ant then that one could ask almost anything of a girl. He stepped out of the cave to block her path and, holding out the pretty blue stone, said, Can you keep a secret?

The girl took the stone, so accepting that it sank into her palm, lodging itself at the base of her fingers. She was filled with a terrifying knowledge – a child bled to bones, a mother who thought it alive and well – and certainty that she must never, ever tell.

So Bereaver still wanders, not knowing that Ant is lost to her. The girl will carry his secret, and when she is no longer a girl, she will give it to another girl, and this sorrow stone will be stolen away in uniform pockets and hidden under the pillows of marriage beds, secreted in diaries, guarded closely by the type of girls who, above all else, obey.

And while Bereaver wanders, River and her women lie catatonic with heartache, dreaming of their children. And when, in the place she is hidden, the surviving god-child cries, their bodies hear her, and their breasts weep, and that, since you asked, is a volcano.

MYSTIC RIVERS

OVID

ARETHUSA

Translated by Kit Andrews

GOLDEN-HAIRED CERES, goddess of the harvest, paused on her journey home and called to Arethusa, "What caused you to flee? How did you become a sacred spring?" Having just recovered her daughter from Pluto and his underworld kingdom, Ceres now longed to hear the story of the beautiful nymph and the lustful river god, Alpheus.

The waters fell silent as their goddess Arethusa lifted her head into the air, and wrung her green hair dry. "I was once one of Diana's nymphs in Achaia," she said, "and none more devoted than I to the virgin goddess of the hunt, diligently crossing forests, eagerly setting traps. And though I never sought recognition for my appearance, I became famous for my beauty. I found no joy in this attention; though other maidens might find delight in such renown, I, ever a country girl, found embarrassing the endowments of my body.

"One hot day, returning from the Symphalian forest, I happened upon a stream. My work had doubled the heat, and the stream flowed so smoothly, without a ripple or a murmur, one could see clearly to the bottom. Each pebble could be counted. The water sustained the willows and poplars on its shores, and they offered shade in return. I approached the stream, soaked my feet, then my knees, and, still unsatisfied, undid my garments, hanging them on the willows, then sinking my entire body, nude, into the water. My splashing in the cool water led me from one bank to another, up and down, around, back and forth, until suddenly I sensed another there.

"Terrified I climbed the nearest bank. In the murmur of the water, I heard the deep voice of Alpheus, the river god: 'What's your hurry, Arethusa? Why the rush?' My clothes stranded on the other bank, I abandoned them in haste. Alpheus pursued me, considering my nudity an invitation. I ran, he chased; I fled, he stalked. I the hunted dove, fluttering; he the hunting falcon, diving. From seashore to mountaintop, from peak to valley, from Orchomenus to Psophis and Cyllene, past the coves of Maenalus, beyond freezing Erymanthus, I kept running. Although his equal in speed, I lacked his stamina. Still, I ran on: through fields, across forested mountains, over boulders, up cliffs. Where paths ended, my flight continued. But so did his pursuit.

"Near the end of day with the sun at my back, I may have glimpsed his long shadow approaching mine, then I was sure I heard his feet, and soon I felt his hot breath on my hair. Worn down by constant flight, I cried out, 'Help me, Diana, or I am done. Save the one you so often chose to bear your bow and quiver.' In answer to my plea, the goddess cast a thick mist over me, frustrating my pursuer. Unable to find me, he began to wander in circles. Twice he called out, 'Arethusa, Arethusa,' and twice, unaware, he came close to where the goddess had hidden me. And what did this poor soul feel? What does the lamb feel when it hears a wolf growling and pacing round the stable walls? Or the rabbit hunched in the bushes, afraid even to twitch its ears when it sees a dog baring its teeth?

"For I was not yet safe. The river god noticed that my footprints led in but not out of my refuge in the mist. He stayed there, watching closely. A cold sweat seized me, freezing my joints. Moisture poured from my hair down my body; with each step my foot left a pool of water. And more quickly than I can now tell you this story, I was changed into a stream. Just as quickly Alpheus recognized in the flowing water the woman he claimed as his. Casting aside his human form, he became again the river, the better to mingle our bodies of water. Diana, though, broke open the earth, plunging me – but not him – into a cavern, through the dark, under the earth, under the sea, until at last I rose again to light and open air, here, as the sacred spring of this island, a place beloved by my goddess, and thus beloved by me."

TAO YUANMING

PEACH BLOSSOM SPRING

Translated by Jin Lei

DURING THE TAIYUAN reign of the Jin dynasty, a fisherman from Wulin paddled his boat far up an uncharted creek, losing track of the distance. Suddenly he beheld a peach grove in full blossom extending at least a hundred yards along both sides of the creek. Maneuvering close to the shore, he noticed, to his amazement, no other trees mixed in among the blossoming peach. The grass was fragrant and undulant, and pale pink petals lay in dreamy profusion. Amazed by this magical scene, and curious about the extent of this mysterious orchard, the fisherman paddled farther upstream.

Beyond the last resplendent trees, he beheld a burbling spring which flowed from a mountainside grotto. Light also seemed to emanate from the aperture in the rock. The curious man tied up his boat and ventured through the opening. At the beginning, the cave was very narrow, barely wide enough for the man to squeeze through. After a dozen more intrepid steps, the space suddenly opened into a shower of light. Before him stretched a vast, fertile plain, with a village comprised of snug houses neatly arranged. There were lush fields, shimmering ponds, mulberry trees and bamboo thickets crisscrossed by well-ordered paths. The sounds of chickens and dogs echoed through the crisp air. Men and women soon appeared, busy in their spring planting. The fisherman noticed the strangeness of their clothing and their hair coiffed in long curls. There were white-haired elders and children, all of whom appeared very happy.

When the people saw the fisherman, they were astonished. They warily approached him and asked from whence he came. The stranger politely answered all their questions. Then they invited him to their homes, set out wine, slaughtered a plump chicken and cooked him a hearty meal. Other villagers heard of this unprecedented visitation and came to ply him with more questions. They also told him about themselves and their origins, which reached back some six-hundred years. "In escaping the tyranny of Qin rule," they explained, "our ancestors fled with their wives and children to this remote place." They went on to say, "We never left, and thus have been cut off from the outside world." Curious about the current era, they knew nothing of the great Han, Wei or Jin dynasties. The fisherman shared what knowledge he possessed, and they listened with great amazement. He told the villagers all the things he knew, and everyone gasped. The friendly people took turns inviting him to their homes, pouring wine and setting out platters of delicious food. After a stay of several days, the fisherman readied himself for his return home and bid the people goodbye. The villagers said to him: "There is no use in telling the outside world about us."

The fisherman slipped back through the narrow passage, found his boat, and paddled downstream, frequently marking the route with a piece of twine or a broken branch. Once he reached the county seat, he hurried to the magistrate's office and told the official everything. The astounded magistrate ordered a team of men to accompany the fisherman and search for the signs he marked, hoping to discover this fascinating place. But they couldn't find the way.

Liu Ziji, the noble scholar of Nanyang, heard this

extraordinary account, and was determined to launch his own expedition. He set off with hopeful excitement, but soon after took sick and died. Since then, no one has dared to search for the village of the Peach Blossom Spring.

TRADITIONAL KALAPUYA

COYOTE FREES WATER FROM THE FROG PEOPLE

COYOTE IS WALKING down the beach. There is a strange smell in the air, and the waves and tide seem different. He notices that the mighty river has run dry, its wide delta now a stinky mudflat. Coyote sits on a driftwood log and scratches his ear. After a while, Coyote is startled by splashes from the ocean.

It's Old Man Salmon, poking up from the surf. His face is bent and pale.

"Hey, Coyote, come here."

Coyote is wary. He's never seen Old Man Salmon looking quite this bad. His skin is flaking off in white patches.

"What's the matter with your face, Salmon?"

"That's what I need to talk to you about, Coyote. You need to help us. The Frog People have built a dam across the river. No water flows. It is past our time to spawn. That is why my skin is falling off. If we don't get up the river soon, the Salmon People will die without children."

Coyote ponders the situation, but his mind is muddled. So he does what Coyote always does when he's confused, he licks his bushy tail. His tail begins to speak.

"Do I taste okay?" his tail asks. "Is something bothering you, Coyote?"

"The Frog People have done a bad thing," Coyote says. "They have built a dam across the river. They are hoarding all the water and blocking the Salmon People."

The tail swishes and Coyote gets closer. Coyote pulls

himself into a circle and tucks his furry ear to the tip of his tail.

"So, here's what you do," the tail commands, laying out the plan.

Coyote digs in the sand and uncovers the old bones of a sea lion. He takes one of the ribs, chews and licks it, then polishes it with his paws and snout until it shines like a dentalium shell, highly prized by the Frog People.

Coyote carries the bone in his mouth and runs, his tail flat out, over the mountains, through the mossy forest, to a large dam made of earth and downed trees. A vast green lake lies behind the dam.

Coyote is panting when he meets the Frog People. He drops the shell and his pink tongue dangles from his mouth.

"Hey, Frog People," Coyote says. "I'm very thirsty. I want a big drink of water. I want to drink for a long time."

Old Man Frog looks at Coyote and the shiny object before him. "Give us that shell," says Old Man Frog, "and you can drink all you like."

Coyote gives him the homemade dentalium and begins lapping up the water.

"Don't worry about me, this might take a while," Coyote sputters between gulps. "I'm parched."

Coyote drinks and drinks and drinks, and the level of the lake begins to drop. Soon he drains half the water into his big belly.

"Hey Coyote," yells Old Man Frog. "If you keep drinking like that, you'll owe us another shell."

"Just let me finish," Coyote says, then plunges his head back in the water.

The Frog People are amazed that anyone could drink this much water. They worry that Coyote might be up to something.

Coyote lifts his soaking head to take a breath.

"Hey," Old Man Frog shouts.

"Just a minute," Coyote says, diving beneath the surface of the lake. Coyote stays down for a long time, digging furiously at the base of the dam until finally it breaches. Water cascades down the canyon, waterfalls spill from dry cliffs, and the river rises, once again joining the sea. The Salmon People begin swimming into the current.

Old Man Frog shouts angrily: "You have lost all our water, Coyote!"

"It's not right for one people to have all the water," Coyote says, shaking off his gray coat. "It needs to run free."

"But where will we live?" Old Man Frog asks.

Coyote is so full of water he looks like an engorged tick. He staggers to a muddy bog and spews a mighty stream from his mouth.

"Frog People, this is your pond. It is not a big pond, but it is yours."

Then Coyote hops on a cedar log floating down the river and rides it all the way to the sea. That night the Salmon People treat Coyote to a great feast. He eats and eats until he falls asleep.

KENNETH GRAHAME

THE PIPER AT THE GATES OF DAWN

From *The Wind in the Willows*

THE WILLOW WREN was twittering his thin little song, hidden himself in the dark selvedge of the river bank. Though it was past ten o'clock at night, the sky still clung to and retained some lingering skirts of light from the departed day; and the sullen heats of the torrid afternoon broke up and rolled away at the dispersing touch of the cool fingers of the short midsummer night. Mole lay stretched on the bank, still panting from the stress of the fierce day that had been cloudless from dawn to late sunset, and waited for his friend to return. He had been on the river with some companions, leaving the Water Rat free to keep an engagement of long standing with Otter; and he had come back to find the house dark and deserted, and no sign of Rat, who was doubtless keeping it up late with his old comrade. It was still too hot to think of staying indoors, so he lay on some cool dock-leaves, and thought over the past day and its doings, and how very good they all had been.

The Rat's light footfall was presently heard approaching over the parched grass. "O, the blessed coolness!" he said, and sat down, gazing thoughtfully into the river, silent and preoccupied.

"You stayed to supper, of course?" said the Mole presently.

"Simply had to," said the Rat. "They wouldn't hear of my going before. You know how kind they always are. And they made things as jolly for me as ever they could, right up to the moment I left. But I felt a brute all the time, as it was clear to me they were very unhappy, though they tried to hide it. Mole, I'm afraid they're in trouble. Little Portly is missing again; and you know what a lot his father thinks of him, though he never says much about it."

"What, that child?" said the Mole lightly. "Well, suppose he is; why worry about it? He's always straying off and getting lost, and turning up again; he's so adventurous. But no harm ever happens to him. Everybody hereabouts knows him and likes him, just as they do old Otter, and you may be sure some animal or other will come across him and bring him back again all right. Why, we've found him ourselves, miles from home and quite self-possessed and cheerful!"

"Yes; but this time it's more serious," said the Rat gravely. "He's been missing for some days now, and the Otters have hunted everywhere, high and low, without finding the slightest trace. And they've asked every animal, too, for miles around, and no one knows anything about him. Otter's evidently more anxious then he'll admit. I got out of him that young Portly hasn't learnt to swim very well yet, and I can see he's thinking of the weir. There's a lot of water coming down still, considering the time of year, and the place always had a fascination for the child. And then there are – well, traps and things – *you* know. Otter's not the fellow to be nervous about any son of his before it's time. And now he is nervous. When I left, he came out with me – said he wanted some air, and talked about stretching his legs. But I could see it wasn't that, so I drew him out and pumped him, and got it all from him at last. He was going to spend the night watching by the ford. You know the place where the old ford used to be, in bygone days before they built the bridge?"

"I know it well," said the Mole. "But why should Otter choose to watch there?"

"Well, it seems that it was there he gave Portly his first

swimming lesson," continued the Rat. "From that shallow, gravelly spit near the bank. And it was there he used to teach him fishing, and there young Portly caught his first fish, of which he was so very proud. The child loved the spot, and Otter thinks that if he came wandering back from wherever he is – if he is anywhere by this time, poor little chap – he might make for the ford he was so fond of; or if he came across it he'd remember it well, and stop there and play, perhaps. So Otter goes there every night and watches – on the chance, you know, just on the chance!"

They were silent for a time, both thinking of the same thing – the lonely, heart-sore animal, crouched by the ford, watching and waiting, the long night through – on the chance.

"Well, well," said the Rat presently, "I suppose we ought to be thinking about turning in." But he never offered to move.

"Rat," said the Mole, "I simply can't go and turn in, and go to sleep, and *do* nothing, even though there doesn't seem to be anything to be done. We'll get the boat out, and paddle upstream. The moon will be up in an hour or so, and then we will search as well as we can – anyhow, it will be better than going to bed and doing *nothing*."

"Just what I was thinking myself," said the Rat. "It's not the sort of night for bed anyhow; and daybreak is not so very far off, and then we may pick up some news of him from early risers as we go along."

They got the boat out, and the Rat took the sculls, paddling with caution. Out in mid-stream there was a clear, narrow track that faintly reflected the sky; but wherever shadows fell on the water from bank, bush, or tree, they were as solid to all appearance as the banks themselves, and the Mole had to steer with judgment accordingly. Dark and deserted as it was, the night was full of small noises, song and chatter and rustling, telling of the busy little population who were up and about, plying their trades and vocations through the night till sunshine should fall on them at last and send them off to their well-earned repose. The water's own noises, too, were more apparent than by day, its gurglings and "cloops" more unexpected and near at hand; and constantly they started at what seemed a sudden clear call from an actual articulate voice.

The line of the horizon was clear and hard against the sky, and in one particular quarter it showed black against a silvery climbing phosphorescence that grew and grew. At last, over the rim of the waiting earth the moon lifted with slow majesty till it swung clear of the horizon and rode off, free of moorings; and once more they began to see surfaces – meadows widespread, and quiet gardens, and the river itself from bank to bank, all softly disclosed, all washed clean of mystery and terror, all radiant again as by day, but with a difference that was tremendous. Their old haunts greeted them again in other raiment, as if they had slipped away and put on this pure new apparel and come quietly back, smiling as they shyly waited to see if they would be recognized again under it.

Fastening their boat to a willow, the friends landed in this silent, silver kingdom, and patiently explored the hedges, the hollow trees, the tunnels and their little culverts, the ditches and dry waterways. Embarking again and crossing over, they worked their way up the stream in this manner, while the moon, serene and detached in a cloudless sky, did what she could, though so far off, to help them in their quest; till her hour came and she sank earthwards reluctantly, and left them, and mystery once more held field and river.

Then a change began slowly to declare itself. The horizon

became clearer, field and tree came more into sight, and somehow with a different look; the mystery began to drop away from them. A bird piped suddenly, and was still; and a light breeze sprang up and set the reeds and bulrushes rustling. Rat, who was in the stern of the boat, while Mole sculled, sat up suddenly and listened with a passionate intentness. Mole, who with gentle strokes was just keeping the boat moving while he scanned the banks with care, looked at him with curiosity.

"It's gone!" sighed the Rat, sinking back in his seat again. "So beautiful and strange and new! Since it was to end so soon, I almost wish I had never heard it. For it has roused a longing in me that is pain, and nothing seems worth while but just to hear that sound once more and go on listening to it for ever. No! There it is again!" he cried, alert once more. Entranced, he was silent for a long space, spellbound.

"Now it passes on and I begin to lose it," he said presently. "O, Mole! the beauty of it! The merry bubble and joy, the thin, clear, happy call of the distant piping! Such music I never dreamed of, and the call in it is stronger even than the music is sweet! Row on, Mole, row! For the music and the call must be for us."

The Mole, greatly wondering, obeyed. "I hear nothing myself," he said, "but the wind playing in the reeds and rushes and osiers."

The Rat never answered, if indeed he heard. Rapt, transported, trembling, he was possessed in all his senses by this new divine thing that caught up his helpless soul and swung and dandled it, a powerless but happy infant, in a strong sustaining grasp.

In silence Mole rowed steadily, and soon they came to a point where the river divided, a long backwater branching off to one side. With a slight movement of his head Rat, who had long dropped the rudder-lines, directed the rower to take the backwater. The creeping tide of light gained and gained, and now they could see the colour of the flowers that gemmed the water's edge.

"Clearer and nearer still," cried the Rat joyously. "Now you must surely hear it! Ah – at last – I see you do!"

Breathless and transfixed the Mole stopped rowing as the liquid run of that glad piping broke on him like a wave, caught him up, and possessed him utterly. He saw the tears on his comrade's cheeks, and bowed his head and understood. For a space they hung there, brushed by the purple loosestrife that fringed the bank; then the clear imperious summons that marched hand-in-hand with the intoxicating melody imposed its will on Mole, and mechanically he bent to his oars again. And the light grew steadily stronger, but no birds sang as they were wont to do at the approach of dawn; and but for the heavenly music all was marvellously still.

On either side of them, as they glided onwards, the rich meadow-grass seemed that morning of a freshness and a greenness unsurpassable. Never had they noticed the roses so vivid, the willow-herb so riotous, the meadow-sweet so odorous and pervading. Then the murmur of the approaching weir began to hold the air, and they felt a consciousness that they were nearing the end, whatever it might be, that surely awaited their expedition.

A wide half-circle of foam and glinting lights and shining shoulders of green water, the great weir closed the backwater from bank to bank, troubled all the quiet surface with twirling eddies and floating foam-streaks, and deadened all other sounds with its solemn and soothing rumble. In midmost of the stream, embraced in the weir's shimmering arm-spread, a small island lay anchored, fringed close with willow and silver birch and alder. Reserved, shy, but full of significance, it hid whatever it might hold behind a veil, keeping it till the hour should come, and, with the hour, those who were called and chosen.

Slowly, but with no doubt or hesitation whatever, and in something of a solemn expectancy, the two animals passed through the broken, tumultuous water and moored their boat at the flowery margin of the island. In silence they landed, and pushed through the blossom and scented herbage and undergrowth that led up to the level ground, till they stood on a little lawn of a marvellous green, set round with Nature's own orchard-trees – crab-apple, wild cherry, and sloe.

"This is the place of my song-dream, the place the music played to me," whispered the Rat, as if in a trance. "Here, in this holy place, here if anywhere, surely we shall find Him!"

Then suddenly the Mole felt a great Awe fall upon him, an awe that turned his muscles to water, bowed his head, and rooted his feet to the ground. It was no panic terror – indeed he felt wonderfully at peace and happy – but it was an awe that smote and held him and, without seeing, he knew it could only mean that some august Presence was very, very near. With difficulty he turned to look for his friend, and saw him at his side cowed, stricken, and trembling violently. And still there was utter silence in the populous bird-haunted branches around them; and still the light grew and grew.

Perhaps he would never have dared to raise his eyes, but that, though the piping was now hushed, the call and the summons seemed still dominant and imperious. He might not refuse, were Death himself waiting to strike him instantly, once he had looked with mortal eye on things rightly kept hidden. Trembling he obeyed, and raised his humble head; and then, in that utter clearness of the imminent dawn, while Nature, flushed with fullness of incredible colour, seemed to hold her breath for the event, he looked in the very eyes of the Friend and Helper; saw the backward sweep of the curved horns, gleaming in the growing daylight; saw the stern, hooked nose between the kindly eyes that were looking down on them humorously, while the bearded mouth broke into a half-smile at the corners; saw the rippling muscles on the arm that lay across the broad chest, the long supple hand still holding the pan-pipes only just fallen away from the parted lips; saw the splendid curves of the shaggy limbs disposed in majestic ease on the sward; saw, last of all, nestling between his very hooves, sleeping soundly in entire peace and contentment, the little, round, podgy, childish form of the baby otter. All this he saw, for one moment breathless and intense, vivid on the morning sky; and still, as he looked, he lived; and still, as he lived, he wondered.

"Rat!" he found breath to whisper, shaking. "Are you afraid?"

"Afraid?" murmured the Rat, his eyes shining with unutterable love. "Afraid! Of *Him?* O, never, never! And yet – and yet – O, Mole, I am afraid!"

Then the two animals, crouching to the earth, bowed their heads and did worship.

Sudden and magnificent, the sun's broad golden disc showed itself over the horizon facing them; and the first rays, shooting across the level water-meadows, took the animals full in the eyes and dazzled them. When they were able to look once more, the Vision had vanished, and the air was full of the carol of birds that hailed the dawn.

As they stared blankly, in dumb misery deepening as they slowly realized all they had seen and all they had lost, a capricious little breeze, dancing up from the surface of the water, tossed the aspens, shook the dewy roses, and blew lightly and caressingly in their faces, and with its soft touch came instant oblivion. For this is the last best gift that the kindly demigod is careful to bestow on those to whom he has revealed himself in their helping: the gift of forgetfulness. Lest the awful remembrance should remain and grow, and overshadow mirth and pleasure, and the great haunting memory should spoil all the after-lives of little animals helped out of difficulties, in order that they should be happy and light-hearted as before.

Mole rubbed his eyes and stared at Rat, who was looking about him in a puzzled sort of way. "I beg your pardon; what did you say, Rat?" he asked.

"I think I was only remarking," said Rat slowly, "that this was the right sort of place, and that here, if anywhere, we should find him. And look! Why, there he is, the little fellow!" And with a cry of delight he ran towards the slumbering Portly.

But Mole stood still a moment, held in thought. As one wakened suddenly from a beautiful dream, who struggles to recall it, and can recapture nothing but a dim sense of the beauty of it, the beauty! Till that, too, fades away in its turn, and the dreamer bitterly accepts the hard, cold waking and all its penalties; so Mole, after struggling with his memory for a brief space, shook his head sadly and followed the Rat.

Portly woke up with a joyous squeak, and wriggled with pleasure at the sight of his father's friends, who had played with him so often in past days. In a moment, however, his face grew blank, and he fell to hunting round in a circle with pleading whine. As a child that has fallen happily asleep in its nurse's arms, and wakes to find itself alone and laid in a strange place, and searches corners and cupboards, and runs from room to room, despair growing silently in its heart, even so Portly searched the island and searched, dogged and unwearying, till at last the black moment came for giving it up, and sitting down and crying bitterly.

The Mole ran quickly to comfort the little animal; but Rat, lingering, looked long and doubtfully at certain hoof-marks deep in the sward.

"Some – great – animal – has been here," he murmured slowly and thoughtfully; and stood musing, musing; his mind strangely stirred.

"Come along, Rat!" called the Mole. "Think of poor Otter, waiting up there by the ford!"

Portly had soon been comforted by the promise of a treat – a jaunt on the river in Mr. Rat's real boat; and the two animals conducted him to the water's side, placed him securely between them in the bottom of the boat, and paddled off down the backwater. The sun was fully up by now, and hot on them, birds sang lustily and without restraint, and flowers smiled and nodded from either bank, but somehow – so thought the animals – with less of richness and blaze of colour than they seemed to remember seeing quite recently somewhere – they wondered where.

The main river reached again, they turned the boat's head upstream, towards the point where they knew their friend was keeping his lonely vigil. As they drew near the familiar ford, the Mole took the boat in to the bank, and they lifted Portly out and set him on his legs on the tow-path, gave him his marching orders and a friendly farewell pat on the back, and shoved out into mid-stream. They watched the little animal as he waddled along the path contentedly and with importance; watched him till they saw his muzzle suddenly lift and his waddle break into a clumsy amble as he quickened his pace with shrill whines and wriggles of recognition. Looking up the river, they could see Otter start up, tense and rigid, from out of the shallows where he crouched in dumb patience, and could hear his amazed and joyous bark as he bounded up through the osiers on to the path. Then the Mole, with a strong pull on one oar, swung the boat round and let the full stream bear them down again whither it would, their quest now happily ended.

"I feel strangely tired, Rat," said the Mole, leaning wearily over his oars as the boat drifted. "It's being up all night, you'll say, perhaps; but that's nothing. We do as much half the nights of the week, at this time of the year. No; I feel as if I had been through something very exciting and rather terrible, and it was just over; and yet nothing particular has happened."

"Or something very surprising and splendid and beautiful," murmured the Rat, leaning back and closing his eyes. "I feel just as you do, Mole; simply dead tired, though not body-tired. It's lucky we've got the stream with us, to take us home. Isn't it jolly to feel the sun again, soaking into one's bones! And hark to the wind playing in the reeds!"

"It's like music – far-away music," said the Mole, nodding drowsily.

"So I was thinking," murmured the Rat, dreamful and languid. "Dance music – the lilting sort that runs on without a stop – but with words in it, too – it passes into words and out of them again – I catch them at intervals – then it is dance music once more, and then nothing but the reeds' soft thin whispering."

"You hear better than I," said the Mole sadly. "I cannot catch the words."

"Let me try and give you them," said the Rat softly, his eyes still closed. "Now it is turning into words again – faint but clear – *Lest the awe should dwell – And turn your frolic to fret – You shall look on my power at the helping hour – But then you shall forget!* Now the reeds take it up – *forget, forget,* they sigh, and it dies away in a rustle and a whisper. Then the voice returns—

"*Lest limbs be reddened and rent – I spring the trap that is set – As I loose the snare you may glimpse me there – For surely you shall forget!* Row nearer, Mole, nearer to the reeds! It is hard to catch, and grows each minute fainter.

"*Helper and healer, I cheer – Small waifs in the woodland wet – Strays I find in it, wounds I bind in it – Bidding them all forget!* Nearer, Mole, nearer! No, it is no good; the song has died away into reed talk."

"But what do the words mean?" asked the wondering Mole.

"That I do not know," said the Rat simply. "I passed them on to you as they reached me. Ah! now they return again, and this time full and clear! This time, at last, it is the real, the unmistakable thing, simple – passionate – perfect—"

"Well, let's have it, then," said the Mole, after he had waited patiently for a few minutes, half dozing in the hot sun.

But no answer came. He looked, and understood the silence. With a smile of much happiness on his face, and something of a listening look still lingering there, the weary Rat was fast asleep.

HERMAN HESSE

THE FERRYMAN

Translated by Hilda Rosner

from *Siddhartha*

I WILL REMAIN by this river, thought Siddhartha. It is the same river which I crossed on my way to the town. A friendly ferryman took me across. I will go to him. My path once led from his hut to a new life which is now old and dead. May my present path, my new life, start from there!

He looked lovingly into the flowing water, into the transparent green, into the crystal lines of its wonderful design. He saw bright pearls rise from the depths, bubbles swimming on the mirror, sky blue reflected in them. The river looked at him with a thousand eyes – green, white, crystal, sky blue. How he loved this river, how it enchanted him, how grateful he was to it! In his heart he heard the newly awakened voice speak, and it said to him: "Love this river, stay by it, learn from it." Yes, he wanted to learn from it, he wanted to listen to it. It seemed to him that whoever understood this river and its secrets, would understand much more, many secrets, all secrets.

But today he only saw one of the river's secrets, one that gripped his soul. He saw that the water continually flowed and flowed and yet it was always there; it was always the same and yet every moment it was new. Who could understand, conceive this? He did not understand it; he was only aware of a dim suspicion, a faint memory, divine voices.

Siddhartha rose, the pangs of hunger were becoming unbearable. He wandered painfully along the river bank, listened to the rippling of the water, listened to the gnawing hunger in his body.

When he reached the ferry, the boat was already there and the ferryman who had once taken the young Samana across, stood in the boat. Siddhartha recognized him. He had also aged very much.

"Will you take me across?" he asked.

The ferryman, astonished to see such a distinguished-looking man alone and on foot, took him into the boat and set off.

"You have chosen a splendid life," said Siddhartha. "It must be fine to live near this river and sail on it every day."

The rower smiled, swaying gently.

"It is fine, sir, as you say, but is not every life, every work fine?"

"Maybe, but I envy you yours."

"Oh, you would soon lose your taste for it. It is not for people in fine clothes."

Siddhartha laughed. "I have already been judged by my clothes today and regarded with suspicion. Will you accept these clothes from me, which I find a nuisance? For I must tell you that I have no money to pay you for taking me across the river."

"The gentleman is joking," laughed the ferryman.

"I am not joking, my friend. You once previously took me across this river without payment, so please do it today also and take my clothes instead."

"And will the gentleman continue without clothes?"

"I should prefer not to go further. I should prefer it if you would give me some old clothes and keep me here as your assistant, or rather your apprentice, for I must learn how to handle the boat."

The ferryman looked keenly at the stranger for a long time.

"I recognize you," he said finally. "You once slept in my hut. It is a long time ago, maybe more than twenty years ago. I took you across the river and we parted good friends. Were you not a Samana? I cannot remember your name."

"My name is Siddhartha and I was Samana when you last saw me."

"You are welcome, Siddhartha. My name is Vasudeva. I hope you will be my guest today and also sleep in my hut, and tell me where you have come from and why you are so tired of your fine clothes."

They had reached the middle of the river and Vasudeva rowed more strongly because of the current. He rowed calmly, with strong arms, watching the end of the boat. Siddhartha sat and watched him and remembered how once, in those last Samana days, he had felt affection for this man. He gratefully accepted Vasudeva's invitation. When they reached the river bank, he helped him to secure the boat. Then Vasudeva led him into the hut, offered him bread and water, which Siddhartha ate with enjoyment, as well as the mango fruit which Vasudeva offered him.

Later, when the sun was beginning to set, they sat on a tree trunk by the river and Siddhartha told him about his origin and his life and how he had seen him today after that hour of despair. The story lasted late into the night.

Vasudeva listened with great attention; he heard all about his origin and childhood, about his studies, his seekings, his pleasures and needs. It was one of the ferryman's greatest virtues that, like few people, he knew how to listen. Without his saying a word, the speaker felt that Vasudeva took in every word, quietly, expectantly, that he missed nothing. He did not await anything with impatience and gave neither praise nor blame – he only listened. Siddhartha felt how wonderful it was to have such a listener who could be absorbed in another person's life, his strivings, his sorrows.

However, towards the end of Siddhartha's story, when he told him about the tree by the river and his deep despair, about the holy Om, and how after his sleep he felt such a love for the river, the ferryman listened with doubled attention, completely absorbed, his eyes closed.

When Siddhartha had finished and there was a long pause, Vasudeva said: "It is as I thought; the river has spoken to you. It is friendly towards you, too; it speaks to you. That is good, very good. Stay with me, Siddhartha, my friend. I once had a wife, her bed was at the side of mine, but she died long ago. I have lived alone for a long time. Come and live with me; there is room and food for both of us."

"I thank you," said Siddhartha, "I thank you and accept. I also thank you, Vasudeva, for listening so well. There are few people who know how to listen and I have not met anybody who can do so like you. I will also learn from you in this respect."

"You will learn it," said Vasudeva, "but not from me. The river has taught me to listen; you will learn from it, too. The river knows everything; one can learn everything from it. You have already learned from the river that it is good to strive downwards, to sink, to seek the depths. The rich and distinguished Siddhartha will become a rower; Siddhartha the learned Brahmin will become a ferryman. You have also learned this from the river. You will learn the other thing, too."

After a long pause, Siddhartha said: "What other thing, Vasudeva?"

Vasudeva rose. "It has grown late," he said, "let us go to bed. I cannot tell you what the other thing is, my friend. You will find out, perhaps you already know. I am not a learned man; I do not know how to talk or think. I only know how to listen and be devout; otherwise I have learned nothing. If I could talk and teach, I would perhaps be a teacher, but as it is I am only a ferryman and it is my task to take people across this river. I have taken thousands of people across and to all of them my river has been nothing but a hindrance on their journey. They have travelled for money and business, to weddings and on pilgrimages; the river has been in their way and the ferryman was there to take them quickly across the obstacle. However, amongst the thousands there have been a few, four or five, to whom the river was not an obstacle. They have heard its voice and listened to it, and the river has become holy to them, as it has to me. Let us now go to bed, Siddhartha."

Siddhartha stayed with the ferryman and learned how to look after the boat, and when there was nothing to do at the ferry, he worked in the rice field with Vasudeva, gathered wood, and picked fruit from the banana trees. He learned how to make oars, how to improve the boat and to make baskets. He was pleased with everything that he did and learned and the days and months passed quickly. But he learned more from the river than Vasudeva could teach him. He learned from it continually. Above all, he learned from it how to listen, to listen with a still heart, with a waiting, open soul, without passion, without desire, without judgment, without opinions.

He lived happily with Vasudeva and occasionally they exchanged words, few and long-considered words. Vasudeva was no friend of words. Siddhartha was rarely successful in moving him to speak.

He once asked him, "Have you also learned that secret from the river; that there is no such thing as time?"

A bright smile spread over Vasudeva's face.

"Yes, Siddhartha," he said. "Is this what you mean? That the river is everywhere at the same time, at the source and at the mouth, at the waterfall, at the ferry, at the current, in the ocean and in the mountains, everywhere, and that the present only exists for it, not the shadow of the past, nor the shadow of the future?"

"That is it," said Siddhartha, "and when I learned that, I reviewed my life and it was also a river, and Siddhartha the boy, Siddhartha the mature man and Siddhartha the old man, were only separated by shadows, not through reality. Siddhartha's previous lives were also not in the past, and his death and his return to Brahma are not in the future. Nothing was, nothing will be, everything has reality and presence."

Siddhartha spoke with delight. This discovery had made him very happy. Was then not all sorrow in time, all self-torment and fear in time? Were not all difficulties and evil in the world conquered as soon as one conquered time, as soon as one dispelled time? He had spoken with delight, but Vasudeva just smiled radiantly at him and nodded his agreement. He stroked Siddhartha's shoulder and returned to his work.

And once again when the river swelled during the rainy season and roared loudly, Siddhartha said: "Is it not true, my friend, that the river has very many voices? Has it not the voice of a king, of a warrior, of a bull, of a night bird, of a pregnant woman and a sighing man, and a thousand other voices?"

"It is so," nodded Vasudeva, "the voices of all living creatures are in its voice."

"And do you know," continued Siddhartha, "what word it pronounces when one is successful in hearing all its ten thousand voices at the same time?"

Vasudeva laughed joyously; he bent towards Siddhartha and whispered the holy Om in his ear. And this was just what Siddhartha had heard.

As time went on his smile began to resemble the ferryman's, was almost equally radiant, almost equally full of happiness, equally lighting up through a thousand little wrinkles, equally childish, equally senile. Many travellers, when seeing both ferrymen together, took them for brothers. Often they sat together in the evening on the tree trunk by the river. They both listened silently to the water, which to them was not just water, but the voice of life, the voice of Being, of perpetual Becoming. And it sometimes happened that while listening to the river, they both thought the same thoughts, perhaps of a conversation of the previous day, or about one of the travellers whose fate and circumstances occupied their minds, or death, or their childhood; and when the river told them something good at the same moment, they looked at each other, both thinking the same thought, both happy at the same answer to the same question.

Something emanated from the ferry and from both ferrymen that many of the travellers felt. It sometimes happened that a traveller, after looking at the face of one of the ferrymen, began to talk about his life and troubles, confessed sins, asked for comfort and advice. It sometimes happened that someone would ask permission to spend an evening with them in order to listen to the river. It also happened that curious people came along, who had been told that two wise men, magicians or holy men lived at the ferry. The curious ones asked many questions but they received no replies, and they found neither magicians nor wise men. They only found two friendly old men, who appeared to be mute, rather odd and stupid. And the curious ones laughed and said how foolish and gullible people were to spread such wild rumours.

The years passed and nobody counted them. Then one day, some monks came along, followers of Gotama, the Buddha, and asked to be taken across the river. The ferrymen learned from them that they were returning to their great teacher as quickly as possible, for the news had spread that the Illustrious One was seriously ill and would soon suffer his last mortal death and attain salvation. Not long afterwards another party of monks arrived and then another, and the monks as well as most of the other travellers talked of nothing but Gotama and his approaching death. And as people come from all sides to a military expedition or to the crowning of a king, so did they gather together like swarms of bees, drawn together by a magnet, to go where the great Buddha was lying on his deathbed, where this great event was taking place and where the saviour of an age was passing into eternity.

Siddhartha thought a great deal at this time about the dying sage whose voice had stirred thousands, whose voice he had also once heard, whose holy countenance he had also once looked at with awe. He thought lovingly of him, remembered his path to salvation, and smiling, remembered the words he had once uttered as a young man to the Illustrious One. It seemed to him that they had been arrogant and precocious words. For a long time he knew that he was not separated from Gotama, although he could not accept his teachings. No, a true seeker could not accept any teachings, not if he sincerely wished to find something. But he who had found, could give his approval to every path, every goal; nothing separated him from all the other thousands who lived in eternity, who breathed the Divine.

One day, when very many people were making a

pilgrimage to the dying Buddha, Kamala, once the most beautiful of courtesans, was also on her way. She had long retired from her previous way of life, had presented her garden to Gotama's monks, taking refuge in his teachings, and belonged to the women and benefactresses attached to the pilgrims. On hearing of Gotama's approaching death, she had set off on foot, wearing simple clothes, together with her son. They had reached the river on her way, but the boy soon became tired; he wanted to go home, he wanted to rest, he wanted to eat. He was often sulky and tearful. Kamala frequently had to rest with him. He was used to matching his will against hers. She had to feed him, comfort him, and scold him. He could not understand why his mother had to make this weary, miserable pilgrimage to an unknown place, to a strange man who was holy and was dying. Let him die – what did it matter to the boy?

The pilgrims were not far from Vasudeva's ferry, when little Siddhartha told his mother he wanted to rest. Kamala herself was tired, and while the boy ate a banana, she crouched down on the ground, half-closed her eyes and rested. Suddenly, however, she uttered a cry of pain. The boy, startled, looked at her and saw her face white with horror. From under her clothes a small black snake, which had bitten Kamala, crawled away.

They both ran on quickly in order to reach some people. When they were near the ferry, Kamala collapsed and could not go any further. The boy cried out for help, meantime kissing and embracing his mother. She also joined in his loud cries, until the sounds reached Vasudeva, who was standing by the ferry. He came quickly, took the woman in his arms and carried her to the boat. The boy joined him and they soon arrived at the hut, where Siddhartha was standing and was just lighting the fire. He looked up and first saw the boy's face, which strangely reminded him of something. Then he saw Kamala, whom he recognized immediately, although she lay unconscious in the ferryman's arms. Then he knew that it was his own son whose face had so reminded him of something, and his heart beat quickly.

Kamala's wound was washed, but it was already black and her body had swelled. She was given a restorative and her consciousness returned. She was lying on Siddhartha's bed in his hut and Siddhartha, whom she had once loved so much, was bending over her. She thought she was dreaming, and smiling, she looked into her lover's face. Gradually, she realized her condition, remembered the bite and called anxiously for her son.

"Do not worry," said Siddhartha, "he is here."

Kamala looked into his eyes. She found it difficult to speak with the poison in her system. "You have grown old, my dear," she said, "you have become grey, but you are like the young Samana who once came to me in my garden, without clothes and with dusty feet. You are much more like him than when you left Kamaswami and me. Your eyes are like his, Siddhartha. Ah, I have also grown old, old – did you recognize me?"

Siddhartha smiled. "I recognized you immediately, Kamala, my dear."

Kamala indicated her son and said: "Did you recognize him, too? He is your son."

Her eyes wandered and closed. The boy began to cry. Siddhartha put him on his knee, let him weep and stroked his hair. Looking at the child's face, he remembered a Brahmin prayer which he had once learned when he himself was a small child. Slowly and in a singing voice he began to recite it; the words came back to him out of the past and his childhood. The child became quiet as he recited, still sobbed a little and then fell asleep. Siddhartha put him on Vasudeva's bed. Vasudeva stood by the hearth cooking rice. Siddhartha looked at Vasudeva and smiled at him.

"She is dying," said Siddhartha softly.

Vasudeva nodded. The firelight from the hearth was reflected in his kind face.

Kamala again regained consciousness. There was pain in her face; Siddhartha read the pain on her mouth, in her pallid face. He read it quietly, attentively, waiting, sharing her pain. Kamala was aware of this; her glance sought his.

Looking at him she said: "Now I see that your eyes have also changed. They have become quite different. How do I recognize that you are still Siddhartha? You are Siddhartha and yet you are not like him."

Siddhartha did not speak; silently he looked into her eyes.

"Have you attained it?" she asked. "Have you found peace?"

He smiled and placed his hand on hers.

"Yes," she said, "I see it. I also will find peace."

"You have found it," whispered Siddhartha.

Kamala looked at him steadily. It had been her intention to make a pilgrimage to Gotama, to see the face of the Illustrious One, to obtain some of his peace, and instead she had only found Siddhartha, and it was good, just as good as if she had seen the other. She wanted to tell him that, but her tongue no longer obeyed her will. Silently she looked at him and he saw the life fade from her eyes. When the last pain had filled and passed from her eyes, when the last shudder had passed through her body, his fingers closed her eyelids.

He sat there a long time looking at her dead face. For a long time he looked at her mouth, her old tired mouth and her shrunken lips, and remembered how once, in the spring of his life, he had compared her lips with a freshly cut fig. For a long time he looked intently at the pale face, at the tired wrinkles and saw his own face like that, just as white, also dead, and at the same time he saw his face and hers, young, with red lips, with ardent eyes and he was overwhelmed with a feeling of the present and contemporary existence. In this hour he felt more acutely the indestructibleness of every life, the eternity of every moment.

When he rose, Vasudeva had prepared some rice for him but Siddhartha did not eat. In the stable, where the goat was, the two old men straightened some straw and Vasudeva lay down. But Siddhartha went outside and sat in front of the hut all night, listening to the river, sunk in the past, simultaneously affected and encompassed by all the periods of his life. From time to time, however, he rose, walked to the door of the hut and listened to hear if the boy was sleeping.

Early in the morning, before the sun was yet visible, Vasudeva came out of the stable and walked up to his friend.

"You have not slept," he said.

"No, Vasudeva, I sat here and listened to the river. It has told me a great deal, it has filled me with many great thoughts, with thoughts of unity."

"You have suffered, Siddhartha, yet I see that sadness has not entered your heart."

"No, my dear friend. Why should I be sad? I who was rich and happy have become still richer and happier. My son has been given to me."

"I also welcome your son. But now, Siddhartha, let us go to work, there is much to be done. Kamala died on the same bed where my wife died. We shall also build Kamala's funeral pyre on the same hill where I once built my wife's funeral pyre."

While the boy still slept, they built the funeral pyre.

TONY BIRCH

THE GHOST RIVER

THE RIVER BOYS camped along the low bank when the weather was on their side. On summer nights they sat by the fire, passed the bottle and cooked a feed, a couple of tins of baked beans or bacon bones in steaming water and bread toasted on an old stove rack. If one of them got lucky with the throwing arm and landed a kill with a fistful of rock, they shared a rabbit on the coals.

Most nights there'd be four or five boys round the campfire, Big Tiny Watkins, Cold Can, the Doctor, Tallboy and Moses, the undisputed boss.

They once had regular names, like you and me, but ditched them and took up with identities that appeared in no public record. The river kept them off the streets and brought them some peace, away from the eyes of the police, who also loved the drink and were notorious for kicking the winos round the streets.

The river boys would end a night's drinking with a tune. They sang to the stars, the moon and, naturally, the river. On warm nights the wind travelled from the north. It swept through the valley, off the water and ran up the hill and carried the river with it.

I'd pick up their drunken choir from my open window, where I perched of a night smoking cigarettes and looking up at the same stretch of sky. The scent of the water, sweet and damp, floated on the warm air. It circled the room, teasing me. I'd take a good sniff and wish I were down on the water with them.

Each of the river boys carried the story of his life; where he'd come from, how he'd sunk low and how he was going to fight his way back to the top, which was nothing more than the drink talking. They spoke one part truth, two parts trickster and, as my father liked to say, "a truckload of bullshit."

Moses was in charge of the campfire, and made the rules on when to light up and when to dampen the coals. He also led the cook-up and the singing. He could play the spoons and the gum leaf and sang country and western as good as a singer on a record album.

He was a man from another time, marching round in his cowboy boots, woollen pants and jacket, and a hat cocked back on his head with a blackbird feather sticking out of the band.

I headed for the river whenever I could, sometimes on my own, but mostly with my closest friend, Sonny, who lived next door, and like me expected to grow up to be an outlaw. We knew the best spots to swim and the death holes to steer away from, where the skeleton tree snags lurked beneath the water, waiting to snatch hold of a foot and never let go. We knew the bridges and trees that were safe to jump from without hitting a submerged rock or a stolen car wreck dumped in the water.

The river had been poisoned over the years, because of all the rubbish and shit dumped in it. Signs had been put up round the waterholes warning swimmers off with skull-and-crossbones markers, frightening off most kids, but not us. Neither of us ever got sick taking in river water and we only ended up with sores full of pus if I went into the water with an open cut.

Any time we heard an animal running through the bush we went chasing after it, whether it was a rabbit, a snake or a wild cat. I never caught one of them cats, and maybe I was lucky I didn't.

Tallboy had once worked as a rabbit trapper along the river and told us that a river cat could wipe out a team of ferrets in a morning and take down a hunting dog if there was a pair of them working together.

"We trapped one of them fellas one night, in a crate we kept to grab the rabbits when they came running out of the burrow with a ferret up the arse. We had this big old Tom in the cage, fangs like a tiger and nuts like bowling balls. The old trapper I worked with back then roped a snare round the cat's neck. Growling and spitting at us, it was. Would have gone us on the spot if we'd freed him. We dropped the cat in a hessian sack along with a rock and tied it up with wire. 'Watch this,' my old mate said and flung the sack in the water. There was a mighty splash and the sack sunk. We waited a bit. And then, bugger me, a couple of minutes went by and I spotted bubbles on the surface of the water. And then the cat, he comes to the top. He swam to the bank and snuck off into the scrub, giving us an almighty growl."

Eventually we knew the river as well as anyone. I could lie on my bed at night with pencil and paper and draw maps of the river, marking every bend and waterhole, the bridges and jumping trees, the empty factories and car wrecks, and the old pontoon floating on forty-fours roped to a wooden landing down river from the campsite.

Moses knew the river better than anybody, and he didn't need no map. He carried every inch of the river in his head. He was also a champion storyteller and we loved listening to him weave a tale. The only story I never got was the one he told over and over again about the river. The more times I heard it the less I understood it.

When he was about to begin the river story Moses would stamp at the ground with the heel of his boot and call out to the birds in the trees, "Listen hard now." He'd clap his hands together a couple of times, make a clicking noise with his tongue and the birds would lift off from the trees in the distance and move a little closer, to the wattles lining the riverbank.

"Back in the old time, before the humans," he would begin, "this girl, the river, she didn't stop her life where she does now, at the mouth at bay there. There is no bay in the time I'm talking with." He'd stop and turn in a circle, flapping his arm about like a bird, and click his tongue again. The birds in the trees would whistle as if he was talking to them.

"All the land was full up." He stuck his stomach out like he was a pregnant woman. "The river, she went on. She went on and she didn't stop 'til she touched the ocean."

He'd pick a stick up from the ground, snap it in two and draw a map in the sand, of a secret river he was sure lived beneath the sea. He'd stamp his foot again and stare everyone around the campfire in the eye. Moses didn't look like any helpless wino when he did that. He was fearsome. He'd slap his thigh as he went on.

"Here's the first lesson. You find yourself out on the bay there, you get yourself in trouble," he'd slap his leg again, "you must be thinking with a sharp eye, search for the quiet water. The still water. Your mother."

He'd draw another swirl in the sand and spear it with the stick.

"She is calm right there. In her heart. The Ghost River, she's there waiting for you. You find yourself in trouble, you look out for her."

The first time I heard the story a shiver went through my

body and I was forced to swallow spit before I could talk. "A ghost river?"

"The Ghost River," he nodded. "All she is. You believe in her, she's there to take care of you. If you're no believer that girl will take you down and teach you a rock-hard lesson. Don't expect her be spitting you back neither. You fuck up on her, you never be coming back."

With the story over Moses would be sweating and shaking. He'd go quiet, sit by the fire and wait for the old Moses to return. I never understood the story the first time he told it, and over the years it only got spookier. I put it down to the drink digging holes in his brain and crippling his body. He slowed down round the fire, could hardly sing a note and ended up blind in one eye.

The next winter was the wettest in years and Moses and the boys were forced to take shelter in the old pumping station downriver. The building was over a hundred years old. In the old days it took water from the river and pumped it up the hill through a pipe for the machines in a woollen mill. The station had shut down long ago along with the mill.

The pumps had stopped running and rusted up. The wooden floor and foundations of the building had rotted away and it had sunk into the riverbed. From the far bank the station looked like a red brick boat somehow floating on the water.

The cellar was flooded out and home to river rats and snakes. They went at each other for a feed, day and night, thrashing about in the oily water. The iron roof had blown off in the wind and the upstairs floor was covered in bird shit half a foot deep. Bats flew into the station on sundown and wrapped themselves in their leather wings and hung from the ceiling rafters until the morning.

The only spot dry enough for the boys to bed down was in the storehouse on the ground floor. They bunked on tables and shelves, under blankets stinking of piss and the grog. They came to of a morning, around the same time as the bats, with their blankets hugging their stooped shoulders, reciting a graveyard cough to get the lungs going.

Over the months of that dark winter the river boys turned grey and mouldy. Eventually the cold and rain and the flooded river got the better of them.

Big Tiny was the first of the boys to go. He slipped over and rolled down the muddy bank one night, whacked his head on a rock and split it open. He tried getting to his feet, fell a second time and rolled into the river.

Tiny's bloated body was found a little over a week later. It was wedged in the branches of a big old tree that had toppled over earlier in the winter and been left to rest half-in-half-out of the water. With his arms outstretched he looked like a man who'd been crucified. The yabbies had eaten his stomach away, the hawks had swooped down and taken off with his eyes, and his skin hung in shreds from his bones.

Moses was quick to pick up how bad his death had upset the rest of the mob. He put his hands together for Tiny and declared that we had to understand that there was good in Tiny's death. In explaining himself he added something more to his Ghost River story.

"When a fella has a clean soul the river takes hold of his body before it's lost, lifts it up and tells it to float along there until it finds a home. Tiny found a home in that old tree. That's why it fell over in the first place, back then, in the wet. That tree was waiting for him to come by."

He gave us the stare and slapped his thigh before going on.

"Now, if a man's soul is dark and dirty, the ghost river

drags that body to the bottom and buries it in the mud. The body is trapped there, like in old Purgatory there, for Mr. Lucifer to come up through the earth and claim that fella for his own self."

He walked round and touched everyone on the forehead, even Sonny and me. "So don't any of you be sad for old Tiny. He had a pure soul, that old boy. All them other fellas feeding on his body after he's gone, the crabs and the birds flying off with his eyes, he'll be seeing us through them. This don't do no harm at all. Not for Tiny."

Cold Can was the next to leave us. He'd never spoken a word any time we'd been down the camp. He always sat close to Moses and nodded in agreement at anything Moses said, even when he was drunk and cursing the world.

Cold Can was crossing the street from the wine shop one night and was knocked down by a truck. He died on the spot. He had no family and no money and was given a pauper's burial.

Moses had a shave and a wash for the funeral. Later that night, when they were sitting round the fire drinking he told the rest of the mob that at the gravesite he'd clammed his eyes shut and willed Cold Can's body out of that coffin and set him free before they could bury him in the ground.

"Where's he now?" Tallboy asked as Moses passed him the flagon. "If he's not in the ground, where the fuck is he?"

"Where would you reckon," Moses shouted, as if the answer was obvious to all of them. "He's gone with Big Tiny, on the ghost river. I put him there. Myself. Be there too, one day. All of us mob."

"Hope so," the Doctor mumbled. "Don't want the Devil getting hold of me. I'm gonna fly with that river," he cackled.

"Damn sure you will, Doc," Moses assured him.

Tallboy inspected the flagon, checking how much they'd drunk, in no doubt that the grog had got them for good.

The Doctor disappeared a week later and was never seen again. Moses had no doubt where he'd gone and said the time had come for the ghost river to call each of them home. Poor old Tallboy fell apart, hearing those words. He felt the river turning against him and wasn't ready to die.

The next morning he hiked the track to the streets above, picked up a decent house brick, lobbed it through the front window of an electrical store and waited for the police to come and arrest him.

It was Tallboy's lucky day. The judge gave him four months inside with a clean blanket and three meals a day.

In the end, Moses was left alone, by his fire. He got lonely and sad and angry. He said we weren't to hang round the river any longer.

"How long you been sitting by the fire here, boys?"

"A couple of years," I answered as Sonny tried adding up on his fingers.

"You spent two years wasting your time with a bunch of no-good drunks? It's time for you to piss off and grow up."

I'd never heard Moses sound so mean. And we didn't want to go anywhere. We were happy on the river. "I like the fire," Sonny protested. "And your stories. Even the ones that aren't clear. You still tell them good."

Moses huffed and puffed and took a swig from his bottle. "Listening days is over. I'm telling the two of you to piss off. Anyhow, I'm going and won't be back. There won't be any stories to listen to."

"Where you going to?" I asked, not really believing what Moses was saying. "We want to be here with you, and be outlaws like you, and Big Tiny and Cold Can."

"No outlaws," he laughed. "You don't need to be like us. We're gone."

I couldn't work out why he was laughing now. I was angry with him, and screaming. "We come to this campfire every chance we get, don't we Sonny?" He was holding his chin in his hands and had tears in his eyes. He tried saying something but couldn't talk.

Moses struggled to his feet, shuffled through the dirt to where I was sitting, in an old car seat. He waved at me to stand up.

When I refused to move he grabbed hold of me under the arms and hugged me tight against his bag-of-bones body. He stunk of the grog and dirt and sweat. But I didn't care. I didn't want him to let go of me. Not ever.

He rocked me from side to side as he spoke. "It's time for old Moses to go with the water, back with my people. Before this river is killed off proper."

"What people?" Sonny called out. "You said you had no people but the river boys."

He kept hold of me. "Oh, I have them, all right. From way back. The Doc and Cold Can too. Even Tallboy. He'll find his way back."

With his palms resting on my chest, he pushed me away. "But not you. Not yet. You got to leave the river. Go away. Time for you to grow. Come back when you men. She'll need you then."

I cannot remember exactly what I said to Moses after that, but I know I told him I hated him, and that he knew nothing and that he was crazy with grog.

I couldn't sleep on account of what I'd said to him and headed for the river the next morning to tell him I was sorry. Moses was nowhere to be seen. He wasn't at his campsite the next day, or the following night after school.

It was months before Sonny and me accepted that Moses was not coming back. On the first warm day of the summer we went for a swim at one of our waterholes and made our way across the public golf course to Phoenix Bridge, our favourite jumping spot.

I always liked to jump first. The drop never frightened me, until I'd leapt from one of the wooden pylons supporting the bridge. As I fell through the air I'd suddenly be gripped by the craziness that I would never find the river and would fall through the sky forever.

But I did hit the water. But not like I always had. Soon as I went in and plunged beneath the surface a shock of cold clawed at my lungs. I knew there was something wrong. I couldn't breathe, in or out. I was sinking into darkness and swallowing poison water.

I was afraid and knew I didn't want to be with the river boys and I didn't want to be an outlaw. But I couldn't help myself. My body was stiff with cold. And then I heard him, Moses, clicking his tongue, stamping his foot and calling to the Ghost River, not to take me but set me free.

Sonny said he'd never seen nothing like it. "I'm looking down from the bridge for you, thinking you'd done your last jump, and then, fuck me, you bob up on the side of the bank like one of them wild cats Tallboy used to speak about. The water lifted you on the bank. How crazy's that?"

I coughed up water all the way home. I felt sick the next morning and told Sonny I wouldn't be going for a swim. I was lying on the couch watching daytime television.

"What about tomorrow?"

"Dunno. I'll see how I'm feeling."

"That'll be two days away from the river. And it's holidays. We haven't done that before. So when we going again?"

"Like Moses said, when it's our time."

ZADIE SMITH

THE LAZY RIVER

WE'RE SUBMERGED, ALL of us. You, me, the children, our friends, their children, everybody else. Sometimes we get out: for lunch, to read or to tan, never for very long. Then we all climb back into the metaphor. The Lazy River is a circle, it is wet, it has an artificial current. Even if you don't move you will get somewhere and then return to wherever you started, and if we may speak of the depth of a metaphor, well, then, it is about three feet deep, excepting a brief stretch at which point it rises to six feet four. Here children scream – clinging to the walls or the nearest adult – until it is three feet deep once more. Round and round we go. All life is in here, flowing. Flowing!

Responses vary. Most of us float in the direction of the current, swimming a little, or walking, or treading water. Many employ some form of flotation device – rubber rings, tubes, rafts – placing these items strategically under their arms or necks or backsides, creating buoyancy, and thus rendering what is already almost effortless easier still. Life is struggle! But we are on vacation, from life and from struggle both. We are "going with the flow." And having entered the Lazy River we must have a flotation device, even though we know, rationally, that the artificial current is buoyancy enough. Still, we want one. Branded floats, too-large floats, comically shaped floats. They are a novelty, a luxury: they fill the time. We will complete many revolutions before their charm wears off – and for a few lucky souls it never will. For the rest of us, the moment arrives when we come to see that the lifeguard was right: these devices are too large; they are awkward to manage, tiresome. The plain fact is that we will all be carried along by the Lazy River, at the same rate, under the same relentless Spanish sun, for ever, until we are not.

Some take this principle of universal flow to an extreme. They play dead – head down, limbs limp, making no effort whatsoever – and in this manner discover that even a corpse goes round. A few people – less tattooed, often university educated – make a point of turning the other way, intent upon thrashing out a stroke against the current, never advancing, instead holding their place, if only for a moment, as the others float past. It's a pose: it can't last long. I heard one man with a fashionable haircut say he could swim the whole length backward. I heard his hipster wife dare him to do it. They had time for such games, having no children. But when he turned and made the attempt he was swept away within the minute.

The Lazy River is a metaphor and at the same time a real body of artificial water, in an all-inclusive hotel, in Almería, somewhere in southern Spain. We do not leave the hotel except to buy flotation devices. The plan is to beat our hotel at its own game. What you do is you do this: you drink so much alcohol that your accommodation is effectively free. (Only the most vulgar among us speak this plan aloud but we are all on board.) For in this hotel we are all British, we are en masse, we are unashamed. We enjoy one another's company. There is nobody French or German here to see us at the buffet, rejecting paella and swordfish in favour of sausages and chips, nor anyone to judge us as we lie on our loungers, turning from the concept of literature toward the reality of sudoku. One of our tribe, an older gentleman, has a portrait of Amy Winehouse on each shin, and we do not judge him, not at all, how could we? We do not have so many saints of Amy's calibre left to us; we cherish her. She was one of the few who expressed our pain without ridiculing or diminishing it. It is therefore fitting that in the evenings, during the brief spell in which we emerge from the Lazy River, we will, at karaoke hour, belt out her famous torch songs – full-throated, already drunk – content in the knowledge that later, much later, when all of this is over, these same beloved verses will be sung at our funerals.

But karaoke was last night; tonight we have a magician. He pulls rabbits from places, unexpected places. We go to sleep and dream of rabbits, wake up, re-enter the Lazy River. You've heard of the circle of life? This is like that. Round and round we go. No, we have not seen the Moorish ruins. Nor will we be travelling into those bare, arid mountains. Not one soul among us has read the recent novel set right here, in Almería, nor do we have any intention of doing so. We will not be judged. The Lazy River is a non-judgement zone. This does not mean, however, that we are blind. For we, too, saw the polytunnels – from the coach, on the way in from the airport – and we saw the Africans who work here, alone or in pairs, riding their bicycles in the merciless sun, moving between the polytunnels. Peering at them, I leaned my head against the shuddering glass of my window and, as in the fable of the burning bush, saw instead of the Africans a mirage. It was a vision of a little punnet of baby tomatoes, wrapped in plastic. Floating just outside my window, in the almost-desert, among the Moorish ruins. Familiar in aspect, it was as real to me as my own hand. And upon that punnet I saw a barcode, and just above that barcode was written *PRODUCT OF SPAIN – ALMERÍA*. The vision passed. It was of no use to me or anyone, at that moment, on our vacation. For who are we to – and who are you to – and who are they to ask us – and whosoever casts the first—

It's quite true that we, being British, could not point to the Lazy River on a map of Spain, but it is also true that we have no need to do so, for we leave the water only to buy flotation devices, as mentioned above. True, too, that most of us voted for Brexit and therefore cannot be sure if we will need a complicated visa to enter the Lazy River come next summer. This is something we will worry about next summer. Among us, there are a few souls from London, university educated and fond of things like metaphors and remaining in Europe and swimming against the current. Whenever this notable minority is not in the Lazy River, they warn their children off the endless chips and apply the highest-possible factor of suncream. And even in water they like to maintain certain distinctions. They will not do the Macarena. They will not participate in the Zumba class. Some say they are joyless, others that they fear humiliation. But, to be fair, it is hard to dance in water. Either way, after eating – healthily – or buying a flotation device (unbranded), they will climb back into the metaphor with the rest, back into this watery Ouroboros, which, unlike the river of Heraclitus, is always the same no matter where you happen to step in it.

Yesterday the Lazy River was green. Nobody knows why. Theories abound. They all involve urine. Either the colour is the consequence of urine or is the colour of the chemical put in to disguise the urine or is the reaction of urine to chlorine or some other unknown chemical agent. I don't doubt urine is involved. I have peed in there myself. But it is not the urine that we find so disturbing. No, the sad consequence of the green is that it concentrates the mind in a very unpleasant way upon the fundamental artificiality of the Lazy River. Suddenly what had seemed quite natural – floating slowly in an unending circle, while listening to the hit of the summer, which itself happens to be called "Slowly" – seems not only unnatural but surpassingly odd. Less like a holiday from life than like some kind of terrible metaphor for it. This feeling is not limited to the few fans of metaphor present. It is shared by all. If I had to compare it with something, it would be the shame that came over Adam and Eve as they looked at themselves and realized for the first time that they were naked in the eyes of others.

What is the solution to life? How can it be lived "well"? Opposite our loungers are two bosomy girls, sisters. They arrive very early each morning, and instead of the common plastic loungers used by the rest of us they manage to nab one of the rare white four-poster beds that face the ocean. These sisters are eighteen and nineteen years old. Their outdoor bed sports gauzy white curtains on all four sides, to protect whoever lies upon it from the sun. But the sisters draw the curtains back, creating a stage, and lie out, perfecting their tans, often adjusting their bikini bottoms to check their progress, the thin line that separates brown stomach from pale groin. Blankly they gaze at their bare pubic mounds before lying back on the day-bed. The reason I bring them up is that in the context of the Lazy River they are unusually active. They spend more time on dry land than anyone else, principally taking pictures of each other on their phones. For the sisters, this business of photographs is a form of labour that fills each day to its limit, just as the Lazy River fills ours. It is an accounting of life that takes as long as life itself. "We both step and do not step in the same rivers. We are and are not." So said Heraclitus, and so say the sisters, as they move in and out of shot, catching the flow of things, framing themselves for a moment: as they are, and as they are not. Personally, I am moved by their industry. No one is paying them for their labour, yet this does not deter them. Like photographers' assistants at real photo shoots, first they prep the area, cleaning it, improving it, discussing the angle of the light, and, if necessary, they will even move the bed in order to crop from the shot anything unsightly: stray trash, old leaves, old people. Prepping the area takes some time. Because their phones have such depth of image, even a sweet wrapper many yards away must be removed. Then their props are gathered: pink flower petals, extravagant cocktails with photogenic umbrellas protruding from them, ice creams (to be photographed but not eaten), and, on one occasion, a book, held only for the duration of the photograph and – though perhaps only I noticed this – upside down. As they prep, each wears a heart-breaking pair of plain black spectacles. Once each girl is ready to pose, she hands her glasses to her sister. It is easy to say they make being young look like hard work, but wasn't it always hard work, even if the medium of its difficulty was different? At least they are making a project of their lives, a measurable project that can be liked or commented upon. What are we doing? Floating?

A three-minute stroll from the back door of the hotel is the boardwalk, where mild entertainments are offered in the evenings, should we need something to do in the few darkling hours in which the Lazy River is serviced, cleaned, and sterilized. One of these entertainments is, of course, the sea. But once you have entered the Lazy River, with all its pliability and ease, its sterilizing chlorine and swift yet manageable currents, it is very hard to accept the sea: its abundant salt, its marine life, those little islands of twisted plastic. Not to mention its overfished depths, ever-warming temperature, and infinite horizons, reminders of death. We pass it by. We walk the boardwalk instead, beyond the two ladies who plait hair, onward a few minutes more until we reach the trampolines. This is the longest distance we have walked since our vacation began. We do it "for the children." And now we strap our children into harnesses and watch them bounce up and down on the metaphor, up and down, up and down, as we sit, on a low wall, facing them and the sea, legs dangling, sipping at tumblers of vodka, brought from the hotel, wondering if trampolines are not in the end a superior metaphor to lazy rivers. Life's certainly an up-and-down, up-and-down sort of affair, although for children the downs seem to come as a surprise – almost as a delight, being so outrageous, so difficult to believe – whereas for us, sitting on the wall, clutching our tumblers, it's the ups that have come to appear a little preposterous, hard to credit; they strike us as a cunning bit of misdirection, rarer than a blood-red moon. Speaking of which, that night there was a blood-red moon. Don't look at me: southern Spain has the highest ratio of metaphor to reality of any place I've ever known. There everything is in everything else. And we all looked up at the blood-red moon – that bad-faith moon of 2017 – and each man and woman among us understood in that moment that there is no vacation you can take from a year such as this. Still, it was beautiful. It bathed our bouncing children in its red light and set the sea on fire.

Then the time ran out. The children were enraged, not understanding yet about time running out, kicking and scratching us as we unstrapped them from their harnesses. But we did not fold, we did not give in; no, we held them close, and accepted their rage, took it into our bodies, all of it, as we accept all their silly tantrums, as a substitute for the true outrage, which of course they do not yet know, because we have not yet told them, because we are on holiday – to which end we have come to a hotel with a lazy river. In truth, there is never a good moment. One day they will open a paper or a web page and read for themselves about the year – 2050 or so, according to the prophets – when the time will run out. A year when they will be no older than we are now. Not everything goes round and round. Some things go up and—

On the way back to the hotel, we stop by the ladies who plait hair, one from Senegal and the other from the Gambia. With the moon as red as it is, casting its cinematic light, we can glimpse the coast of their continent across the water from our own, but they did not cross this particular stretch of ocean, because it is even more treacherous than the one between Libya and Lampedusa, by which route they came. Just looking at them you can tell that they are both the type who could swim the Lazy River backward and all the way round. In fact, isn't this what they have done? One is called Mariatou, the other Cynthia. For ten euros they will plait hair in cane rows or Senegalese twists or high-ridged Dutch braids. In our party, three want their hair done; the ladies get to work. The men are in the polytunnels. The tomatoes are in the supermarket. The moon is in the sky. The Brits are leaving Europe. We are on a "getaway." We still believe in getaways. "It is hard in Spain," Mariatou says, in answer to our queries. "Very hard." "To live well?" Cynthia adds, pulling our daughter's hair, making her yelp. "Is not easy."

By the time we reach the gates of the hotel all is dark. A pair of identical twins, Rico and Rocco, in their twenties, with oily black curls and skinny white jeans – twin iPhones wedged in their tight pockets – have just finished their act and are packing up their boom box. "We come runner-up *X Factor* Spain," they say, in answer to our queries. "We are Tunisia for birth but now we are Spain." We wish them well and goodnight, and divert our children's eyes from the obscene bulge of those iPhones, the existence of which we have decided not to reveal to them for many years, or at least until they are twelve. At the elevators, we separate from our friends and their children and ascend to our room, which is the same as their room and everybody's room, and put the children to bed and sit on the balcony with our laptops and our phones, where we look up his Twitter, as we have every night since January. Here and there, on other balconies, we spot other men and women on other loungers with other devices, engaged in much the same routine. Down below, the Lazy River runs, a neon blue, a crazy blue, a Facebook blue. In it stands a fully clothed man armed with a long mop – he is being held in place by another man, who grips him by the waist, so that the first man may angle his mop and position himself against the strong yet somniferous current and clean whatever scum we have left of ourselves off the sides.

ELIF SHAFAK

ZALEEKHAH

from *There Are Rivers in the Sky*

BY THE RIVER THAMES, 2018

INSIDE THE BLACK CAB that Uncle Malek arranged for her, Zaleekhah looks out of the window, watching the pedestrians, the cyclists, the restaurants flash past in a stream of blurred lights. London for her has never been a capital of solid, sturdy architecture and historical monuments and leafy public parks but rather a city carved by water, smoothed by tide and flow, an ever-expanding reservoir of fluvial memories, some obliterated, others repressed, still others forcefully gushing, like its many rivers and their tributaries.

They are everywhere – the ghost streams.

There is the mysterious River Fleet, for instance – the largest and most important of London's subterranean rivers, the "hollow stream." Once a broad tidal basin and an important artery bringing goods and business into the capital, it has repeatedly endured abuse at the hands of humans, choked and polluted with discarded carcasses and putrefying offal from the meat markets and tanneries lining its banks – next, all at once, it was deemed too filthy, too malodorous, too unpleasant to look at and therefore no longer of use. A solution was found to hide it from sight, cover its ugliness under stacks of bricks. It lay buried for about 250 years, until it was rediscovered and reopened – only to be buried again. A legendary river, then an open sewer, then an aimless canal, then an open sewer again and, eventually, forgotten by almost everyone. Still alive, though. A watery specter that refuses to die.

Then there is the River Effra in South London, concealed and culverted, nowadays a conduit for drainage and waste matter, silently coursing under not only houses and offices but also cemeteries, whence it sometimes unearths and carries off buried coffins. There is also the Tyburn, a source of delicious fresh salmon in the distant past, though barely remembered these days, as it flows unseen and unheard underneath celebrated urban landmarks. The Walbrook, once a sapphire-blue river running through the Roman fort of Londinium into the Thames, shimmering like the wing of a dragonfly, provided residents with clean water; now it only feeds into a malodorous sewer.

Then there is the quaint and charming River Westbourne – "the royal stream." When Victorian engineers could not find a way to build a Tube station above the river, they made the river run through the station instead. Today, invisible to thousands of commuters, hidden in plain sight, it pours through a pipe above the platforms in Sloane Square Tube station, after being entombed in London clay to make way for the prosperous terraces of Chelsea and Belgravia above. It has survived storms, and even a bomb blast in the Second World War. They are all there, roiling beneath the cement pavements and the tarmacked streets, rumbling and rushing under strata of concrete and bricks, buried under sediments of history and the weight of amnesia.

Sitting back, Zaleekhah closes her eyes momentarily, as if hoping to hear the water through the noise of the traffic. On a sudden impulse, she leans forward and says to the driver, "Excuse me!"

The man, busy chatting to someone on the phone, doesn't answer immediately.

"Sorry!" Zaleekhah says, louder. "I've changed my mind. Can you take me somewhere else?"

Now she has his full attention. He looks at her through the rearview mirror. "The postcode was for the houseboats by the shore. So you're not going to Cheyne Walk?"

"Yes, I was, but I'm not now." She gives him the name of a district in Southeast London instead, a street of converted warehouses.

He nods, though in the driving mirror she can see his eyes tinged with a trace of suspicion.

The crepuscular light has drained into darkness by the time Zaleekhah arrives at a dull ochre, two-story brick building in Bermondsey. A metal sign on the door reads *Centre for Ecology and Hydrology*. A not-for-profit, independent institute for research in biogeochemistry, water studies and biodiversity. Its flat roof, bland functionality and absence of ornament stands in stark contrast with the luxurious elegance of Uncle's house.

Opening the door, she steps into the corridor and inhales the familiar smell of disinfected floors. The entire space is divided economically into small rooms and modest cubicles, except for the larger common areas, which are reserved for team meetings. A few items are dotted around here and there: Post-it notes, inspirational quotes, postcards pinned to corkboards; mugs with funny sayings, succulents in ceramic pots . . . The universal simplicity of office objects. Zaleekhah does not find the effacement of individuality, if that is what it is, unappealing. It is a place designed for collective endeavor, not for personal gratification.

She walks slowly, her footsteps echoing in the empty building. The last door on the right displays her name – *Dr.*

Zaleekhah Clarke. For a moment she stares at the plaque. Upon getting married, she took her husband's surname. Now it will probably have to change again. Women are expected to be like rivers – readjusting, shapeshifting.

It is perhaps easier to justify the end of a relationship – both to yourself and to others – when there is a definite, tangible cause, no matter how painful. But it is harder to grasp the gradual evaporation of love, a loss so slow and subtle as to be barely detectable, until it is fully gone. Now she feels like a passenger on a sleeper train who awakens and draws back the curtains, only to find an unfamiliar landscape that had been there all along. She cannot pull the curtains closed again.

She is almost thirty-one years old. She has no children, no parents. This time last year she was certain that her husband was her family. Their colleagues always commented on how perfectly matched they were, which was meant as a compliment, and also the politest way of saying neither could have found anyone better. It was true, though: they seemed like a good couple, and there were times when they really were – *if only she'd had the capacity for happiness*. But she also knows that the fabric of their marriage had worn thin in many places. All it needed was one sharp tug for it to tear.

Zaleekhah lets herself into her office, which is small and spartan but clean. On the opposite wall there is a poster – a black-and-white picture of a single drop of water. At first glance, it seems to be plunging from a great height into a lake or an estuary, but it could equally be emerging from the depths of an ocean, ascending toward the skies.

Apart from this image, the walls are bare. Her research papers are arranged in folders on the desk, alongside a jar of pencils, all neatly sharpened. A fiddle-leaf fig droops listlessly by the window; it has stayed in its original, stunted form even though she has done her best to take care of it. On the left side is a slate-colored sofa – also heaped with papers and folders. Good thing Uncle has never visited her workplace. He would have found it depressingly drab. But she loves her job, and cherishes this space she can call her own.

She moves aside the clutter on the sofa. Under a scratch pad, attached with a paperclip, as if it were an afterthought, she sees a note.

HOW TO BURY A RIVER

1. Build concrete troughs along both sides of the riverbed.
2. Add a roof to the troughs.
3. Encase the river completely on three sides, turning it into one long, winding coffin.
4. Cover the roof with earth, making sure no trace is visible.
5. Build your city over it.
6. Forget that it was ever there.

Zaleekhah doesn't remember when she wrote this; she must have scribbled it in a moment of distraction. She crumples the paper and tosses it toward the bin, narrowly missing it.

On a shelf behind her desk, amid clusters of books stacked every which way, is an arrangement of photographs in silver frames. In the first she is with her husband, on their honeymoon in Marrakech. Sitting under a tree whose pomegranates droop ripe and rubicund above their heads, after a stroll through the souks in the medina, they look carelessly happy, spent and sunburnt. The next picture is a slimmer and younger version of herself, taken at her university graduation party. A palpable pride in her features, she leans over a sumptuous table, in the company of Uncle Malek, Aunt Malek and Helen, glasses held aloft in a toast. Beside that is a photo of her parents. Her father sports his customary charming smile, his eyes crinkling at the corners. Sitting by his side, her mother beams at the camera, her hair draped over one shoulder in a long, dark braid. She wears a green dress cinched at the waist, the soft curve of her belly suggesting the early months of pregnancy. This is how her mother would have looked, Zaleekhah assumes, had she ever appeared in her dreams.

The fourth frame – smaller in size – is tucked away at the back of the shelf, not easily visible. A photo of Zaleekhah at a conference in Dublin with a tall, slender man in his fifties. Her mentor, her colleague, her friend. Professor Berenberg was an eminent hydrologist, biochemist and climate scientist. Highly respected in his field, he was known not only for his brilliant intellect and contribution to the discipline but also for his kindness and generosity toward staff and students. They collaborated on various projects for long years – until he left the lab, alone and publicly disgraced.

Toward the end of his life, the professor became preoccupied with a hypothesis he referred to in his notes as "aquatic memory." He argued that, under certain circumstances, water – the universal solvent – retained evidence, or "memory," of the solute particles that had dissolved in it, no matter how many times it was diluted or purified. Even if years passed, or centuries, and not a single original molecule remained, each droplet of water maintained a unique structure, distinguishable from the next, marked forever by what it once contained. Water, in other words, *remembered.*

Consumed by this hypothesis, Berenberg dropped all other research. Expanding and diversifying his team, he hired biologists, chemists and immunologists to work alongside hydrologists. He was convinced that if they could prove that water possessed some kind of memory, this would have groundbreaking implications, not only for hydrology and biology but also for medicine, homeopathy and conventional attitudes toward healing. Satisfied with his results, he submitted his findings to peer-reviewed scientific journals – and one agreed to publish his paper.

The backlash was almost instant. A tide of skepticism followed. His arguments were found to be weak, his conclusions insufficiently supported by evidence. It did not help the professor's case that independent researchers could not verify his results when they repeated his experiments under similar lab conditions. Skepticism gave way to disbelief, disbelief to rejection and rejection to ridicule. Berenberg did not back down, insisting on the validity of his method. The more he held his ground, the more he was lambasted. His reputation tarnished, he was forced to endure a swift downfall. Old friends stopped calling him. Young researchers distanced themselves. Shunned, he lost his lab and funding. Still he carried on doggedly, moving to the basement of his home; and when his last remaining grants ran out, he covered all the costs of his research out of his own pocket. There he worked with limited means and barely any staff – until one morning, two years ago, he was found dead on the floor, felled by a heart attack.

Ever since then, he has been a ghost river in Zaleekhah's life, pushed into the dark recesses of her past. She rarely, if ever, mentions his name, although she thinks about him often. Aquatic memory has been a contentious subject for her – professionally and personally. Her husband believed that the late professor, though well intentioned, was misled by his own unconscious confirmation bias, seeing in the findings what he simply wished to see. Whereas Zaleekhah is convinced that more studies are needed to understand water and its many anomalies, and until then it would be as absurd to conclude that Berenberg was deluded as it would be to suggest he was triumphant.

Following the death of the professor, without telling anyone, Zaleekhah continued his experiments for a while. The results were often confusing, neither stable nor clear. At times, she felt on the verge of proving the hypothesis. At others, the data were so weak she doubted the proposition altogether. With such wide variation, it was impossible to submit anything definitive to respected journals. Despite her disappointment, she carried on testing and tenaciously recording the results – until her husband found out.

"Are you out of your mind? Why are you wasting your time with a failed hypothesis?"

"I just want to see where the research will take me."

"Isn't it obvious? It'll take you nowhere. It's poetic nonsense – not science."

"Maybe they're not worlds apart – science and poetry, I mean."

The glare in his eyes, the sudden withdrawal of his patience. "I don't know what you're trying to do, but please stop it – for your own good. Unless you want to risk your job? I've never understood why you took the guy seriously. I'm sorry, but he was pathetic. He was clearly losing his mind."

That is when Zaleekhah told her husband. Speaking slowly, she explained to him how much the deceased scientist meant to her and how she was not ready to let go of the theory of aquatic memory. She said she missed working with

Berenberg and then she said something that she thought she would never voice out loud: Berenberg was her mentor at first, and a close colleague and a good friend, but, somewhere in between these stages, for a passing time, she had also been in love with him.

"In love?"

"Yes, but that was before I met you. Before we got married. I'd known him for a long time."

Few things harden the human heart as fast as jealousy. Cold and commanding, it settles quickly in the warm spot left by affection, chilling it with its bitter touch.

"All these years you were working with your ex-boyfriend, and you didn't even think to tell me?"

"He was never my boyfriend!"

"What was he, then?"

"Nothing. He was just—"

"Special?"

"No, not like that. He was different – okay?"

"Different from me, you mean."

"Brian, that's not what I'm saying—"

The silence that followed did not surprise her. But she was not ready for his anger, which felt too close to hatred.

"I can't believe you've kept this from me when you know how much I've given up for you."

Once again, there it was, their one unresolvable debate, always ready to rear its head.

"Why are you bringing this up now? Because you knew when we got married I never planned to have children."

"You never even *wanted* to want them!"

She looked at him, expecting him to hear the awkwardness in his own words. But in that moment, he lifted his chin and said, "You wouldn't have my child, but I bet you would have had his."

A few minutes later Zaleekhah packed a few belongings, put them in a cardboard box and left.

She will sleep in the lab tonight again. As long as she has her sleeping pills, she does not mind. With the water from a Thermos, she swallows two pills. Then she rummages in the cupboard for a blanket that she keeps for times like this. She takes out the book she borrowed from Uncle Malek. She was planning to start reading it tonight, but her eyelids are closing. So instead she wraps her cardigan around it. *Nineveh and Its Remains* will be her pillow. Maybe she will dream of human-headed, bird-winged *lamassus* feathering earthwards from laden clouds.

She switches off the lights. In the dark, she is ambushed by a memory – unbidden and unexpected. They were packing his things, the two of them, the day Berenberg left the office. The temperature had fallen that morning, breath condensing in front of their eyes. She asked him if he ever regretted studying "aquatic memory," given the price he paid for choosing such a controversial subject.

"Not for one second. I wanted to research an unknown property of water, and I treasured every moment of it."

"But it cost you so much."

"True . . . but you and I both love the work we do and that love is beyond all personal success or failure. You'll pick up where I've left off, and, if you falter, someone else will take on your research. We do this to keep scientific inquiry going – with or without us."

Thinking about these words now, Zaleekhah curls into herself and hugs her knees. The sofa is shorter than she is, but that's not the cause of her discomfort. She feels guilty for never having told Berenberg how much he meant to her and she feels guilty for telling her husband how much Berenberg meant to her. She was silent when she should have spoken; she spoke when she should have been silent. Either way, guilt is her most loyal companion. And regret, too – not so much for her acts as for her failure to act. She was drawn to Berenberg's dedication and perseverance, a devotion so selfless as to seek only the good of its object, an unreasonable commitment perhaps more commonly observed in ancient mystics and ascetics than in the modern workplace.

As she closes her eyes, waiting to descend into a drugged sleep, she can hear a gentle lapping in the distance. They are all there. The lost rivers of time, out of sight and out of mind but notable in their absence, like phantom limbs that still have the power to cause pain. They are here and everywhere, eroding the solid structures on which we have built our careers, marriages, reputations and relationships, evermore flowing onwards – *with or without us*. Zaleekhah knows she may not be one of them, but she will always be attracted to people who are pulled toward something bigger and better than themselves, a passion that lasts a lifetime, even though it will consume them in the end.

ACKNOWLEDGMENTS

ANONYMOUS: "La Llorona" (Mexico, traditional). Translation copyright © Jaime Marroquín Arredondo 2024. Reprinted with permission.

LESLEY NNEKA ARIMAH: "What Is a Volcano?" from *What It Means When a Man Falls from the Sky: Stories* by Lesley Nneka Arimah, copyright © 2017 by Lesley Nneka Arimah. Used by permission of Riverhead, an imprint of Penguin Publishing Group, a division of Penguin Random House LLC. All rights reserved. "What Is a Volcano?" from *What It Means When a Man Falls from the Sky*, Riverhead Books, 2017. Tinder Press, Headline Publishing Group Limited.

TONY BIRCH: "The Ghost River" originally published in *The Guardian*, 7 November 2013, Copyright Guardian News & Media Ltd 2024. Reprinted with permission. Reproduced with permission of Tony Birch.

ERSKINE CALDWELL: "Warm River" from *We Are the Living*, Viking, 1933. Published by Little, Brown, Hachette Group. Peters, Fraser, Dunlop.

KUNIKIDA DOPPO: "River Mist" (Japan, 1898). Translation copyright © Naoko Ishikura Smith, 2024. Reprinted with permission.

OLEKSANDER DOVZHENKO: "Easter Flood" from *The Enchanted Desna*, published privately in Ukraine, 1957. Translation copyright © Dzvinia Orlowsky and Ali Kinsella, 2024. Reprinted with permission.

SALWA ELHAMAMSY: "By the Nile". Copyright © by

Salwa Elhamamsy, 2022. Reprinted with permission from the author.

E. M. FORSTER: "The Road from Colonus" (1904), taken from *Collected Short Stories*, Penguin, 1947, by permission of Peters, Fraser, Dunlop.

ERNEST HEMINGWAY: "Big Two-Hearted River" first published in *In Our Time* (1925). From *The First Forty-Nine Stories* published by Jonathan Cape.

HERMANN HESSE: "The Ferryman" by Hermann Hesse, from *Siddhartha*, copyright © 1951 by New Directions Publishing Corp. Reprinted by permission of New Directions Publishing Corp. "The Ferryman" from *Siddhartha* by Hermann Hesse, translated by Hilda Rosner (Peter Owen Ltd, 1954), reproduced by permission of Pushkin Press.

ELIZABETH JANE HOWARD: "Three Miles Up" from *Mr Wrong*, first published by Pan in 1993, an imprint of Pan Macmillan. Reproduced by permission of Macmillan Publishers International Limited. Copyright © Elizabeth Jane Howard 1975. Reprinted with consent from Jonathan Clowes Limited.

ZORA NEALE HURSTON: "Magnolia Flower" (1925) from *The Complete Stories*, Harper Perennial Modern Classics, 2008. Joy Harris Literary Agency, Inc.

GUY DE MAUPASSANT: "On the River" (France, 1876). Translation copyright © Chloë Hughes, 2024. Reprinted with permission.

CORMAC McCARTHY: "The Dark Waters" first published in the *Sewanee Review*, vol. 73, no. 2, Spring 1965. Reprinted with permission of the editor.

ALICE MUNRO: "The Found Boat" from *Something I've Been Meaning to Tell You* (1974). Copyright © Alice Munro 1974. Vintage Books, London. Copyright © 1974, copyright renewed 2002 by Alice Munro. WME Agency.

HUYNH QUANG NHUONG: 1,980-word selection titled: "So Close" from *The Land I Lost* by Quang Nhuong Huynh, illustrated by Vo-Dinh Mai. Text copyright © 1982 by Huynh Quang Nhuong. Illustrations copyright © 1982 by Vo-Dinh Mai. Used by permission of HarperCollins Publishers.
OVID: "Arethusa" (Greece, 8 CE). Translation copyright © Kit Andrews, 2024. Reprinted with permission.
ELIF SHAFAK: "Zaleekhah" from *There Are Rivers in the Sky* by Elif Shafak, published by Viking Penguin. Copyright © Elif Shafak. Excerpt(s) from *There Are Rivers in the Sky: A Novel*, by Elif Shafak, copyright © 2024 by Elif Shafak. Used by permission of Alfred A. Knopf, an imprint of the Knopf Doubleday Publishing Group, a division of Penguin Random House LLC. All rights reserved.
ZADIE SMITH: "The Lazy River" from *Grand Union: Stories* by Zadie Smith, copyright © 2019 by Zadie Smith. Used by permission of Penguin Press, an imprint of Penguin Publishing Group, a division of Penguin Random House LLC. All rights reserved. "The Lazy River" from *Grand Union: Stories*, Penguin Press, 2019. Rogers Coleridge & White.
RABINDRANATH TAGORE: "The River Stairs" (India, 1884) translated by Jadunath Sarkar. The Modern Review, Vol XII, No. 7–12, 1912, Calcutta. Reprinted with permission from the Estate of Sir Jadunath Sarkar.
TAO YUANMING: "Peach Blossom Spring" (China, 421 CE). Translation copyright © Jin Lei, 2024. Reprinted with permission.
Illustrations by Paul Gentry used by permission.

Titles in Everyman's Library Pocket Classics

African Stories
Selected by Ben Okri

Bedtime Stories
Selected by Diana Secker Tesdell

Berlin Stories
Selected by Philip Hensher

The Best Medicine: Stories of Healing
Selected by Theodore Dalrymple

Cat Stories
Selected by Diana Secker Tesdell

Christmas Stories
Selected by Diana Secker Tesdell

Detective Stories
Selected by Peter Washington

Dog Stories
Selected by Diana Secker Tesdell

Erotic Stories
Selected by Rowan Pelling

Fishing Stories
Selected by Henry Hughes

Florence Stories
Selected by Ella Carr

Garden Stories
Selected by Diana Secker Tesdell

Ghost Stories
Selected by Peter Washington

Golf Stories
Selected by Charles McGrath

Horse Stories
Selected by Diana Secker Tesdell

London Stories
Selected by Jerry White

Love Stories
Selected by Diana Secker Tesdell

Music Stories
Selected by Wesley Stace

New York Stories
Selected by Diana Secker Tesdell

Paris Stories
Selected by Shaun Whiteside

Prague Stories
Selected by Richard Bassett

River Stories
Selected by Henry Hughes

Rome Stories
Selected by Jonathan Keates

Scottish Stories
Selected by Gerard Carruthers

Shaken and Stirred: Intoxicating Stories
Selected by Diana Secker Tesdell

Stories of Art and Artists
Selected by Diana Secker Tesdell

Stories of Books and Libraries
Selected by Jane Holloway

Stories of Fatherhood
Selected by Diana Secker Tesdell

Stories from the Kitchen
Selected by Diana Secker Tesdell

Stories of Motherhood
Selected by Diana Secker Tesdell

Stories of the Sea
Selected by Diana Secker Tesdell

Stories of Southern Italy
Selected by Ella Carr

Stories of Trees, Woods, and the Forest
Selected by Fiona Stafford

Venice Stories
Selected by Jonathan Keates

Wedding Stories
Selected by Diana Secker Tesdell

Saki: Stories
Selected by Diana Secker Tesdell

John Updike:
The Maples Stories
Olinger Stories